...what readers are saying...

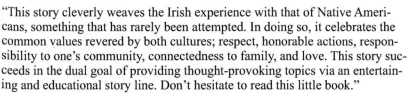

"...a well-paced story that inspires a recognition of the importance of family. I wrote down the words that constitute the main theme of the book say them to my two son
                    Kathy Leege, W   and Mom, Eau Claire, WI

"This story cleverly weaves the Irish experience with that of Native Americans, something that has rarely been attempted. In doing so, it celebrates the common values revered by both cultures; respect, honorable actions, responsibility to one's community, connectedness to family, and love. This story succeeds in the dual goal of providing thought-provoking topics via an entertaining and educational story line. Don't hesitate to read this little book."
                    Rick Koziel, Director, Beaver Creek Reserve, Outdoor
                    Education Facility, Eau Claire County, WI

"The connections to many unknown bits of American history and Plains Indian culture made this a fascinating story. High school students will love it and so will their teachers. It is a teaching story and a great read."
                    Judy Dekan, Principal, Augusta Public Schools, WI

"I loved this book, and I learned some American History, too. I usually only read sci-fi, but this story kept me interested. I'm recommending it to my friends."
                    Mimi Lea, High School Student, Chippewa Falls, WI

"...a story that reminded me of how much we have been given by our ancestors, no matter where they originated. Some of my French-Canadian forbearers came from the places portrayed in this story. It made me proud."
                    Mark Gagnon, Ironworker, Local 512, St. Paul, MN

"*The Crook'd Staff* is a creative way to present some American history and cultural anthropology to a broad range of readers. It succeeds in doing just that. The plot and characters cause the reader to reflect on our country's past, and the suggested bibliography is evidence of the author's extensive familiarity with the topics. This book ranks with the best stories in this genre and a sequel needs to be written."
                    Eddie Fox, Music and Literary Reviewer, Madison, WI

"This book has great characters. They were believable and so was the plot. I liked the way the story moved along. There was a lot of history I didn't know. I wish this was the kind of book we were required to read at school more often."
                    Brian Wells, High School Student, Eau Claire, WI

"...so many twists and turns that I gave up trying to figure out where this story was going to go next. I read a lot and this is a must-read little book that was thoroughly enjoyable."
                    Lou Recine, Software Tester, Eau Claire, WI

For Bruce + Barb

The Crook'd Staff

Pete Roller

The Crook'd Staff

An Adventure of Ireland and America

Peter E. Roller

Tiyospaye Publishing
Fall Creek, Wisconsin

First Edition, 2006
First Printing, June 2006

LCCN: 2006903587

ISBN—10: 0-9785-0353-8   Paperback
ISBN—13: 978-0-9785-0353-6

ISBN—10: 0-9785-0354-6   Hardcover
ISBN—13: 978-0-9785-0354-3

ISBN—10: 0-9785-0351-1   Recorded book
ISBN—13: 978-0-9785-0351-2

ISBN—10: 0-9785-0352-X   Teacher's Guide
ISBN—13: 978-0-9785-0352-9

ISBN—10: 0-9785-0350-3   e-Book
ISBN—13: 978-0-9785-0350-5

Published by
Tiyospaye Publishing
8965 Hwy. 12   Suite #44
Fall Creek, WI 54742
http://www.tiyospayepublishing.com

Pages formatted by
Obsessive Formatting & Design
207 Wilson St., Suite C
Newton, IL 62448
618-562-7263

Printed in the United States of America by
Graphic Image Group, Inc.
526 Crescent Blvd., Suite #362
Glen Ellyn, IL 60137
http://www.giginc.com

TABLE OF CONTENTS

ACKNOWLEDGMENT
INTRODUCTION
DEDICATION
PROLOGUE

ACKNOWLEDGMENT

Writing this novel has taken me on an interesting journey. At times I just couldn't seem to find the words to describe the scenes I had in my mind. Then at other times, I neglected to remember that the reader does not have the same longstanding connection with these characters as I do, and so some things that I thought were obvious needed to be explained.

I was fortunate to have a number of people to help me through those situations. They were my readers, and I want to acknowledge them. They include history and American literature teachers, friends, and high school students who acted as my "trial market readers." Many of them made great suggestions on how I could make the story better. I thank them for taking the time to read the book in its early stages and for giving me their comments. (Thanks Len, Mark, Lou, and Lori; Bobbi, Nancy Jean, Kathy, Lisa, Catherine, John, and Terry; Mimi, Colin, Brian, and Nathan.)

I also relied on two of my historic re-enactor colleagues to verify certain little facts that I wanted to include in my story. They have a lot of knowledge about the Fur Trade Era that is difficult for the average reader to acquire, and I have used their personal expertise whenever I could. (Thanks Tom and Dan.)

Of course, a very special thanks goes to my wife, Susan, who put up with my disappearance for long hours as I wrote and rewrote, and for giving me invaluable insights and suggestions for making certain parts of this story clearer. Without her understanding and support, this little story would never have gotten to print.

There are a number of special authors I want to credit, and I have listed them in a brief bibliography. I want to acknowledge their scholarship and the creative, often sensitive treatments they have given to their subjects. Their research and books have taught and inspired me, and I thank them now. If you want to know more about some of the things I have referenced in this story, you might start with those books.

A wonderful friend, Beverly Fletcher Kitzmiller, my major editor, did an extraordinary job of proofreading the manuscript. Her thirty-plus years of teaching grammar and punctuation to high school students was a key element in the final composition of the book.

Another long-time friend, Sharon Poppleton, was responsible for the MS Word formatting of the manuscript. Her talents stem from her long career as a high school business education teacher. I needed her talents so that I kept my sanity.

I thank you both for your significant contributions to my effort and for being astute readers as well.

In conclusion, I want to acknowledge all of the websites, books, and articles I consulted which gave me a clearer understanding of the publishing process, as well as certain historical events I wanted to include. The historical and personal connections I discovered as I researched and wrote were astonishing. The internet is a powerful tool. But so are real libraries. There is nothing quite like a printed book.

Peter E. Roller
Tiyospaye Publishing   2006

INTRODUCTION

I have had this story in me for a very long time. People have encouraged me to write it down, and so I have. It might best be told some evening around a campfire, or sitting inside a tipi with a candle or two burning. I have told parts of it in that atmosphere, and it seems to have a strong effect on the listeners.

This is not the story of my ancestors. I would like to think it could have been. All of the main characters are fictional, and their names are also fictional, although I do know people with the same first or last names. But there is absolutely no attempt to connect the events of this story with any of them, and no resemblance to them was intended, nor should it be inferred.

While the references to actual historical events and people are also fictional in that I have invented parts of the story around them, I have tried to be accurate in connecting the dates, places and real historical figures to my characters. There is a list of characters at the start of each Part and some Maps and some Family Trees at the end of the book to help the reader.

I also want to point out that my characters are depicted the way they are simply because I want them to be that way. Sometimes they have thoughts and opinions quite different from those that would have been the more common perspectives of their neighbors in that time period. While my characters' attitudes are historically accurate, some of them are, admittedly, out of the mainstream.

The most noticeable example of this is in my depiction of the trading relationship between the Native Americans and two of my main characters. Fur trade history actually reveals an exact opposite picture of these economic alliances. I have purposely reversed this because I do believe that there were some white traders who did trade honorably. However, they were few and far between.

I have also used some Ojibwe, Lakota, and Cheyenne words and other cultural references. If they are deemed incorrect or inappropriate by those Native American readers, I beg forgiveness. It was not my intention to insult or improperly portray their ancestors or cultures. If I have done so, I say again that it was not intentional, and I beg forgiveness.

The Crook'd Staff is not a light, happy romance. Nor is it a dry, ponderous history of Native Americans or European immigrants. It is the story of some young Irish kids who came to America under very different and difficult circumstances and who achieved success in very different ways. It is a story of honor, of responsibility, of choices, of community, and of family. I hope my readers will find inspiration in the major themes.

I have often said: "If you know where our nation and its citizens have come from and what they've experienced, you might have a better sense as to where we ought to be going. Without an eye toward the future, history is just a bunch of fading memories of the past. So, celebrate the past, but let it teach you. Those who came before us did not have it all that easy. They have given us much."

Please read this story with that in mind. But remember: It is a fiction story. I have always loved to dream.

Peter E. Roller   2005

DEDICATION

For my daughters, Amy Elizabeth and Sarah Anne

Thanks for always remembering whose kids you are.

You have always made me proud!

PROLOGUE

"I have an idea that some men are born out of their due place.

Accident has cast them amid certain surroundings, but they have always a nostalgia for a home they know not....

Sometimes a man hits upon a place to which he mysteriously feels that he belongs.

Here is the home he sought, and he will settle amid scenes that he has never seen before, among men he has never known, as though they were familiar to him from his birth.

Here at last he finds rest."

From <u>The Moon and Sixpence</u>
    by W. Somerset Maugham, 1919

PART ONE

Ireland: 1823

List of Characters in Part One

Michael Ryan—peasant farmer in County Tipperary,
    Ireland
Mary Patterson Ryan—his wife

>   Evan Ryan—their eldest son
>   Ana Ryan—their daughter
>   Timothy Ryan—their youngest child

Thomas O'Leary—peasant farmer and close neighbor
    Elizabeth Kelly O'Leary—his wife and good friend of
        Mary Ryan

>   Catherine O'Leary—their eldest daughter
>   (Little) Thomas O'Leary—their son
>   Catherine O'Leary—their youngest child

Patrick Hughes—peasant farmer and neighbor
    Zoe O'Toole Hughes—his wife

>   Patrick Hughes—their son

John Burke—owner of a public house in the nearby
    village

Daniel Murphy—local blacksmith
    Adam Murphy—his son

Father Sean—Catholic priest in the local parish

Brandon McCombs—area peasant farmer

Shamus O'Toole—area peasant farmer

Percival—British soldier

Map for Part One in Appendix I

CHAPTER 1
...soap, and the smoke of firewood...

It was dark! He heard them coming down the lane. Oh, how he hated them, the way they strutted and swore. And especially the way they treated the Irish girls.

"Come, give us a kiss, ya Irish trollop," the one had said to his younger sister, Ana. He boiled again as he remembered the night just two weeks earlier. He had done nothing while the officer grabbed the girl and pulled the twelve-year-old into an unwanted embrace.

Luckily, the girl had been able to pull away from the man's drunken grip and had darted over the fence, disappearing around a building. But the boy had done nothing, and the memory shamed him again as he thought of it. When they told their parents about the incident, his father's look was all that Evan needed to understand that more was expected of him.

* * * * * * *

Evan Ryan was a strong lad for his fourteen years. His father depended on him to care for the ponies and for the few sheep and goats the family kept on the little farm. Now, as he stood quietly in the shadows of the shed, he wondered what his father would want him to do in this situation.

It was clear that the British soldiers had drunk too much. They reeled as they walked, and their singing was slurred. But it trailed off as they neared the farmhouse.

"We ought to go in there and get us one of them colleens," he heard one say. In the soft light coming from the small window, Evan could see that he was a cruel-looking man with a sword hanging off center and swinging more across his back than from his hip.

"You're always looking for them young girls," the biggest one laughed. "Ya can spend your money with the whores in Dublin and not be in trouble. Let's be off now, Percival."

"I've already done that, and I am in trouble. I've still got the pox," he snarled. "Them young ones won't give ya nothing."

Evan cringed. The farmhouse was the home of their close neighbors, the O'Learys. Suddenly, he understood the danger Catherine was facing.

The O'Leary girl was his age, and they had grown up together. He had always teased her, and she had teased back just as capably. They had an easy way with one another, almost like that which exists between a close brother and sister. But he had noticed over the past year that she now always blushed a little whenever he looked directly at her.

He also knew that he had been looking at her more and more often. It seemed that he couldn't help it. Her green eyes always sparkled, and her soft, light-red hair seemed to shimmer in the sunlight. He had noticed a certain new plumpness about her that he had never really paid any attention to before. He realized that he had been experiencing new feelings about her that were confusing to him.

He remembered that there had been that one afternoon just two days earlier when they had chanced to meet in the common pasture as he was rounding up the small flock. With nobody else around, he found himself talking with her differently than he ever had before.

It had not been the talk of children, the way it had been in earlier years. It was quite adult-like. Evan had inquired about Catherine's mother, Elizabeth. The woman was soon to have another child, and he knew it would be his mother, Mary, who would attend her. The skills of a midwife were all that Irish farm women had on such occasions.

"Aye, she is very close to her time," Catherine had said that day in the field. "The baby is ready to come any time, Mother says. I hope it's a girl."

Then she had asked if he had ridden the young pony that she knew was ready for the saddle.

"Not yet" had been his reply. Evan's father, Michael, raised racing ponies as a source of cash.

"Be careful," she had said quite seriously. "I wouldn't want to see ya with your arm in a sling. Ya wouldn't be able to dance with me next Saturday at the festival. Ya will be there, won't ya?" Her tone had not been teasing, but hopefully questioning.

Evan knew he was turning crimson, and to compose his thoughts, he looked away quickly, kicking at a big ewe. Then he turned back to the girl, and with a deep breath said, "I will be there, and I would be proud to dance with ya, Catherine."

I feel funny inside. He noticed.

Now it was Catherine's turn to blush. In her hesitation, he threw all caution to the wind, the strange feeling within him even stronger.

"There is no other girl in all of Ireland who I would rather dance with," he had said, looking directly into her eyes. She had looked down, and to soften the moment, he had added, "But, ya'll have to teach me how."

She laughed quickly, a laugh that was both relief and happiness. *Oh Evan! Do ya not understand how I feel about ya?* She thought.

"Let me show ya right now," she said.

She had dropped the shepherd's crook she was carrying and smiled. *The sheep will not run away!* She thought.

And I will learn to dance with ya! He smiled inwardly.

* * * * * * *

Now he stood in the shadow of the shed watching the British soldiers, and the thoughts of that time just two days before came swirling in his mind.

On that sunny afternoon in the pasture, he had held Catherine gently in his arms in the dance position, and she had showed him the steps. He had quickly learned them. Then he remembered that suddenly the stepping was over, and that they were standing looking into one another's eyes. For a moment, they had just stared at one another.

She was so lovely there in his loose arms, like a feather that he had guided easily once she had shown him the steps.

He remembered the best part. She had risen up on her toes and kissed him on the mouth. It was just a quick kiss, but a kiss nonetheless. Then she had pulled slightly back and looked up at him inquisitively, waiting for him to make the next move.

He had leaned in toward her and gently pulled her to him. She had smiled and blushed, but still looked up at him and gave no resistance. He could feel their bodies touching, and it almost took his breath away.

Catherine! Oh how my heart bursts for you! Evan's mind had reeled with the passion of the moment and the feeling of the girl's softness in his arms. She had smelled of soap and the smoke of firewood, and he loved it. He very slowly had lowered his face to hers. Her eyes sparkled in the sunlight and then fluttered shut as she waited for his kiss. He closed his eyes, and their mouths met again. This time the kiss was much longer, and their bodies became almost as one. Evan had never felt this way before, and he was lost in the pure pleasure of the moment. It seemed so right. She felt so good pressed against him.

And then, slowly, the kiss was over, and she had stepped back and out of his arms. She turned away from him, and, picking up the sheep staff with the crooked end, she walked briskly toward her farm.

He had remained frozen to the spot looking after her as she left him. Then, after she had gotten a few paces away, she had suddenly turned and pointed at him.

"I love ya, Evan Ryan. Remember that! There will be nobody else in all my life but ya!" she half-shouted.

Then she had turned back toward her house and began to run. The boy had watched her as she went across the field and disappeared over the hill. He had been stunned.

Could it be true? He had thought. *She loves me! She said it.* Then he had raised his face up to the sky and shouted, "And I love ya, too!"

* * * * * * *

The noise of the soldiers in the lane snapped him out of his brief dreaming. He knew Catherine was alone in the house caring for her brother, Little Thomas, while her mother and father were at Evan's house. It had been as far as they had gotten on their return trip from the village when the woman's labor pains had begun in earnest.

"Go to the O'Learys and tell Catherine not to worry," his father had said, gently pushing the boy out of the house.

And now he stood in the darkness of the shed's shadows as these drunken British soldiers staggered up the lane. *What should he do? What could he do? What would he do?*

CHAPTER 2
...and did the sheep watch?...

Catherine was joyous, almost giddy as she came into the little house. Elizabeth looked up and saw the glowing cheeks of her daughter.

"Running hard gives ya good color, girl," she said smiling. "Are the sheep all right?" Thomas O'Leary was known to have one of the finest, small flocks in the area, and both Catherine and Little Thomas learned early the expectations of their father.

"Aye, they are, Mother. And I spoke with Evan," she answered quickly. She knew her mother was aware of her fondness for the Ryan boy, a fondness born of growing up next to him and of knowing him perhaps better than he knew himself. Now, with the regularity of her power which, like the moon, came to fullness every month, her feelings for Evan had become different, but perhaps more recognizable.

"Ah, did ya now?" her mother said. "And will ya dance with him on Saturday?" she asked.

"Aye! I showed him how to do the steps, and he is a fast learner," she answered.

"And did the sheep watch?" Elizabeth asked laughingly.

"Aye, and they saw me kiss him, too," Catherine answered. She had always had an easy and open relationship with her mother, one that most girls her age abandoned when they reached the changing years.

"Ya did the kissing, did ya? And did he kiss ya back?" she asked.

"Aye, he did, and then I ran away." She left out the part about the second, more passionate kiss and what she had called out back to him.

"Well, my my!" Then she paused, thinking about what she would say next.

"They are a good family, those Ryans. I think he would make a good husband in a few years. Just be slow with him, Catherine. Boys and men need time to understand us women," she quietly said. "Often, they never do," she added.

Catherine smiled and looked down. She had observed her parents and their relationship, but with different eyes these past few years. Her father, Thomas, was clearly the head of the family, but she had noticed how her mother seemed to really be in control.

"Mother, I only want to make a place for myself in this world with a husband as fine as Father. I have known Evan all my life. If ya think he would make a good husband some day, I won't let go of what I feel for him," she responded.

Then, as if to change the subject, she asked, "Will ya and Father go to town tomorrow?"

"No, probably in two days. Your father still has to finish getting ready for the market."

"And the baby?" Catherine asked.

"I think it wants to be born. Maybe the wagon jolting will bring on the time," she said. "Just be ready to take care of Little Thomas when the baby comes."

Two days later Catherine's parents left in the late morning for the village about an hour's journey to the east. The little village was on the main road between Limerick and Cork. It was not very large, but it still had a small church, a public house and a few tradesmen's shops that served the local farmers for many miles around.

* * * * * * *

While Thomas O'Leary had some repair work done by Murphy, the blacksmith, his wife visited with a seamstress friend in the woman's front yard. By the middle of the afternoon, Elizabeth walked slowly along the narrow main street intending to trade fresh vegetables for some cloth to make a nightdress for the new baby.

As she passed John Burke's pub, a young and very drunken British soldier came roaring out of the doorway nearly knocking her down. Instead, he was the one who tripped and sprawled in the dust.

"Bloody Irish whore," he cursed, as he got unsteadily to his feet. "I'll teach ya to trip a British soldier."

He raised his hand to strike the woman when suddenly, from out of nowhere, a burly priest, Father Sean, stepped between the two.

"Ya'll not strike this good woman, young man," he calmly said. His voice was not loud, but full of authority. "Can ya not see she is heavy with child? Does the King know that his soldiers go about attacking defenseless women? Would your commanding officer like to know of your vileness? Will ya stand before God and defend your drunkenness?"

The soldier's hand dropped drunkenly to his side.

"Papist pig!" He almost spat out the words and lurched back into the tavern pushing past the priest and the still-shaken woman.

"Ya'll be fine, Missus O'Leary. Don't bother about him or his fellows!" assured the good Father. "Soon I'll be baptizing your new little one, aye?"

"Aye, Father Sean. It'll be soon for my time is quite near," she said.

Within two hours, the O'Learys were back on the road. As they neared the Ryan farm, the jolting wagon had brought about the expected result. Elizabeth O'Leary was in the full work of labor.

CHAPTER 3
...leave her alone...

Mary Ryan was known as a good midwife, a skill she had learned from her mother, Sarah Patterson. The Pattersons had lived in County Cork for two generations. The original family members had been among those Scots the English landlords had brought to their lands in southern Ireland to work the fields and pay rent, too.

Mary had met Michael Ryan quite by chance in Cork. Now they lived near his home village in the area to the northwest of Cork in County Tipperary. She had loved this big, gentle Irishman from the first, and even though marrying him meant moving away from the Pattersons, she did so gladly.

They raised most of the food they needed, and a good portion of their extra cash was supplied by the racing ponies that Michael bred and trained. He usually made a trip to Cork or Waterford on the Celtic Sea coast every year or two just to sell one to the British gentry who came there specifically to buy race horses.

Irish ponies from Tipperary were known to be fast, and his reputation as a good breeder and trainer always resulted in top money, even though the old Penal Laws prohibited Catholics from owning horses worth more than five pounds sterling. Still, those hated laws were being relaxed by the British occupation forces, and Michael was able to earn a good sum with every sale.

Mary Ryan's midwife skills also added to the family's larder; the families she assisted reciprocated with gifts of vegetables, some fresh fish from the local streams, or a sheep. Now it was Elizabeth O'Leary who needed Mary's skills. The midwife was ready to help her close neighbor and good friend deliver her third child.

"Bring her to our bed and get me hot water," she instructed as Thomas O'Leary came through the door half-carrying his wife. "The little one will be here soon enough."

For a few minutes, the room was a flurry of activity as the candles were lit, and the laboring woman was made somewhat comfortable on the bed. Mary turned to her husband and gave a stern nod of her head. Michael took Thomas by the arm and moved toward the door.

"Let's go into the barn for a spot and let these women do their work," he said gently. Then he turned and faced his own children.

"Evan, go to the O'Learys and tell Catherine and Little Thomas what is happening. Then get back here quickly and see that the ponies have feed and water." His tone was commanding but not harsh. "Timothy, ya come with us. Ana, stay and help your mother."

* * * * * * *

The ponies were still in the field, so Evan ran the entire way to the O'Learys. It was almost two kilometers. It was getting darker now, and there was no moon. But he knew the way well and soon saw the small light coming from the O'Leary front window.

It was when he neared the O'Leary outbuildings that he heard them coming up the road toward him. He slipped into the shadows of the first shed. He could hear the British soldiers talking very clearly.

The soldiers were quiet for a few moments. Then he heard the voice of the ugly one whose face was partially illuminated by the light coming out from the window. He was clearly the most drunken of the three.

"I'm going in that place and get me something," he sneered. Evan saw the soldier's silhouette as he half-staggered toward the door.

The boy realized the peril Catherine was facing.

Catherine, my Catherine. He thought.

Evan crept closer, staying in the shadows of the shed, and crossed quickly into the sheep pen near the farm house. *What should I do?*

He thought about yelling to Catherine, but it was too late for that. He saw the door open and the light stream out as the soldier pushed into the front room. He heard Catherine's short scream of alarm.

It was almost as though Evan was acting on instinct rather than from a well-reasoned plan. Slipping through the sheep-pen fence, his hand suddenly came in contact with the shepherd's stick that Catherine had carried the day before in the pasture. It was a sturdy, wooden staff about two meters long with a curved hook at the top. He grabbed it and raced across the short distance separating the house from the pen. Staying close to the front wall of the farmhouse where the shadows were deep, he burst through the half-open door.

"Leave her alone," he shouted, as he entered the small house. He raised the butt end of the staff, holding it with two hands, the crook part down. The drunken and surprised eyes glared at the boy, and then with a snarl, the soldier jeered at him.

"What have we here, now? Looking for a fight with a British soldier, are ya?" the soldier said.

"Just get out. We've done nothing to ya. Leave us alone." It did not even sound like Evan's voice. He moved closer to Catherine, trying to position himself between her and the soldier.

The Redcoat suddenly brought his right hand from behind his back. In it was the short sword that had been hanging awkwardly out of place from its usual spot on his hip.

"A stick against my blade? Ya Irish bastard! Ya think ya can stand and do battle with me, do ya?" he barked in a challenging tone.

"Ya have no business here. We've done nothing to ya. Just go. Please, sir," answered Evan. The last word stuck in his throat. It was too good for this man.

"Nay, boy! I'll get what I've come for, and my blade is out and won't go back 'til I've blooded it a bit." With that, he lunged drunkenly toward Evan, the sword coming across in a wobbly arc.

Evan deflected it easily, and, not knowing what to do next, he quickly hooked the soldier's left ankle with the curved tip of the crook. He yanked, and the man lost his balance and went down. The boy stepped on the blade arm, and raising his staff again, brought it slashing down on the side of the soldier's head. Then he heard Catherine's voice again.

"Evan!" she screamed.

Half-turning back toward the door, he was suddenly grabbed by a huge soldier and saw that a third man was coming through the doorway.

"Strike the King's men, will ya?" the big man growled into Evan's ear. His bear-hug grip was like a vise, and the boy was powerless to move. Behind him, the last soldier grabbed Catherine and began to wrestle the struggling girl down onto the dirt floor.

The first soldier staggered to his feet holding his head and a bleeding ear.

"Bastard!" he yelled and struck the boy with a closed fist across the face. Again and again, he hit Evan until the big soldier dropped the boy unconscious to the floor.

"Enough!" the bigger one said. "He's had enough."

* * * * * * *

The cold water dripping on his battered face brought Evan back to partial consciousness. He ached everywhere, and he could barely open his mouth. Blood streaked his shirt, and his lips and eyes were badly cut and starting to swell.

"There ya are now, son," his father's voice registered in his brain.

"Catherine!" he managed to say through clenched teeth. Then he lapsed into a world that was neither sleep nor consciousness.

CHAPTER 4
...understand what has happened...

When Evan finally did awake, it was morning. He was lying in his own bed slightly propped up on pillows. The bruising discolored his swollen face, and he did not look much like the son his parents remembered from the evening before.

Where was Catherine? He tried to get up, but his head throbbed painfully. His sister, Ana, came into the room.

"Drink this," she said as she offered a cup of tea and sat down on the bed next to him. It was not too hot and sweeter than he liked. But it felt good in this mouth.

The girl was very quiet. Unnaturally quiet.

"Is Catherine all right?" the boy managed to say through his swollen lips and still partially clenched jaw.

Ana got up quickly and left the room. Within a few moments, Michael Ryan stepped into the boy's view. His father was pale and looked as though he had not slept all night. His hands shook as he moved a chair to the bedside.

The older man remembered a scene quite like this some twenty-five years earlier when his uncle had told him of his own father's death at the hands of the British. It had been in a massacre that had followed the unsuccessful Irish Rebellion of 1798. The French fleet had not landed as planned in order to support the Catholic and Presbyterian Irishmen who had attacked the Anglican Irish and British forces in the area north of County Tipperary. His father, Charles, a surrendered prisoner, had been hacked to death.

Now he sat down, and with his own uncle's words on that day so long ago clearly in his mind, he looked at his young son. Then he began to speak, softly and very slowly, as if he was choosing his words carefully.

"Listen to what I am going to tell ya, Evan. I want ya to understand what has happened," he said, and then paused. He took a deep breath.

"Catherine is dead. Those soldiers killed her. We found ya late last night when ya did not return from the O'Learys to take care of the ponies."

His voice was quiet, but steady. He stopped speaking, and Evan saw that his father's lower lip quivered.

The boy tried to comprehend what he had just heard. It couldn't be. *No! No! She kissed me just two days ago and taught me to dance. No! No!*

"Dead?" he asked through his clenched, swollen mouth. Michael nodded.

"Noooooooo!" Evan screamed, and somehow his jaws opened. "No!" He tried to rise up out of the bed, but his father's hand steadied him. Then came the vomit. Again and again, he coughed it up, until there was nothing left but the dry heaving, and the warm tears that flowed unceasingly down his swollen cheeks until they, too, were dry.

* * * * * * *

Over the next few hours, he was told the whole story in bits and pieces, interrupted by his father's chores and the intervals in the telling that Michael gave his son so that the lad could digest all that he was saying and sleep, too.

What had happened was simple enough. Elizabeth O'Leary had a hard labor, but it went fairly fast. By midnight, she had delivered a healthy little girl. She was still in the next room but would be returning to her own home tomorrow with the baby. And yes, she knew of Catherine's death.

The night before, when Evan did not return from the O'Learys as instructed, his father had ridden over to see where he was. He had found the farmhouse door open and Evan lying unconscious on the floor.

Lying near him was Catherine. It was clear that she had been raped and, in the violence of the act, her throat had been crushed, and she had suffocated.

Michael had dripped water on his son's battered face, and, seeing that the boy was not in immediate danger, he had ridden back to his farm and then returned with Thomas O'Leary and his wagon. Together they had covered Catherine and prepared to bring Evan back home. It was only then that they remembered Little Thomas. They found him hiding behind one of the beds, his eyes fixed in a vacant stare and his body still trembling. The little boy had managed to say two words, "British soldiers." He had seen it all.

Father Sean was being summoned, and Catherine's funeral would be held in two days.

* * * * * * *

Michael gently awakened his son. It was almost evening, and the boy had been sleeping for most of the afternoon.

"There are neighbors here who want to speak with ya," he said. "Come outside with me, Evan."

He helped Evan get out of the bed. The boy ached all over, and his face was terribly bruised and swollen. He went outside with his father where three men stood waiting.

"Can ya tell us what they looked like, these British?" John Burke asked. He owned the pub in the village and was considered somewhat of an intellectual man because he had learned to read and write.

"I saw the one who beat me," answered Evan. "The others I only got a glimpse of."

"What did they look like?" he asked again, pressing the boy.

"The one I saw best was about Father's height but more slender. He had a sharp, pointed nose and a scar on his right cheek just under his eye. He was very drunk, and he was the one who was going after Catherine." Evan felt the anger beginning to build once again within him.

"I told him to leave, that he had no business in the house, and I even addressed him as 'Sir.' But he would not listen," Evan continued. His eyes began to tear up, and his voice got louder with the recollection of that night.

"What happened then, Evan?" asked Daniel Murphy, the local blacksmith.

"He came at me with his sword. I dodged it when he swung it at me, and I used the herding staff to pull his feet out from under him. When he went down, I hit him on the side of the head. That's when the second one grabbed me and held me while the first one got up from the floor and beat me." He tried to stay focused on the question, but he started to tremble from the memory of the event.

"Did ya see the one who held ya or the other one? And are ya sure there was only three of them?" Burke went on with the questions.

"I know that the one who held me was very big and strong. I only glimpsed his face from the side. He had a funny smell about him. I would recognize it if I ever smelled it again. I really didn't see the third man's face clearly, but he was a British soldier, too. They all were. I hate them," he said in a voice that started to crack.

"Aye, son! Ya did what ya could, Evan," said Daniel Murphy. "Ya did more than many grown men could or would have done."

"Aye! Your father and all of us are proud of ya," said Adam Murphy, Daniel's son.

"We know who those soldiers are," said Burke. He waited for Evan to understand the meaning of what he had just said.

"How can ya know this?" Evan asked, wiping his eyes and suddenly becoming much calmer upon hearing this new information.

Burke reached into his pocket and pulled out a brass button. It was stamped with a regiment number and a British lion.

"Only one group of soldiers wears these buttons. Thomas O'Leary found it on the floor. Catherine must have pulled it off one of their coats when she fought them. We know she put up a struggle. There was skin and a little blood under her fingernails." Burke was silent, waiting.

Oh God! Why didn't I do more? Then he thought, *That would be Catherine. Catherine. My Catherine. And now ya are gone from me forever. Forgive me, Catherine. I should have done more!*

Then he looked up and growled, "Bastards! British bastards! I'll kill them!" The boy was overcome with a cold rage he had not ever had before and which he did not recognize in himself. He had no tears in his eyes when he said the words, and his voice was steady.

The three men exchanged glances. They had seen this chain of events a number of times before. Then the older Murphy spoke.

"We'll be going to Cork in a month or so. Perhaps we can settle the score for Catherine. Would ya care to come along, Evan?" he asked.

"Will my father be going, too?" the boy replied, looking at his father and then back at the blacksmith.

"Oh, I think so! Him and Thomas O'Leary, for certain," said Murphy.

Almost as if they had rehearsed it, the three men suddenly turned and walked away from Evan. He watched them going down the lane toward the O'Leary farm. Then he turned and went back into his own home with his father.

CHAPTER 5
...a paler shade of light red...

Elizabeth O'Leary was grief-stricken at the loss of her eldest child. But she was strong; she had to be. Their lives would go on. There was Little Thomas to bring out of his shock and vegetables to harvest and the winter coming not too far off and a new baby. Her head reeled with the thought of it all.

She had seen this before, mainly as a child, this killing of Irish peasants with no law to stop it or punish the guilty ones. It had been going on for generations. Catholics and Presbyterians killed by the Anglicans and British troops, the occupiers moving unheeded throughout the countryside disarming the local farmers and then stealing their crops and animals, raping their wives and daughters, and torturing or killing whomever they pleased for whatever the reason. It would never end, so it seemed.

Now the great sadness had entered her own home. She needed to be strong. She would attend her daughter's funeral mass, and she would name this new baby after Catherine. It was proper, and everyone would understand and laud her for keeping the memory of her firstborn alive in the new daughter's name. Elizabeth O'Leary would be strong. She was strong.

* * * * * * *

Funerals always began and ended at the home of the deceased. With the help of neighbor women, Elizabeth got the little house ready as best she could, even supervising the preparation of Catherine's body.

Everyone said that Catherine looked beautiful, "like a child of God." There were no marks to reveal the trauma that had caused her death because of the high-collared dress Elizabeth had chosen for her daughter's burial clothes.

Crowds of neighbors filled the little farmhouse and

spilled out into the front yard. They were a strangely quiet group. When Evan arrived at the wake that evening, he noticed that the crowd silently parted to let him pass, and the men took off their hats to him. It was strange, and he felt uneasy about it as he entered the main room.

Inside, the full reality of Catherine's death immediately struck him. The candlelit interior was much brighter than it normally would have been. Catherine's coffin had been placed in the center of the front room and stood at waist height on two raised planks. Evan moved slowly toward it and stood quietly, his swollen eyes never leaving Catherine's face. He choked back the tears, and he felt sick.

Can I ever find someone as beautiful as ya? He thought as he looked down at her. *Can I not just see your eyes one more time? Who shall I dance with now? I love ya, Catherine. I will always love ya.* Then he noticed that her hair seemed to be a paler shade of light-red.

* * * * * * *

While it was not uncommon for there to be a good deal of wailing and loud crying at Irish funerals, it was surprisingly quiet in the O'Leary house. Many of the neighborhood women knelt by the coffin and said the Rosary.

The news had traveled fast, and all of the families in the surrounding area had come. Most brought food. Jugs of wine and ale, and a few bottles of whiskey were placed on the sideboard. The men drank freely but did not inebriate themselves as they might have if one of their adult peers had passed away. It was plain that they were showing respect for the dead girl and the way in which she had died.

But there were murmurings among the men. When will these British leave us alone? What right do they have coming onto our lands and doing these things with no law to stop or punish the offenders? These were old questions, and there were men present who felt that they knew the answers. A free Ireland is what they wanted, what they needed, and what was rightfully theirs to have. Some day they would make it happen.

* * * * * * *

Long after dark, Michael approached his son.

"We must leave now, Evan," he said softly. "The O'Learys and others will keep the watch all night."

His eyes filled with tears once again. He softly touched Catherine's arm and then her hair. Then he left.

* * * * * * *

The next day, as the funeral procession moved to the little village church, Evan walked close to the coffin which rested on one of his father's wagons. He kept his hand on it for the entire way. The O'Learys rode behind in their wagon because of Elizabeth's recent delivery. The new baby was in her arms and was surprisingly quiet.

The mass was short. Father Sean said the words, but Evan did not hear most of them. Only once did a thought register in his mind when the priest also referred to Catherine as a "child of God" who was "now with the Lord."

Where was God to help her three days ago? Why did not Michael the Archangel swoop down to protect her from the swine who had raped and killed her? Why did God give a boy with a shepherd's crooked staff such a responsibility? Why had God failed Catherine in her greatest moment of need? I failed you, Catherine.

He turned away when the men began to fill in the grave.

CHAPTER 6
...a silent tribute...

Evan sat in the front room of his house staring blankly at the wall. It was still late summer, and it was not cold. Still, he felt cold. Life would go on, but he knew it would never be quite the same again.

It had been the hardest day of his life. He had buried the only girl he had ever loved and before that love could ever come to fulfillment. And he had discovered that he harbored a coldness and rage that was totally new to him.

His thoughts were interrupted by the creaking of the door. He looked up as Catherine's younger brother, the one called Little Thomas, stepped quietly into the room. His shock had worn off, and he no longer trembled. But his eyes seemed different.

He was only seven years old and not a large boy. He stood motionless next to the partly open door and waited.

"Come in, Little Thomas," Evan said softly. The boy shut the door and sat down in a chair across from Evan. For a while, neither of them spoke, nor did they look directly at one another.

Then the little boy began to speak very quietly, almost in a whisper.

"I saw what ya did. They didn't know I was there in the room. I saw that ya tried to help my sister, and ya would have if them other two hadn't been there."

Evan did not respond. Suddenly, the images of three nights before began rushing into his head. The little boy continued.

"I saw it. I saw it. She fought them as good as she could. I never knew a girl could fight so hard. She scratched them and bit them and kicked and hit..." his voice was becoming louder and more agitated, "...and the one put his knee on her throat to hold her steady while the other ones...."

"Which one?" Evan looked up at the boy and screamed the words at him.

Little Thomas jerked back, clearly frightened by the unexpected outburst, and he began to shake again. He looked wide-eyed at Evan, not knowing what to do. His trembling increased, and his tears began flowing rapidly as he choked and gasped for breath.

"Which one? Which one held Catherine down?" Evan yelled. He was standing now and starting to cry with almost the same intensity as when his father had first told him of Catherine's death.

"Which one, Little Thomas? Which one held her down?" he screamed again as he began moving toward the boy, his fists clenched tightly shut.

"The one that held ya and then the one ya hit with the staff," the little boy sobbed out the words, his eyes wide with fright as he held up his arms defensively as though expecting Evan to strike him.

Evan, still crying, stared mutely at the boy and then slowly went the last few steps to him. Kneeling down, he put his arms around Little Thomas. They held one another and wept, their bodies shaking almost in unison.

"Thank ya, Evan," the little boy sobbed. "Thank ya for what ya did." In Evan's tight embrace, his trembling began to lessen.

What I did? I didn't do enough. Catherine is dead. She is gone forever. Oh God! Forever!

Suddenly, with that thought, his tears stopped; the cold rage seemed to take over his body. He patted Little Thomas on the back and gently pushed him away. Then he got up off his knees, walked over to the wall, and stood facing away from the boy.

They were quiet for some time. Little Thomas got up out of the chair.

"Will ya come home with me? I don't want to walk alone. There is food there," he said.

Evan turned and smiled. "Aye, Little Thomas, I will."

Together, they went out of the house to the horse corral where Evan mounted bareback and pulled the boy up behind him. In a short time, they were at the O'Learys.

* * * * * * *

There were still many neighbors sitting and standing around talking. The food was good, and the boys discovered that they were actually hungry.

As they ate, Evan noticed that the many neighbor women seemed to be looking at him, and when he met their gaze, he saw that they would nod at him in recognition. While they did not smile at him, there was a sad, soft kindness to their faces as they exchanged glances with him. It was almost like a silent tribute, and it unnerved him just as it had the night before at the wake when the older men took off their hats to him. It seemed so strange.

A short time later, after he had eaten, Evan was standing in the front yard and talking with the younger Murphy. Suddenly, one of the neighbor men walked over to Evan and, removing his hat, shook the boy's hand. He was followed by another and another until it became a steady stream of hand-shakers. It seemed to go on and on.

Most of the men said nothing. A few simply said his name in greeting, while others added "ya are a brave lad." The last one to come up to Evan was Thomas O'Leary.

"Thank ya, Evan," he said quietly and pulled the boy to him.

In the brief embrace, Evan thought. *Thank ya for what? For letting Catherine be raped, and killed? I failed your daughter. I failed you. I failed myself. Oh Catherine!*

Then the odd greeting was over, and John Burke was the only man left to greet Evan. Darkness was descending, and the crowd was thinning out. Burke shook his hand and said, "Come with me."

The boy followed him, and they walked away from the O'Leary farm buildings toward the forested hills that stood to the west of the first small pasture. Neither spoke as they crossed the field.

The woods were dark, but Burke seemed to know precisely where he was going. Deep into the trees, he suddenly slowed his steps. He moved to the right off the trail they had been following. About ten meters into the dense undergrowth, he stopped.

"What I am about to show ya will remain forever locked in your head. Ya will never reveal this to anyone. Not to any living soul. Do ya understand, Evan?" he asked.

"Aye, Sir! I do," the boy answered, looking directly at the older man, although in the darkness, he could not quite make out the man's face.

Burke parted some of the bushes and tangled vines and stooped low, almost crawling. Suddenly, a small opening in between some rocks appeared directly to their left, and he slipped through it. Evan followed him.

Using a steel striker and piece of flint, Burke quickly sent a shower of sparks onto a piece of charred cloth. A tiny bit of tinder suddenly burst into flame, and he lit a candle from it. The soft light revealed that they were in a small cave just tall enough for them to stand erect. While it was not very big, it was large enough to hold perhaps six or seven men.

Burke scraped the ground with his foot until he uncovered the corner of a piece of oilcloth. He handed the candle to Evan and carefully rolled the heavy cloth back. Under the canvas were flat boards which the man then spread apart just enough to reveal the hole underneath and the contents which lay buried in the cave's floor. The pit was stacked with muskets, pistols, lead, and cow horns that certainly contained gunpowder. It was a stash of weapons. He pointed down at them.

"Ya are now the tenth man to know of this place. Some day these British will pay for their crimes," he said. "When that day comes, men like ya will be part of the rebellion. I know it, Evan Ryan. I've seen it in your face. Ya are one of us now. We will protect our homes and families at all cost. Do ya understand me, Evan? We will protect our homes and families. Erin Go Bragh!" he added in old Gaelic. Evan knew that it meant "Ireland Forever!"

Burke replaced the boards and oilcloth and then smoothed the dirt over the floor of the small cave. Using a leafy branch, he rubbed out their footprints as they backed out. Soon they were walking back toward the O'Leary farm. Once again, neither of them spoke.

* * * * * * *

Evan rode home that night with Ana behind him on the pony. She clutched him tightly and laid her head against his back. His mother and father followed in their wagon with Timothy.

Later, as he and his father were unhitching the dray horse and putting it and Evan's pony into the corral, his father spoke.

"A lot has happened these past three days, Evan. The O'Learys will never be the same again. And I doubt that ya will be the same either."

Michael had never spoken this way to Evan. It seemed to be more of the type of conversation that happens between two men, not between a man and a boy.

"No, Father, I will not be the same. I am not the same. I feel it already," Evan replied.

"I saw ya talking with the Murphys and Burke. They are good men, but remember this: the things ya are experiencing now will be with ya all your life, and the things ya do now will affect ya for the rest of your life. Choose what ya do very carefully, and the harder it is to choose, the greater will be the effect it will have on your life."

Evan did not respond, but he thought, *I know, Father; I understand. And I still want to kill them. But Father, do ya know about the weapons in the cave?* He dared not ask.

CHAPTER 7
...I'll not dance with any girl...

Father Sean completed the mass. It had only been a few years since he established the parish. The British Penal Codes that had prevented open Catholic worship in Ireland for many years had been relaxed. His congregation was growing.

This is so much better than the way it used to be. He thought. He remembered the days not fifteen years earlier when he had to conduct mass using a boulder in a field as the altar. The rocks were always referred to as "shepherd's rocks" by the farmers. The name hid their real purpose from the British authorities. Now he had a real church. It wasn't much, only room for the altar and perhaps twenty people. But the front of the building was left open so that more could stand outside and participate. He smiled as he looked out at his parishioners.

It was surprising that so many of them were present, it being only a few days after the O'Leary funeral. And it had been the festival weekend in the village, and that usually meant there would be fewer men in attendance. But the inside and the front grounds of the tiny church on this particular morning were packed with local Catholics, and most of the area men seemed to be there, too.

* * * * * * *

On the previous evening, the dancing had been spirited, and the musicians had kept up the reels and jigs until late into the night. Hundreds of families attended, but for the close neighbors of the O'Learys, the mood was less festive.

Evan Ryan stood at the outside of the circle of dancers. His face was still a little swollen and definitely discolored, but it was returning to its more normal appearance. He watched many of the dancers fumble with steps and thought, *Catherine and I were better dancers. Much better! Oh Catherine!* He felt an ache deep within him.

His thoughts were interrupted by a girl's voice.

"Want to dance, Evan?" It was the daughter of John Burke, the pub owner. She was two years younger than Evan but a big girl, and the word was that she was already "old for her age." At least, that was the gossip among the young men of the area.

"I don't know how," he answered.

"Oh, come on! I'll teach ya," she said smiling prettily.

"No, I can't, and I won't," he answered and his voice was so cold and flat that she frowned and then turned and walked away.

I'll not dance with any girl but my Catherine, he thought. Then it struck him. *I can't ever dance with her again.* He turned away from the dancers.

"Evan!" It was the voice of the priest. He was usually present at the festivals, but he never danced.

"I wanted to speak with ya and did not have the chance the other day at Catherine's funeral," he said.

"Aye, Father Sean?" Evan answered.

"I understand that ya were there the night Catherine was killed and that ya tried to protect her. That was very brave of ya!" the priest said. Evan did not respond and looked down at his feet.

"I know these things must be hard for ya, but I want ya to be comforted by the knowledge that Catherine is with the Lord now. It was her time, and He called her to Him," went on the priest.

"We can't always have things the way we want them to be. The Lord works His wonders in mysterious ways," said the priest. "Remember that, Evan." The boy looked up at the man but said nothing. The priest turned and was gone.

>   *So, the Lord wanted Catherine, and so He made her die in a terrible way just so He could have her? And we should not question the mysterious workings of this Lord who loves us? What did she ever do to deserve such a short life?* Evan thought.

* * * * * * *

When Father Sean looked out at his flock on that Sunday morning, Evan Ryan was not there.

CHAPTER 8
...Erin Go Bragh...

There were ten of them altogether: Michael and Evan Ryan, Thomas and Little Thomas O'Leary, Daniel and Adam Murphy, John Burke, and three farmers from their neighborhood, Brandon McCombs, Shamus O'Toole, and Patrick Hughes.

They traded off walking and riding in the two wagons filled with fresh produce and the few blacksmith implements the Murphys had made for selling in Cork. It was an active port, usually full of British gentry and soldiers, too.

It was a two-day journey into the city, and they stayed one night in the shed of a farmer they all knew, a relative of Shamus O'Toole. This farm was a regular stopping place for the men from Evan's village, and the man was always glad to get the latest news from the area farther west.

By the afternoon of the second day, they had arrived in Cork. The group rented a room in a cheap inn where they all ate a good meal and then turned in for the night. All except the Murphys. They slept under the two loaded wagons, just for security.

On the next day, they sold all of their goods within the first six hours. Then they split up into small groups and went their own ways for the remainder of the afternoon.

Michael took the time to visit the race track just to keep up his contacts. His racing ponies were much in demand, but he would not have one, or maybe two, ready for sale until the following autumn. Evan was with his father, and so were the two O'Learys.

* * * * * * *

The group met at a different inn that evening, one unknown to Evan. They sat together toward the rear of the room and ordered their meals. While the mutton and potatoes were only fair, at least the ale was tasty.

The pub was a busy place, but it was dark and musty. The odor of the beeswax candles burning everywhere did little to mask the smell of the spilled ale and the food scraps which lay about on the floor.

They looked up when a commotion at the front of the pub interrupted their conversation. A small squad of British soldiers had entered the tavern. The men were loudly ordering ale, and their speech was affected by whatever they had already drunk.

Evan was sitting with his back to the front of the room and had not turned around to observe the red-coated group. Little Thomas's eyes suddenly grew wide, and the boy began to shake.

"Little Thomas, are ya all right?" Evan asked, noticing the boy's agitation. The other men in the group stopped eating and looked up at the little boy.

The older O'Leary leaned close to his son and quietly asked, "What's wrong, Little Thomas?"

The boy raised his finger and pointed toward the soldier group. "It's him," he choked out. "That's the one who hurt Catherine."

Evan grew cold. He looked across at his father and began to rise from his seat on the rough bench.

Michael Ryan, who was sitting next to Thomas O'Leary, quickly reached across the narrow table and grabbed Evan's arm. He sternly said, "Stay where ya are."

He took off his slouch hat and handed it across the table. "Put it on now, son, and pull it low over your forehead," he said. "Do not turn around."

Then he nudged Patrick Hughes, who was sitting on his other side, and very quietly said, "Change places with Evan."

To Evan he added, "Come to this side of the table, and keep your head down as ya do it. And don't be lookin' at them soldiers."

The two quietly exchanged places. Evan sat down next to his father and kept his head lowered as he had been instructed. The hat covered his face very effectively in the dimly-lit room.

"Are any of those soldiers the ones from the O'Leary place?" his father asked in a whisper. "Look up slowly and carefully."

Evan looked up under the brim of his father's hat and scanned the faces of about a dozen British soldiers. His eyes settled on a beak-nosed man with an ugly scar running down from his right eye. The coldness inside him grew stronger.

"The one on the left next to the barmaid is the one who beat me," he whispered.

"Are the others here, too?" his father asked.

Evan searched the other faces. The other two were not there as far as he could tell. He hadn't seen them too well that night, so he shook his head.

His father turned to Thomas O'Leary and whispered something that Evan did not hear. Evan was not shaking; he was not afraid; he was not uncertain about his identification, but he was cold.

Is this why all ten of them had come to Cork? Is this why Little Thomas is with us? Is this why we came to this particular inn? Did these men know something that they weren't telling him? He thought.

Michael Ryan looked at the others across from him and said, in a very quiet voice, "We will all stay right here and finish eatin'. One of the men who killed Catherine is among those British soldiers. We will wait for the right time. Tonight there shall be justice for Catherine O'Leary. Erin Go Bragh!" He said the last words just under his breath.

They were barely audible, but each of the men at the table heard him very well.

Not one man moved or spoke. Then Brandon McCombs smiled and said, "I'm going to enjoy this very fine last supper." John Burke snickered at the religious joke, and the group began eating again. Only Little Thomas seemed to have no appetite.

Within a quarter of an hour, their dinners had been eaten.

* * * * * * *

"More ale, gentles?" asked one of the barmaids. She was a tall, rather homely woman in her early twenties. "And was not the mutton good?" she continued.

"It is always good when it is butchered right," said Burke. "And give us one more round of this fine Irish ale so that we can remember this night rightly."

The nine mugs of ale came back quickly, and they settled their bill with the barmaid. The men drank slowly, and their conversation was very hushed. They spoke with one another about things they already knew the answers to, asking questions and feigning interest in the quiet answers that only served to take up time and not yield any important or new information. Clearly, they were biding their time, and all the while they kept their ears tuned to the activities of the soldiers at the front of the pub.

Finally, the soldier that Evan and Little Thomas had pointed out stood up. In a loud voice, he proclaimed that he was going out into the alley to "water the Irish cobblestones" and that maybe some colleen would find him with his pants down.

With a roar of laughter, the remaining soldiers watched him go through the door and into the street. They failed to take notice of the four men and a little boy who moved past them and out the door. They also never saw that the rear of the inn was also empty, the others from Evan's table having exited through a back door.

In the alley, the British soldier stood half in the shadows and urinated against the wall, his buff-white knee britches unbuttoned. Just as he was finishing, he suddenly found his arms being pinned behind him by two much bigger men.

"Aye, what do ya bloody think you're doing?" he cursed. "Take your bloody hands off me ya filthy peasants."

A kerchief quickly went around his mouth and was tied soundly at the back of his head. Then the two men behind him spun him around to face away from the dark alley. The light from the street revealed the man's face quite clearly. An ugly scar ran down from under his right eye and disappeared beneath the kerchief that was now keeping him from speaking.

Michael Ryan stepped in front of the man and asked quietly, "Do ya recognize this boy?"

He pushed Evan in front of the soldier and slid the slouch hat off of his son's head. The light from the street illuminated Evan's face.

"Do ya know this lad?" he asked again.

The soldier's eyes betrayed him. There was no need for him to even nod.

"Are ya sure this is the one?" Michael said to his son.

Evan never answered his father. He was experiencing the coldness that, since Catherine's death, had become part of him. His response came with his moving fist, which he slammed into the jaw of the restrained man. Another blow broke the soldier's nose, and blood began to run down the front of his uniform. A third blow came quickly and caught the soldier squarely in his covered mouth.

Michael stopped Evan from striking a fourth time. With a calming hand on his son's arm, he motioned to the others, and they all began walking deeper into the dark alley away from the street. The tight grip of the two farmers behind the soldier easily controlled him, and they half-pushed, half-carried him along.

They had gone only a few steps when John Burke said, "Wait, let me check his buttons."

He pulled a small folding-knife from his pocket, and quickly the button was held up and compared with the one found on the O'Leary floor a month earlier.

"It's the same," Burke announced.

The group moved deeper into the alley and around two corners pushing the struggling soldier before them. For additional security, Burke walked back toward the front of the pub. His way with words would certainly distract any soldiers who might come looking for their comrade.

In the alley, nobody spoke. The soldier was plainly frightened now that the odds were not in his favor. His nose still bled heavily, but with his arms pinned securely behind him by O'Toole and McCombs, he was helpless to stop the flow.

Michael was the first to speak. He merely said, "This is for my son who ya beat almost to death." He hit the soldier squarely below the ribcage. The man would have doubled over but could not. Then Michael struck him again, this time lower in the stomach, and then again.

Evan still felt cold, and yet he was strangely calm and detached from what was taking place. He felt no joy, no relief, no pity; only coldness.

The soldier was moaning now and was slumping so badly that the two farmers could no longer hold him up easily. They let him slip to the ground where he lay curled, holding his stomach and trying to put one hand on his broken nose.

Daniel and Adam Murphy rolled the man onto his back, and each took one of his arms and wrenched it out at his sides. Then they stood on the soldier's arms so that it looked as though he had been crucified onto the rough cobblestones that paved the alleyway.

At that moment, Little Thomas unexpectedly stepped forward and leaned over the man close to his face.

"I saw what ya did to my sister. Ya killed her." He spat out the words. The soldier looked up and saw the little boy and a look of perplexed non-recognition played across his eyes.

Thomas O'Leary gently pulled his son away from the soldier. He leaned down.

"Ya never saw him in the room, did ya?" he asked. "Take off the kerchief," he said to O'Toole.

* * * * * * *

Inside the pub, the British soldiers continued their drinking. Then one got up and said, "I'm going to see where Percival is. He shouldn't be this long in the alley."

Outside, after peering into the vacant alley, he approached Burke, who was idly standing up against the front of the building near the door.

"Hey, Irish! Did ya see a British soldier come out here?" he asked.

'Nay, but I thought I saw one going off that way with a young lady, don't ya know," replied Burke, who then nonchalantly lit his pipe.

"Aye, that sounds like Percival," the Englishman said.

The soldier went back inside, and a moment later Burke heard a roar of laughter from the front of the pub. He smiled and then turned into the alley and walked away from the street. In less than a minute, he had joined the others.

* * * * * * *

One by one, each of the men from County Tipperary knelt down and delivered one stout punch to the soldier's mid-section. With two men always holding his arms out, there was little he could do to protect himself. Even with the kerchief untied, the man only groaned with each blow that broke ribs and bruised internal organs.

Then Little Thomas stepped up and delivered a hard kick to the man's crotch. He howled with pain and vomited onto the ground. He was still conscious but unable to do anything more than lie there.

The group stepped back waiting for Evan and Thomas O'Leary to add their punishment. Evan shook his head and walked away. As if it had been planned, the men all followed him, leaving Thomas O'Leary alone with the beaten soldier.

Catherine's father stood over the man who was now trying to stop the bleeding from his nose.

"When I tell the rest of my squad what ya've done, they'll have their way with ya. Count on that, ya bloody Irish scum," he managed to rasp out the words.

Thomas leaned down close to the man and quietly said, "Well, then, we must not let that happen now, must we? Ya raped my little girl, and ya killed her. In our land, that is a crime, and the punishment is death."

As he said the words, he was pulling a long and very sharp dagger out of his boot. It was a knife that he used to slit the throats of sheep and goats, and he knew how to use it effectively. Without a moment's hesitation, he plunged it up into the man's chest just below the breastbone. With a quick motion to the right and left, the sharp, two-edged blade severed the main arteries coming out of the man's heart.

The soldier's eyes opened wide in surprise, and his hands grasped at the knife. His legs thrashed a few times, and blood gushed wildly from his mouth and nose. Then his legs were still, and his eyes became fixed in a wide-open, blank stare.

Thomas O'Leary wiped the knife on the soldier's coat and put it back into his boot.

"Erin Go Bragh!" O'Leary muttered as he walked away.

Nothing was said and not a question was asked when Thomas O'Leary met his friends a few minutes later. He simply grimaced at Evan Ryan and nodded. The evening was never spoken of by any of them ever again.

PART TWO

America: 1827—1828

List of Characters in Part Two

Michael and Mary Ryan—peasant farmers in County
　　　Tipperary, Ireland

　　　Evan, Ana, and Timothy Ryan—their children

Patrick Hughes—neighbor peasant farmer, son of Patrick
　　　and Zoe Hughes

English landlord—owns the lands on which the Ryans live

(Little) Thomas O'Leary—son of Thomas and Elizabeth
　　　O'Leary

Robert Delaney—originally from Dublin, Ireland;
　　　carpenter in Cincinnati, Ohio
　　Mollie O'Rourke Delaney—his wife

　　　　William Delaney—their son
　　　　John Delaney—their son
　　　　Robert Delaney—their son
　　　　Elizabeth Anne Delaney—their daughter

Lieutenant John Baker—officer in the U.S. Army; from
　　　New York State

Zachary Taylor—commander of Fort Snelling

Lawrence Taliaferro (pronounced "Tolliver")—Indian agent
　　　at Fort Snelling

John O'Toole—Hudson Bay Company clerk; originally
　.　from County Tipperary, Ireland

Antoine Toussaint—Montreal blacksmith
　　Marie Toussaint—his wife

Hole-in-the-Day—Ojibwe man

Patterson—a Scot from the Selkirk colony

Map for Part Two in Appendix I

CHAPTER 9
...I hope ya'll dance...

It was dark. Evan Ryan lay in bed in the tiny second room of the Ryan farmhouse. His little brother, Timothy, shared the bed with him and slept soundly, as did their sister, Ana, who had her own bed adjacent to the one of her brothers. The house was very small, but it was comfortable and relatively warm in the winter months. Michael and Mary Ryan had their bed in the main room.

The house was not much more than a two room hut built of rock and sod, and it was nothing fancy. The Ryans raised their own food, depending on the garden and flock for all their needs. It was mainly potatoes that they ate, with an occasional cabbage, turnip, or onion. On rare occasion, they butchered a sheep or a goat. Cash for other things came from the annual or biannual sales of race horses. Michael, his father, was known as having the fastest and best at the track in Cork.

I still miss her. Evan thought as he lay there. Catherine, his first and only love, was dead as the result of a savage rape by British soldiers. He thought of her constantly, and he still carried an enormous guilt that he had not done enough to save her from the terrible attack on the night that she died.

None of the other girls in the area interested him in the slightest. He never called on any of them, never walked with them, and never danced with any of them at the festivals which were held periodically in the village just a few miles away.

Not that he didn't look at them and find many of them attractive, and they him. To be sure, he noticed them as they danced, and occasionally he caught their scent when they had rubbed mint or flower petals on their necks and passed near to him. But most of them had given up asking him to dance. He seemed inaccessible.

He never met any of them after mass either. In fact, he had not been to church even once since Catherine's funeral, and that had been four years earlier. The words of the priest had been hollow for him.

Most of the farm people in that area northwest of Cork were Roman Catholic. Even his mother, Mary, who had been an Anglican in the south of Ireland in the area just west of the seaport of Cork, had converted almost twenty years earlier when she married Michael.

It all confused Evan, this religious separation. Both of the churches, Anglican and Catholic, had priests; they both practiced the sacraments, and they both told the same stories about a Jewish carpenter they called the "Son of God." Most Irish peasants knew very little about Church doctrine, and many were only mildly familiar with the rituals.

"A child of God," had said the priest about Catherine when he had performed her funeral service.

* * * * * * *

The next evening after supper, Evan found himself alone with his mother.

"Have ya thought more about leaving Ireland and going to America?" she asked him. She had planted the idea in her eldest son's mind months earlier, and they had talked about it often when they were alone. Now, with a trip to Cork planned for later in the week, she wanted him to more seriously consider leaving.

"Aye, Mother, I have. There is nothing for me here," Evan replied. "I have skills that I can use anywhere in the world, and America is full of opportunity."

He was referring, among other things, to the blacksmith skills he had acquired over the past few years by working often at the side of Daniel and Adam Murphy. They had taught him the rudiments of the craft, and he could shape iron and forge-weld pieces together quite handily.

He had also learned to make iron arrow points and repair black powder weapons, although those repairs were always done in secrecy.

Evan could also use the bow and arrow, and he was an excellent marksman with this old type of hunting tool. It was the only weapon most farm families possessed because many years earlier all of the Catholics in Ireland had been stripped of their muskets and powder by the British. That was one of the reasons the Irish Rebellion of 1798 had been so disastrous for the Irish. They had to fight with pitchforks, clubs, and arrows, while the British soldiers and Irish Anglicans were armed with Brown Bess muskets and cannon. His grandfather, Charles Ryan, had lost his life because of this disparity.

But Evan knew of the cache of illegal arms, and he understood that in due time there would be a use for them.

And, of course, Evan Ryan was an excellent horseman. He could help deliver foals when necessary; he could break a young horse, and he rode with the ease of any boy who had grown up on the backs of these animals. He even knew some trick riding moves and often demonstrated them to the delight of his younger brother, Timothy, and some of the neighbors who visited periodically.

"Aye, Mother," he repeated. "I have thought much about America."

Mary Ryan was quiet. She knew her son was now a man, and while it pained her to think of him leaving, she understood that she must encourage him to take his chances away from Ireland and the hard, peasant farm life that she and Michael had always known.

"When ya go to Cork this week, why don't ya see what the passage to America will cost?" she said. "Some of the young men from our area are leaving. Perhaps you'll meet up with those that ya know. If ya have the chance, take it and go, son."

* * * * * * *

Three days later Evan and his father got ready to leave for the city. They were taking two racing ponies, and they anticipated that the sale would be easy.

It was a two day trip to Cork, and they would once again spend the first night in their friend's shed. Then, if they traveled quickly, and if the sale was quick, they would make it back to the O'Toole farm late on the night of the second day. Three days would be all they would need to be away from their own little farm. This time it would be different.

* * * * * * *

Mary was quiet, and both Ana and Timothy sensed their mother's tension. She watched her husband and eldest son put the final things on the back of one of the horses.

"I have the feeling I shall never see ya again," she said to Evan as he turned toward her after adjusting the small pack on the horse.

Ana and Timothy could not believe what they were hearing. Neither of them had any idea about Evan's thoughts about leaving. They listened incredulously as their mother spoke to her eldest.

"If ya go, always remember us, Evan. Remember our names even when our faces begin to fade from your memory," she said. "Live well in America and make us proud."

Ana's breath caught in her throat, and a little cry signaled her shock.

She was a delicate girl of sixteen now, and the farm work was hard on her. Evan had often done some of the heavier chores that were really hers to do just because he knew they were difficult for her.

Evan turned toward his sister, a shocked look of disbelief plainly registered on her face.

"Ya are leaving?" she asked.

"Aye, Ana, if I can," he replied.

"But..." she started to say when he interrupted.

"Ya'll be fine, if ya are careful. Ya must take care of yourself, though," he said, enfolding her in his arms.

May God forbid that ya should die the way Catherine did! He thought.

They stood quietly. She began to weep softly, burying her face in his chest. He pulled back, and holding her at arm's length, he smiled and said, "Nay girl. Don't be crying for your old brother. Be happy for him. He's going to America, and some day he'll be rich."

"What am I to do without ya around," she said between her tears. She loved her big, older brother and suddenly understood that perhaps he would not be around any more to help and, if need be, protect her.

Hugging her to him a bit harder, he whispered, "Just always be on guard for your own safety."

Then he paused and said very quietly, "And do this for me: please tell the O'Learys that I shall never forget them or their Catherine."

The girl nodded and sobbed harder. Evan held her until her weeping began to calm.

He gave her a little squeeze, and then, releasing her, he turned to Timothy. The boy was now ten and a bright lad who was a quick learner.

"Take over my work, Timothy, and help Father all ya can. Some day ya'll be making the trips to Cork yourself," he said. He smiled at the boy and hugged him quickly. The ten-year-old was silent, absorbing it all.

Then, he turned back to his mother.

They embraced. "Mother!" It was all he could say.

"Some day, Evan, I hope ya'll dance," she said. Ana heard the words, and the ache in her stomach grew stronger, and she began to sob silently again. She knew exactly what her mother meant.

Oh! He still loves Catherine so. Ana thought.

For a few moments, the mother and son stood holding one another. Then Evan grabbed the bridle of one horse and started walking down the road away from the farm, not waiting for his father. He knew they were watching him, but he did not look back. He could not look back.

* * * * * * *

True to their expectation, the sale of the two horses was very quick.

"We've done well, Evan," said his father. "Just a bit over twelve pounds sterling for the pair. Shall we go now to the docks?" he asked, knowing full well the answer.

The port of Cork on the Celtic Sea separating England and Ireland was always full of trading ships. Many mills were beginning to spring up in the city, and cloth was a major commodity. The Industrial Revolution had hit southeastern Ireland and was changing the lives of many.

It was just past midday when the Ryans walked along the piers. Large bundles of cotton and flax were being unloaded from the ships that had just come in from the southern American states. Smaller bundles came off the boats coming from the northern reaches of North America, and most were stamped with the letters "HBC" and a number.

"Those must be Hudson Bay Company furs," said Michael. The packs were tightly tied, and all of the seams were sewn shut preventing any certain identification of the contents.

Finally, they arrived at a ship that was clearly in the process of loading. Bundles of manufactured goods were being slid and rolled up the gangplanks. Barrels of axe heads, iron bars and lead, cases of wine and high spirits, and even kegs of gunpowder went into the hold of the vessel.

"Hey Irish, want to work?" shouted a man in a frock coat who stood on the pier with a ledger book in his hand. He was recording the various cargo items being loaded.

"Is this ship going to America?" Michael inquired.

"Aye, it is. To Kanata," the man replied using the old Huron Indian name for the land north of the St. Lawrence River that was still controlled by England.

"Does it take passengers?" Michael continued.

"Perhaps," the man answered. "Who wants to go?"

"This lad," Michael spoke up, gesturing toward Evan.

"Aye! We could find a place for him if he had five pounds sterling," he said, certain that these peasants would not have anything close to such wealth.

Michael stepped forward. "Do you have need of a blacksmith on board?" he asked. "The lad can do that work."

"Aye, we do need one for the passage over and back. Can he fix broken rings and make flat iron pieces?" the man inquired, now plainly interested. He was the bursar for this Hudson Bay Company ship that was loading for the trip to Montreal, and he had just been told that the blacksmith they normally hired was laid up in Cork, sick with fever.

Michael exchanged glances with his son.

"The lad is good, kind sir. He can do that work easily and quickly. Hire him for the trip across, and ya won't be sorry," he replied.

"But he'll jump ship in Montreal, and I'll be stuck for a smithy on the return," the bursar said. He knew full well that the ship could make one crossing back to England without a blacksmith.

"Would three pounds in your pocket change your mind?" Michael asked quietly.

* * * * * * *

For over fifty years, the British had controlled most of North America with the exception of the eastern seaboard, which had successfully separated from England. That war for American independence had been costly in revenue, and the control of the land to the north of the new United States was vital to the English treasury.

The northern part of North America, Canada, was controlled by the British through the trading empire of the Hudson Bay Company. Huge numbers of furs and vast quantities of other raw materials, particularly lumber, came into England and into other continental European ports. The taxes on these goods, both the imports and the exported manufactured goods, provided a large part of England's revenue.

Another part of that national revenue came in the form of land taxes which the Irish farm families had to pay to their landlords, most of whom were absentee Englishmen. While the Penal Laws had been relaxed considerably by the 1820s, Irish peasants still lived a hard life.

What right do those who do not work the land have to collect money from those of us who do? Evan had often thought. It was a major reason why he had made the decision to leave Ireland, and now he stood on a dock in Cork listening to his father bargain with the bursar.

* * * * * * *

The bursar's eyes opened a bit wider, and he carefully considered his answer. He paused and scratched in his ledger. *Three pounds sterling in my pocket. Maybe I can get more!* He thought.

"This ship sails within the hour. Is he ready to go?" he asked.

"Aye, he is," answered Michael. "What passage fare would be reasonable if he works as a smithy for ya on the trip across?" He wanted it plainly understood that this would be a one-way trip.

"If he works and causes no trouble, I'd take four pounds sterling, Irish," the bursar replied, still not believing these peasants would have even that much money.

"Done!" said Michael quickly and reached into his shoulder bag to retrieve part of the money he had just made from the sale of the two horses.

"Father, no," said Evan just under his breath. But it was too late, and the transaction was completed in an instant.

The bursar was clearly surprised. He counted the money being offered, and then said, "Aye! Get your things, lad, and join the others up top. They are getting ready to haul up the sails shortly."

The bursar smiled at Michael. "Take a few minutes with the lad," he added. The man was a father himself and understood precisely what was happening before him.

Well, not all the British are cold, unfeeling bastards! Thought Michael.

Evan and his father stood on the dock. They were silent for a time, and then Evan spoke.

"Ya've known of my wish to go to America?" he asked.

"Aye, son, I have," Michael answered.

Then my talks with Mother have been shared with Father. Mother is a remarkable woman, to be sure. But does Father really approve? He wondered.

"Ya have taught me much, Father. I won't be forgettin' it. Give me your blessing on this, will ya?" he said quietly.

"Aye, son, I do give ya my blessing. Your mother and I have hoped ya would leave some day. Now, ya shall go. Just remember what I told ya when Catherine was killed," Michael said.

"About my actions, father?" Evan asked.

"Aye, son! The choices ya make when ya are young will be with ya all your life. And the harder it is to choose what ya will do, the more important will be its effect on ya. Remember that always," Michael said.

Evan had heard these words before from his father, and now the man was once again passing them on to his son. He had said the words slowly, almost as if they were sacred.

And in a way, they were sacred. Michael Ryan could give his son no great tracts of land, no flocks that covered the hillsides, or no fields of potatoes and other crops to make him a rich and powerful man. He could only give him the example of hard work and a few simple rules for living so that his son might have a chance at a good life wherever he was.

"I will, Father, I will," said Evan.

"Make us proud, son," Michael said as the two men embraced warmly. Then he turned and walked away from his eldest son. It was abrupt, only so that Evan could not see the tears forming in his father's eyes.

Ya are a good son, Evan! Michael thought, as he moved along the dock. *Live well in America! Remember that ya are a Ryan and make us all proud!*

CHAPTER 10
...a true flower of Ireland...

It was very early in the morning when Mary Ryan prepared the meal for her two remaining children. Once again, she worried about the safety of her husband and eldest son. Cork was a big city, and danger was always present there, much more so than in their small village in County Tipperary.

Still, she knew that her husband and son had to make the trip; there were two racing ponies to sell.

"Be careful, Michael," she had said to her husband. "Come back quickly. I do not like to be alone with Ana and Timothy."

It was the morning of the third day, and she knew that by nightfall Michael could possibly be back. But she somehow knew that he would be alone. Evan, her firstborn, would be on his way to America.

"Mother," said Ana, interrupting her thoughts. "Will Evan really go to America?"

"Aye, girl, he will. If the opportunity presents itself, he'll go for certain." She was sure of her intuition, and there was no reason to soften the words for her daughter. Ana might be delicate of build, but she was strong of character. Like her mother!

* * * * * * *

Ana Ryan was a true flower of Ireland. She was not tall, nor was she raw-boned like many of the neighbor girls her age. In fact, she was rather slender, and the farm work was always hard for her. It was one of the reasons why her older brother had usually done the more difficult chores for her.

She was a very pretty girl, if one took the time to really look at her. Her eyes were blue, and her hair was a light shade of brown, becoming even more blonde in the summer sunlight. She had a straight nose and very white, even teeth. And her complexion was flawless, smooth, and not ever too sunburned.

"Ya remind me of my mother, Sarah," said Mary once. "Ya look more Scottish than Irish." Then she had laughed, and Ana had blushed.

But her pretty face was not her most outstanding quality! Instead, it was the quiet and demure way in which she carried herself. When speaking with adults, she had the habit of looking down, never meeting their eyes. And when she laughed, she always covered her mouth with her hand.

She was soft-spoken and appeared shy and for that very reason, while other girls her age were dancing and carrying on at the village festivals, Ana was usually passed over by the local boys. They almost never asked her to dance, and none of them came to call either.

Only one boy, Patrick Hughes' son, who was named for his father, had seemed to notice her. It happened at mass the last Sunday morning not a week earlier. Their eyes had met as they left the little church, and he had smiled at her and nodded. No words were spoken between them, but his eyes told Ana of his interest in her.

* * * * * * *

"What do ya think of the Hughes family?" she had asked her mother on the way home from church.

"Aye, the Hughes. They're good folks, Ana. And their son, Patrick, is a fine lad," her mother answered. "Why do ya ask?" she said, correctly guessing the reason for her daughter's question.

"I was only wondering," Ana responded. "He smiled at me when we were leaving the church last Sunday. I was only wondering."

Careful, girl. Mary thought. *Sounds like me the first time I saw your father.*

* * * * * * *

He came as expected. The wealthy Englishman who owned the land being farmed by Michael Ryan and his family appeared as he always did in the early autumn to collect his rent.

"Have you got the money, Ryan," he asked when Michael met him at the gate to the front yard of the modest farmhouse.

"Aye, most of it, sir," Michael answered. "I'm a bit short this year, but I have a good wagon-load of potatoes and onions ya may have to make up the difference."

The money he had paid to the bursar for his son's passage to America reduced his cash, and he knew that he needed to come up with a full rent payment.

"I have no need for that," he said. He was not a hard man like many of the English landlords, and he had come to know the Ryans fairly well from his annual visits. This time he had another idea in mind.

"I would like to take your daughter to England with me," he said. "My wife is often bed-ridden, and she could use an upstairs maid. If the girl comes with me and works for us, the rent will be forgiven for this year and the next."

Unlike earlier times, the English no longer simply kidnapped Irish peasants for whatever the reason. Some of the more reputable landlords were trying to have a more congenial relationship with their tenants.

Michael was shaken. He had not seen this coming, and the idea of what amounted to two years of work as an indentured servant for his daughter had never entered his mind.

"May I have some time to speak with Ana and her mother?" he asked.

"Aye! Do so, and I shall return in two days. I've not long here in Ireland, and I'd like to take the girl with me when I leave from Cork. I have noticed her these past few years, and she seems bright and hard-working." He did not add that Ana was also growing into a very pretty young woman whose manner was quiet and respectful. *She'd make a good upstairs maid!* He thought. *Very good indeed!*

* * * * * * *

Timothy was out at the pens doing chores, and Ana and her parents sat at the table in the main room of the little farmhouse.

"What do ya think?" Mary asked her daughter.

"My feelings are mixed, Mother," Ana answered. "I would go if it helped ya and Father. I'm not sure I want to be away from ya."

"Is there any other reason to hold ya here?" Mary asked, knowing that her daughter just might have an interest in Patrick Hughes, the neighbor boy who was just a few years older than Ana.

"Aye, there is!" Ana said. "There are some who I might never see again." She said the words softly and lowered her eyes like she always did when speaking with adults about things that were very personal or important.

"Ya must choose for yourself, Ana. Your brother is gone, but we will make do without ya," her mother said. "Think about it. The landlord will be back in two days, and we can owe him the rest of the rent if need be. But remember! The choices ya make when ya are young will be with ya all your life. And the harder it is to choose what ya will do, the more important will be its effect on ya."

After Ana left the room, Mary looked at her husband.

"Do ya think we are doing right by allowing Ana to take this position with our landlord if she chooses to?" she asked.

Michael was thoughtful for a time.

"I don't like the idea of Ana being an upstairs maid. But he mentioned his sickly wife, and he has always been a decent chap to us. I think his motives are proper," he answered. "But it must be Ana's choice."

* * * * * * *

Ana Ryan could not sleep. For two nights, she tossed in her bed with the prospect of becoming an "upstairs maid" for an English lord running through her mind.

What does it mean? She thought. *If I go, it will help Father. Perhaps I should go! But if I stay, I will see Patrick, and perhaps I will like him. Mother said they can make the rent somehow if I stay.*

The whole thing disturbed her greatly. By the morning of the second day, she had come to a decision.

* * * * * * *

Just as he had said he would, the landlord returned very early in the morning.

"Have you made up your mind about the girl, Ryan?" he asked immediately. Just then, Ana stepped out of the farmhouse. She carried a small parcel that contained her meager belongings.

"It looks as though you have," he said smiling. "It's a good choice, Ryan. I can use this girl, and your rent this year is now forgiven and all of next year's as well. Are you ready, girl?"

"Yes, sir," Ana replied softly, her eyes cast down at the ground. Then she turned and embraced her mother, who had come out of the little house behind her.

Mary Ryan held her daughter. "Remember what Evan told ya," she said. Ana nodded, fighting back the tears as best she could.

"Aye, Mother, I will. I shall be safe. Tell Patrick that I am so sorry to be leaving," she said. It was all she could say, and she turned away. She stooped to quickly hug her brother, Timothy. He was taking it all in and was silent.

Her father, Michael, gave her a brief embrace and suddenly she was on the wagon moving away from the little peasant hut she had always known. She kept looking back until it was out of sight.

I have made this choice, and it is hard to do. She thought.

* * * * * * *

Michael watched his only daughter until she was out of sight. Then he turned to his wife.

"Have we done right to let her go?" he asked.

"Aye. We have," she answered. Then she added in a voice that was strong with conviction, but tinged with pain.

"We have strong children, but now two are gone."

Then she put her hands to her face and wept. It was a scene young Timothy would never forget.

CHAPTER 11
...a new life was about to begin...

Patrick and Zoe Hughes' only child moved through the thick underbrush. He followed Little Thomas O'Leary. It was well past sundown, but the darkness was illuminated by a nearly full moon that seemed to dodge in and out of the night clouds.

"Here it is," said Little Thomas. He was now eleven and still quite small for his age. He was a very quiet lad, but smart. He was frequently gone from the house during the night and seemed to know everything that was going on in the area. And, he usually kept to himself, even in the company of other boys his age. The death of his older sister four years earlier still plagued him. The neighbors said that it had changed him and that his eyes always "looked different." They seemed to have a vacant, unemotional appearance.

The two ducked into a small opening between two rocks. Little Thomas struck a flint and steel, and in a moment they had a candle lit which illuminated the small cave in which they stood. The younger boy quickly uncovered the cache of weapons hidden under the dirt of the cave's floor. He took out two black powder pistols, two small leather bags of lead balls, and two smaller horns of gunpowder.

"We'll find good use for these," he said, and then covered up the pit again.

* * * * * * *

It had been in the late afternoon of the very day that Ana Ryan had left with the landlord when young Patrick Hughes came to call on her. It was the first time he had ever done so, and he was surprised to discover that Ana was gone. He was very clear about his intentions when he spoke to Michael and Mary Ryan.

"I shall go after her. I'll not threaten your agreement with the Englishman, but I shall follow her," he had said.

"My intentions are honorable, sir, and I will try to persuade her to become my wife some day soon, even if I must go to England myself and work for the man, if that's what Ana agrees to."

His words came rushing out and caught Ana's parents totally by surprise. But his honesty was at once apparent, and Mary quickly said to the big farm lad,

"Then go to Cork and do what ya need to do."

* * * * * * *

Patrick was on the road to the port city, the unloaded pistol concealed under his loose peasant shirt. The small parcel he carried strapped across his back contained a few articles of clothing wrapped around the powder horn and the small bag of ammunition.

He had never fired a pistol or musket before, but he had been told the procedure of loading and cautioned about the possibility of misfiring. Not many men in his neighborhood admitted to being familiar with such weapons, and his inquiries had been met with many negative responses. Then, he had spoken with John Burke and had asked him about how to load and shoot the weapons.

Patrick had worked occasionally for John Burke at the tavern. He was very bright and had learned the basics of handling money. He knew the different denominations and how to make change, and he understood the concept of banking, although he had never been inside a bank. While he could not read, he could recognize the meanings of the written signs inside the little tavern and the names on the various bottles. These skills would serve him well, and sooner than he could have imagined.

Burke smiled when he heard Patrick's request, and then spent some time with the nineteen-year-old out behind the pub where their talking would be safe from other ears. Even in 1827, the threat of British retaliation for owning illegal weapons was still paramount in the minds of many Irishmen. Neither of them knew that Little Thomas had been hiding nearby and had heard their entire conversation. He had gained an understanding of the weapons as well.

* * * * * * *

Patrick traveled all night and arrived in Cork the next afternoon. He began by searching the inns for signs of the landlord and Ana Ryan. He came up with nothing, and even though he had been without sleep for over a day, he moved to the dock area, inquiring about which ships were leaving for England.

Then he saw her. He almost didn't recognize the girl; it was getting late in the evening, and the ship was scheduled to leave on the tide which was just coming into the harbor.

Ana was standing at the railing of a vessel bound for Liverpool. She looked different. Her clothes appeared new, and her hair was styled in a manner that he had never seen. She was looking across the dock and recognized him immediately. Her face registered a look of shock, and then, composing herself, she gave him a nod. With a discrete gesture, she pointed to a man standing about a meter away from her looking off in a different direction. Her expression had changed from happy disbelief to one of strained concern.

Turning toward the man and seeing that he was now walking slowly away from her engaged in a conversation with another Englishman, she once again looked at Patrick who was standing on the dock below her. Using her hands, she gestured for him to wait. Then she moved silently away from the Englishman toward the gangplank.

In a few moments, she was on the dock standing next to her neighbor, the boy she thought she might have feelings for and whom she never ever expected to see in Cork. Or perhaps ever again, for that matter!

"Patrick, what are ya doing here," she said. They had moved and were standing behind some large stacks of packaged goods out of view of the Englishman.

"I couldn't bear to have ya leave, Ana," he blurted out. Then he reached for her, and they melted into each other's arms in a close embrace that was more of relief than anything else.

She smells so sweet! He thought.

Oh my! He smells like he has been on the road for days! But he came here for me! How wonderful! Ana thought.

For a moment, they held one another; it was the first time they had ever touched at all or even spoken for that matter. Then, a commotion on board the sailing vessel interrupted them, and they peered around the stack of bundles. The Englishman was yelling loudly and pointing at the merchant officer who was higher up at the helm of the ship. The naval man shrugged his shoulders, and the Englishman moved toward the gangplank.

"If ya don't want to go, Ana," said Patrick, "ya don't have to. Come with me now, and we'll run! Your mother and father know I have come for ya."

He looked directly into her eyes. His eyes were questioning, pained and frightened, but full of affection.

Patrick Hughes was not a handsome man. He was a big, strong boy for being only nineteen and a little on the rough side. But his direct gaze into Ana's eyes was as honest as his words.

Mother always said that a man's eyes told you what was in his mind and heart. Ana thought.

The girl hesitated. She wanted to stay in Ireland, but she had agreed to go to England as an upstairs maid in exchange for two years of rent-free living for her parents. But now she felt that there would be more expected of her by the landlord than either she or her parents had originally envisioned. Michael and Mary Ryan might be peasant farmers, but their values were high for themselves and their children.

As she stood looking up at Patrick, she remembered what the last day had been like.

* * * * * * *

Ana and the English landlord had arrived in Cork early in the evening of the previous night. The wagon had been pulled by a double team of horses, and the trip had been accomplished in one long day of travel from the Ryan farm.

The girl had been taken to a ladies' salon where she had bathed, and her hair had been cut and put into a very tight wrap. New clothes were provided for her, and when she looked in the mirror at the final result, she almost did not recognize herself.

She emerged from the establishment alongside the English landlord. She looked more like a middle class lady than a simple Irish farm girl. Every man who passed her on the street leered. Their looks unnerved her, and she did not like or appreciate the attention.

Then the landlord had taken Ana to an upper class inn where they had enjoyed a fine dinner. She had refused the wine and high spirits offered by her new employer and drank only tea. She had been quiet during the meal. This was all so very new to her.

After dinner, he escorted her to another inn where he had provided her with her own room.

"I must take leave of you now," he said. "There is a game I must attend. I feel that my luck is very good tonight."

The Englishman then left. He had taken up his lodging in a better inn a few blocks away. Ana spent the night in peaceful sleep, her door bolted soundly.

The next morning she had awakened and was, at first, frightened by the strange surroundings and the sounds from the street below. She washed, put on the new clothes, and went down to the main room below. The English landlord was already sitting there.

"Ah, Ana," he said. "You look lovely. I was very successful last night at gambling. I'm sure it is due to your presence here. Tonight, we shall be on the ship to England, and soon you shall be my special upstairs maid." He said the word "special" with a peculiar tone, and he had a strange look in his eyes.

By midday, they were on board the ship, waiting for it to sail on the evening tide. Ana was struck with the clear understanding that a new life was about to begin for her. In fact, it had already begun, and she was not sure she wanted it.

* * * * * * *

Patrick's eyes searched her face. She was frightened and confused about her potential trip to England, and yet she was comforted by the unexpected concern and tenderness evidenced by the arms and words of Patrick Hughes.

She paused, and then simply said, "I do not want to go to England. I will go with ya, Patrick."

His eyes softened. "Then we shall run. I don't want to go there either," he said. He took her hand, and they walked briskly away from the docks and down the first alleyway they came to.

As they moved quickly down the narrow passageway, they heard footsteps behind them. Looking over his shoulder, Patrick saw the Englishman running after them. They started to run, too, and he pulled Ana along with him. It was getting darker now, and Patrick was not sure where he was. He turned at the next intersection. The second alley led them back to the docks.

"What shall we do?" said Ana, who was running out of breath.

"I don't know," answered Patrick.

The sound of a cannon firing signaled that the tide was ready to carry those outgoing vessels into the sea. Many of the merchant ships still practiced the old naval custom of shooting powder charges as they prepared to sail, and the sounds of many muskets now began to fill the air. Setting sail was like a celebration.

The Englishman rounded a corner and approached the couple.

"So, you intend to leave, do you?" he said. "I'll not have it. You'll come with me now, girl." He grabbed for her.

Patrick stepped in front of the man and deflected his reach for Ana.

"Nay, Sir. She's not going," he said.

The Englishman looked at the young man and laughed.

"You are not going to stop Ana from leaving, and if you think you can, I'll have the authorities take you. Is that what you want?" he said. His voice was starting to take on a threatening sound.

"Now, leave her with me and be gone," he barked.

He moved forward to grab Ana's arm again.

"No," said Patrick forcefully, and he unexpectedly struck the man hard in the jaw. The Englishman staggered, his knees buckled and a look of shock and surprise spread across his face. Patrick struck him again, and he went down onto the dock.

They were in a little hollow square formed by packs and barrels of goods, and they were out of sight from any ship's deck. The edge of the nearly deserted dock was to their left, and seawater lapped at the pilings. The sound of musket volleys continued to make a racket.

"We must go. Now!" said Patrick. The couple turned back toward the alleyway and began to walk quickly away from the Englishman, who was now trying to get up onto his knees. From out of the darkness in front of them stepped a familiar figure.

It was Little Thomas O'Leary. The boy gave no sign of acknowledgement as he passed them. His eyes were focused straight ahead of him. They stopped and watched him kneel behind the Englishman, who was holding his face and still trying to get up. Then Little Thomas turned toward them and waved them away.

As Patrick and Ana turned and walked back down the darkening alley away from the dock, the sound of a single pistol shot went unrecognized in the din of the blank rifle volleys still being fired all along the waterfront.

* * * * * * *

A few minutes later Ana and Patrick were joined by Little Thomas.

"The Englishman will make no more trouble for ya," the boy said. His voice was flat, and his eyes had that strange, vacant look for which he had become known.

The boy held out a long and very heavy money belt. "Take this. I have his other purse. There's plenty in it for me to buy more weapons, sure enough."

"And this fell out of his coat sleeve," he added, holding up a playing card.

Patrick took the thick leather belt with the hidden pocket on the back side and began to open it. Ana looked down and watched him fumble with the lacing. When they looked up a moment later, Little Thomas had disappeared.

* * * * * * *

Patrick and Ana were astonished. They had never seen so much money. It appeared to be hundreds and hundreds of pounds sterling. Patrick quickly closed the belt's rear pocket and concealed the bulky strap beneath his shirt. He took Ana's hand, and they began moving out of the alleyway into the streets of Cork.

* * * * * * *

They walked slowly around the city all night long, afraid and not knowing quite what to do next. They talked quietly, and by the time morning had come, their plan was set.

They stopped first at a clothing store where Patrick bought three outfits of men's wear that appeared to be of the same quality as the new apparel Ana was wearing. Then he went to a men's barber shop where he had a bath, a shave, and his hair trimmed in the latest fashion.

Ana sat in a small inn across the street, sipping tea and waiting for him. When he came up to her table a little more than two hours later, he looked entirely different

* * * * * * *

Ana Ryan and Patrick Hughes spent that next night in the same middle class inn where they had met after his transformation. They ate an early dinner there, and then went up to the room they had rented.

There was only one bed, and it was awkward at first, with each of them taking off their street clothes. Patrick put on a new nightshirt he had purchased, and Ana wore only her shift. Sleep came to them almost instantly because they were so fatigued by the events of the previous day and night. For Patrick, it had been more than two days that he had not slept.

The next morning the couple awoke at almost the same moment. Ana was snuggled up against Patrick's arm with her head on his chest. Her stirring brought him out of his sleep.

She looked up at him and smiled. He smiled back at her, and then quickly got out of the bed and moved to the dressing area at one corner of the room. It was partially shielded from view by a self-standing, painted screen.

He put on his new clothes and stepped back into her view. Passing before the mirror that hung over the small chest, on which sat the wash basin and pitcher of water, he caught sight of himself. Once again, he was surprised at his new appearance.

While Ana used the dressing area, Patrick washed and then sat on the bed. He counted the money in the belt more carefully. It was a staggering amount of paper money, well over three thousand pounds British sterling.

"Did you say that your landlord was a gambler?" he asked Ana.

"Aye!" she answered.

"Well, he must have done very, very well last night," Patrick said. "This is a huge amount of money."

* * * * * * *

He had left his peasant clothing at the barber shop, but kept the small bundle containing the pistol and its needed supplies. This special bundle he had placed unopened in a medium-sized piece of leather luggage that he had also purchased at the clothing shop. It held the pistol and small powder horn nicely, as well as the other clothing items he had bought. Now the luggage sat on the floor next to the bed.

He buckled the money belt securely to his body under his shirt and buttoned up the waistcoat. Then he stood.

"We have enough money to go to America if ya want," he said to Ana. "But, we can speak of that later. Right now, I'm hungry and I need to eat."

Boys! Always hungry! She thought and then smiled.

They went downstairs and sat at a table on the first floor of the inn to have a late morning meal.

"What do ya think, Ana?" he asked between bites. "About America?"

"I shall go where ya take me," Ana said lowering her eyes.

"Aye, Ana. I want to marry ya if ya'll have me. I shall try to be a good husband to ya and treat ya right all my life," he replied.

Ana did not know what to say. *I think I like him, but I hardly know him.* She looked down at her plate, feeling the redness flush up her neck and across her face.

Then, not pressing her for an answer, he added in a very hushed voice, "We must leave Ireland, I fear. We have enough money to buy our passage, and I think we should leave as soon as we can. Will ya go with me?"

The choices ya make when ya are young will be with ya all your life. Her mother's words rushed into her thoughts.

Ana Ryan softly answered, "Aye!"

* * * * * * *

Late afternoon found them on board a passenger ship bound for New York City in America. It was a ship that had left England and made the one stop in Cork before crossing the Atlantic Ocean. It was called a clipper ship and was noted for its speed. Patrick had paid the entire one-way fare for each of them. They occupied a first-class cabin, and they still had a very large amount of money in paper notes remaining. They would need to masquerade as a young, middle-class, Irish couple going to America. It hardly seemed possible.

CHAPTER 12
...Queen City of the West...

Cincinnati was a fairly large city in the 1820s, and it bustled with activity. Located on the northern bank of the Ohio River, it was a natural stopping place for the many boats coming down the river on the way to the Mississippi, and it was a focal marketplace for the region's farmers.

Most of the boats were a flatbed, raft-styled craft with a rear rudder for steering. They were poled along when the current was not strong enough. The rafts were large enough to hold one or more family's goods under a shelter that was usually built in the middle of the boat. While not a fast means of transportation, river traffic was increasing steadily every year, and the number of emigrants moving west was swelling. The various types of crafts often needed repair.

Because the "Queen City of the West" was a major place for making the necessary repairs to the vessels, carpenters and blacksmiths were always in demand. Robert Delaney possessed wood-working skills.

Originally from Dublin, he had come to America just before the Irish Rebellion of 1798. Being a Catholic in that city had been difficult, and he distrusted all of the Anglicans and British who were in control.

Arriving in New York, Robert had made his way to Cincinnati and had apprenticed himself to a master carpenter who primarily did flatboat repairs. While not a large man, he had a good eye for wood, and he quickly developed the more specific skills necessary to become an asset to his employer.

However, his most important attribute was his ability to size up a job and accurately predict the amount of time and material it would take to complete the work. His employer, James Wilcox, came to depend on Robert for his keen business eye and his gregarious, friendly rapport with the traveling families whose rafts needed servicing. Largely due to Robert's talents and personality, the Wilcox business was good.

Robert married a local girl, Mollie O'Rourke, and the children came quickly. They were all sons, three of them until the birth of Elizabeth Anne. Born in 1810, the little girl was, at first, the light of the household.

"She is the first Delaney girl in three generations," Robert proudly exclaimed as he showed off his little daughter to neighbors. But while her special status in the family was never threatened, it was expected and understood that her brothers would take over the business.

* * * * * * *

By 1820 Robert's apprenticeship had long expired and, because Wilcox was a bachelor who had no children and was getting on in years, the business quite naturally began to be controlled by the Delaneys. It was financially very successful, and the Delaney family enjoyed a standard of living that was a bit above that of most laboring and trade families in the city.

By the time James Wilcox died in 1822, the boat repair business was slowly being supplanted by furniture-making. Many of the farm families from Ohio and Indiana who sold their produce in the river city often lacked some of the finer pieces of household furniture. The Delaney's shop was noted for its high quality. It was still called "Wilcox and Company," but it was totally a Delaney enterprise, and it was beginning to ascend to even greater heights.

One by one the Delaney sons married, and for little Elizabeth Anne, life revolved around her mother. The girl was her mother's constant companion.

Her mother, Mollie, was a kind, little woman who practiced the arts of midwifery, and her special talents were much sought after in the tradesman community surrounding the Cincinnati dock area.

But by the time Elizabeth Anne had reached her teenage years, she found her life less and less satisfying, and she saw no prospect for a successful marriage. By 1827, she was seventeen, and while small for her age, she had become a lovely young woman. Many of the local tradesmen's sons came to call on her, but she was uninspired by their talk of how they were "doing well in father's business" and hoped to "inherit a good place in the world."

Make your own place in the world! She always thought when she listened to their comments that were designed to impress her. *Don't depend on your father for your future.* They bored her so.

And she began to feel increasingly alone in the world. She would not inherit any of the Delaney furniture business because it would pass to her brothers. None of the illiterate men in her immediate neighborhood interested her. After all, she had learned to read and write and do numbers, and she had been taught the midwife skills by her mother.

I can make my own place in this world! She thought.

* * * * * * *

By 1827, Indiana and Illinois Territories had both already become states, and this signaled that the lands to the west were open to emigrants wanting to own their own land and who were willing to take a chance with the elements and the Indians.

The American government had already surveyed much of the land between the Atlantic seacoast and the Mississippi River. The British troops that had once occupied the major forts in the Great Lakes area were long gone, replaced by American army units. Many of these American soldiers traveled on the Ohio and Mississippi rivers to their new assignments.

It was one of these soldiers, a young officer named John Baker, who first caught the eye of Elizabeth Anne.

* * * * * * *

John Baker had been born in New York State near Albany. He was from a moderately wealthy family of merchants, and his early education was accomplished by hired tutors who were boarded in the Baker home. He was a smart boy, and because his father had been a Revolutionary War veteran, he quite naturally gravitated toward a military career. He signed up with the United States Army at the age of eighteen and did his military training at West Point on the Hudson River.

His leadership skills were recognized right away, and John rose to the rank of lieutenant. As an officer who specialized in engineering, the basic course offered at West Point during those years, he understood that if he were married he would gain certain benefits that were not offered to the rank-and-file soldiers in the regular American army. However, his first duty assignment had come so quickly that he had had no time to find a suitable wife in New York. He was still a single man when he began his trip down the river and into the west.

John arrived in Cincinnati in September of 1827, and as was common, his boat stopped for repairs. He first saw Elizabeth Anne when she brought the noontime food to her brothers, and he was attracted to her immediately. Not only was she small and pretty, he found that she was quite comfortable speaking with him and that her conversation was neither trivial nor patronizing. She was very different from the many other young women he had met in recent years.

* * * * * * *

Lieutenant Baker was not hard-drinking and uncouth, the way most of the other soldiers in his command were. Rather, he was extremely mannerly when in the presence of women and girls. His rough, military personality only came to the surface when he was with his troops.

It was one of the reasons Elizabeth Anne was swept off her feet by this handsome young officer. Within two days, they were walking about the city together. She even invited him to dinner on a number of evenings, and it was clear that both of her parents liked the congenial young officer. The couple's fondness for one another was growing by the hour.

It took almost two weeks for the carpenters to finally declare that the flatboat was unworthy of any further repairs. The military company was transferred onto one of the new steam-driven paddlewheel boats that had been built in Cincinnati. It was scheduled to leave the next day on its trip down the Ohio River and then up the Mississippi to St. Louis. Autumn was in full color, and the boat needed to get to its final destination in Minnesota far to the north before the winter ice locked up the waterways.

* * * * * * *

John and Elizabeth Anne sat on the front porch of her home on the evening before his departure.

"Will you meet me at Fort Snelling next spring and become my wife?" he suddenly blurted out during a lull in the conversation.

It caught the girl totally off-guard. She liked this young officer. She liked him a great deal. He was good at conversation, and he had read all of the great books, it seemed. He was handsome, kind, and most importantly for Elizabeth Anne, John Baker was making his own place in the world, and she sensed that he would be successful.

Elizabeth Anne needed to fulfill her own destiny, by herself and by her own choices. She had long ago decided that she would not be stuck as a tradesman's wife in this river city that was so full of drunkenness and uneducated dock workers.

"I will," she answered after a pause, "if my father will approve." She might have been her own woman, but she respected certain proprieties that she knew needed to be honored.

He kissed her. It had been a soft kiss—one that spoke of the promise of a new life. Then they went into the house to speak with Elizabeth Anne's parents.

*　*　*　*　*　*　*

The meeting with Robert and Mollie Delaney was short.

"I do give you my blessing. Who will do the marrying?" Robert asked. "How will you get there safely, girl?"

"The fort commander has the civil authority to perform marriages, sir," John replied.

"I suppose I'll take a boat, Father," the girl answered. The next morning Elizabeth Anne watched John Baker's paddlewheel leave the dock area. She waved and called out, "Watch for me in spring." The young lieutenant smiled and waved back. Then he was gone.

*　*　*　*　*　*　*

Later that day, Elizabeth Anne and her mother sat talking.

"You will make a life for yourself," said Mollie. "You have always been a bit headstrong and certain of your own abilities, and you have always been able to hold your own against your older brothers. You have an independent streak in you that I have watched grow stronger every year. And you are often impetuous. I'm not surprised that you will be leaving."

"You have taught me so much, Mother, and I know I can always use those skills," she said, referring to the midwife procedures with which she was very familiar from first-hand experience at the side of her mother.

"Yes, those many nights when you were with me delivering babies will some day serve you well," her mother answered. "Military wives will always have children, so you will be able to put your skills to frequent use. And you are good at it."

"John seems to be a considerate and kind man," the girl said, changing the subject. Her mother nodded in agreement.

Then the daughter added, "But it may take some time for me to learn to love him. I think that it often takes a while for real love to come about between a man and a woman."

Mollie smiled. Her only daughter was wise beyond her years.

* * * * * * *

The Cincinnati Diocese covered a very large area and was dominated by Irish, Polish and German Catholics. Many of its member parishes and various convent orders were springing up all across Ohio, Indiana and Illinois. One of the first things the Church had to do was to familiarize its members with the basic doctrine. Many were immigrants and knew nothing about the doctrine and rituals. By 1819, St. Xavier Catholic Church had been built in Cincinnati. It had only a few hundred members.

There was also an effort to spread the Church into the northwestern territories known as Wisconsin and Minnesota. Churchmen were going regularly into the new territories, and with luck, Elizabeth Anne would be able to travel safely to John Baker's duty assignment at Fort Snelling. It was a new military post located in the Minnesota Territory at the confluence of the Mississippi River and the St. Peter's River. Catholic influence was already well-established in that area.

A visit with their local priest yielded some important information. It seemed that there were two new priests coming to Cincinnati from the east, and they would be going into the Minnesota territory in the spring. Along with them would travel a number of Grey Nuns who would be setting up a convent near St. Anthony's Falls. Elizabeth Anne could travel with them. It would be safer that way. It was great news because her father's concern for his daughter's safe travel would be satisfied.

* * * * * * *

All throughout the winter months, the mother and daughter prepared diligently for the latter's leaving. Certain family things that Mollie wanted Elizabeth Anne to have were packed carefully into a leather case called a portmanteau. The girl's clothing and some new wool blankets were bundled into a square canvas pack which was then sewn shut and tied with rope around the outside. By the time spring had come, the young girl was ready for her journey.

"I want you to have this," Mollie said to her. She placed a small crucifix on a chain around her daughter's neck.

"Do what you must do in your life, but remember us always," she said.

Elizabeth Anne hugged her mother.

I won't forget you, but I can't wait for the boat to leave. She thought. *I will have a totally new life.* Little did she know that it would be a journey that would take her to new places and to a life she could never possibly have imagined.

CHAPTER 13
...Is there something wrong with me?...

What am I doing? Here I am going to a place I know nothing about to become the wife of a man I have only known for a fortnight. What am I doing? Then Elizabeth Anne smiled.

It was the spring of 1828, and she was traveling on a flat-bottomed paddlewheel steamboat. She was to meet Lieutenant John Baker and become the military wife of an officer in the United States Army. She was excited.

She was not traveling alone. In the company of two priests, the nuns having changed their plans and stayed in St. Louis, she still felt reasonably safe. And quite by chance, she had met a girl who was her same age and who appeared to be with her husband. She had met the couple on the docks in Cincinnati as the paddlewheel was loading firewood, and now the three of them had struck up a warm friendship as they traveled together. They were all headed for the same destination.

Elizabeth Anne learned that the young couple's names were Ana and Patrick Hughes. They were from Ireland, they said, and had been in the United States for only a short time.

From their speech, Elizabeth Anne was fairly certain that they were probably uneducated farmers. But their clothes appeared relatively new, and they seemed to have plenty of money. It was curious, and Elizabeth Anne wondered how such young and, she presumed, illiterate immigrants could afford the luxury of steam travel.

* * * * * * *

"Have you been in America long?" she asked Ana quite nonchalantly as they sat on the bow deck of the paddlewheel. It was very late in March, and the weather was almost balmy. The sun was comfortable, and the breeze brought new smells as the boat moved upriver from St. Louis. Patrick was at the rear of the vessel, and the young women were alone. Their conversation was very private.

"We arrived in New York late last fall from Ireland. The crossing was a bit rough, and we was sick much of the time. This is smooth traveling compared to our crossing," Ana answered. She spoke softly, as was her habit, and did not look directly at Elizabeth Anne.

*　*　*　*　*　*　*

It had been exactly as she had stated. Ana and Patrick had purchased their passage on the dock at Cork, and the ship had left that very same October day of the previous year. It had been a fairly fast crossing on the clipper ship, but the Atlantic was always rough that time of year, and not being accustomed to sea travel, they had both spent most of the time in their cabin. They had taken almost all of their meals there and so never spent much time with the other passengers.

Anyway, they had both felt uncomfortable conversing with people that were clearly a few steps above their social strata. After all, they were engaging in a bit of a charade, and they worried that they might be found out for who they really were. There was also the question of the large amount of money Patrick carried.

The passage across the Atlantic had been hard on them for another reason. It had to do with the close sleeping arrangement in the tiny cabin. Although they had traveled first class, their cabin was very small, and they had spent weeks together in the confined space. There was little that they did not know about one another by the time they reached New York City, and their friendship had been established easily and naturally.

Still, Patrick had not touched her in any way beyond a chaste kiss. While she slept under the covers of the small bunk, he had remained on the outside, simply pulling the blanket over him as the weather got colder. Very often, he had gotten up and paced the floor of the tiny room rather than succumb to his desires. The same thing happened during the winter months they spent in New York. It had been difficult for them both.

Why does he not touch me? Ana often thought. *Is there something wrong with me?*

Then Ana began to think of it as an indication of just how kind and thoughtful this Irish lad from her own neighborhood in County Tipperary really was. She was falling desperately in love with him as the weeks passed.

* * * * * * *

"How long have you been married?" Elizabeth Anne asked, probing for more information that might clear up her assessment of the young couple.

"Actually," said Ana shyly, dropping her eyes and voice even lower, "we have not yet had the blessing of the Church. Patrick mentions it often."

"Well, there are two priests on board. I will be your witness if you like," Elizabeth Anne responded. The two young women had grown fond of one another, and Ana knew of the other girl's plan to wed an American Army officer at Fort Snelling.

"I would like that. We have both waited for the right moment. Would ya speak to the Fathers for me?" Ana asked. She was thinking of all those nights of frustration sleeping next to Patrick, and neither one touching the other in an intimate way.

When will he truly make me his wife? She had often thought.

* * * * * * *

Elizabeth Anne had spoken to both the priests, and Father Clement had offered to perform the ceremony. The next afternoon it took place on the bow of the boat as it moved gracefully along the river.

"I shall always love ya," Patrick said to her later in the evening when they were alone in their quarters. "I shall protect ya, and I only ask that ya be my friend always."

"Isn't that what we agreed to before the priest?" answered Ana, surprised at her own boldness. She smiled and looked directly into his eyes. "And I do love ya, too, Patrick. Very much."

She reached for him, and this time the kissing did not stop. Ana Ryan and Patrick Hughes soon became man and wife, and there was nothing wrong with Ana Ryan Hughes.

CHAPTER 14

...I shall avenge you...

If the passage across the Atlantic had been hard for Ana and Patrick on the clipper ship, it was fifty times more difficult for Evan Ryan. The ships were not the same. Theirs had been a sleek, fast-moving vessel designed to make the trip across the Atlantic in as short a time as possible. Evan's ship was the older style that lumbered slowly through the seas. It carried cargo, and time was less important than the successful, safe delivery of the manufactured goods that packed the hold.

More importantly, the couple traveled in first class accommodations, while Evan worked as the ship's blacksmith. Evan could never have guessed that his younger sister was making the same journey at about the same time that he was.

Evan had said goodbye to his father on the dock at Cork and boarded the large cargo ship. It had been difficult to leave the man who had taught him so much over the past eighteen years. But he knew that this was the right choice, and he was glad to be going to America.

The merchant marine officer on the top deck had shown him the quarters below where he stowed away his small parcel of personal belongings. Then Evan went immediately to the blacksmith forge in the rear hold just to look things over.

The blacksmithing area was not large. A supply of charcoal in barrels stood adjacent to the forge. It had a foot bellows, and there were the necessary hammers, tongs and other tools of that trade hanging nearby. The entire forge area was raised from the floor of the ship on a foot of sand. Evan understood at once the reason for this; fire on board a ship of the ocean was the most feared of all calamities. There was no place to go if the ship caught on fire and burned to the water line.

The ship lurched as the sails filled, and the nightmare for Evan began. Within six hours, it was rounding the southeastern coast of Ireland and moving toward the dark, open Atlantic. By then, he was sick, and while it got better as the days went by, he was never entirely well.

* * * * * * *

The hold where he slept stank of rotting produce. The open slop buckets into which the crew vomited, urinated, and defecated daily added to the stench. Only the burning forge offered Evan any relief from the foul odors, and he was glad to be busy.

Most of the time, he worked at the forge. He mended broken rings used in the rigging, and he crafted all kinds of special iron pieces that were needed "up top." He usually saw only the maritime officers who came below to order the repair work or the new pieces from him. He was good at his work and fast, and the officers complimented him on his efforts. He was so busy that only during the evening hours was he able to venture up onto the deck.

It was on one such night that he saw the man. He almost did not recognize him, but the coldness came over him at once, and he was sure of his first thoughts.

It is the soldier that held me that night. He thought. *The bastard helped kill Catherine.*

Evan Ryan had been only fourteen when he had tried to protect the neighbor girl, Catherine O'Leary. He had been unsuccessful, and the girl had been savagely killed in the attack. Now, one of those responsible for her death was on the ship.

He was sure of his identification, even though he had never directly seen the soldier's face that night four years earlier. The man had been big, and his steel hold on Evan had immobilized the lad while another soldier had given him a severe beating. Evan had managed to turn just enough to get a side-look at the man. He had seen enough of his face to be sure that this was the same man. But it had been the smell about the soldier that Evan had never forgotten.

Evan went back down into the hold to his hammock where he slept. He turned toward the wall of the ship and tried to sleep, but the words of his father coursed through his head denying him any rest.

"The choices ya make especially when ya are young will be with ya all your life. And the harder it is to choose what ya will do, the more important will be its effect on ya. Remember that always." Evan was awake most of the night.

* * * * * * *

Over the next few days, he purposely stayed at his forge. Most of the food was prepared on another deck, and a young Irish boy named John brought the wooden bowl to him twice a day. The big ex-soldier never ventured into Evan's part of the ship, and for that, Evan was glad. He began to forge a special piece of iron bar.

He really had no need to worry that he would be recognized because now Evan looked quite a bit different than he had that night at the O'Leary farmhouse. His beard had grown full, and although he kept clean-shaven, his hair was longer and darker, and his jaw had taken on a more squared look. He had filled out and stood nearly six feet tall. His arms were powerful from all the farm work he had been accustomed to, as well as the blacksmithing hammering he had done under the tutelage of Daniel and Adam Murphy.

But even though his physical appearance had changed somewhat, the biggest change was in the coldness he had acquired as a result of Catherine's death. That coldness had once again taken over his very being, and it drove him on as he labored hour after hour at the hot forge.

He had considered his father's words, and his decision had been made. Four years earlier, Thomas O'Leary had given his daughter some justice. This time Evan Ryan would be the one to exact the retribution. Catherine would be avenged.

* * * * * * *

"Who are the officers on the deck above us?" he had asked John. His Irish friend was only a year younger, but this was his second voyage to North America, and the lad knew a great deal. He worked as a galley helper and waited on the officer's tables at their mess some two floors above.

"Most are British seamen," John answered. "But some are former British soldiers, especially artillerymen. They are the ones the company hires to defend the ship if there is an attack by an enemy ship or by pirates. We've got a squad of them with us, don't ya know."

"What do those men do with all their time?" Evan asked.

"Most of the time they clean the cannon, and every day or two they fire practice shots," John replied. "But most of the time they just get in the way. Why do ya ask?"

"Oh, I was just wondering," Evan said.

* * * * * * *

Over the next few days, Evan continued to work on the flat piece of metal when he was not mending ship hardware. By heating and re-heating it, pounding it, and then grinding it on the wheel that sat adjacent to the forge, he was slowly turning it into a very sharp knife.

His friend, John, brought him a piece of wood that had formerly been a used as a lanyard tie-down. It was a wooden peg, and it was thick. It had been broken and was in the refuse pile only because it could be burned in either the below-deck cooking fire or at the forge. These wooden pegs were correctly called belaying pins, and Evan was able to cut it. Then, by using a drill that was part of the blacksmithing tools hanging near the forge, he fashioned it into a handle for his new blade.

Evan had observed that these naval pegs were used all over the railings on the top side of the ship and that the seamen were very skilled at throwing them. In fact, they often competed with one another and bet heavily on the outcome of their throws at a circle target drawn on one of the exterior cabin walls. It was a necessary skill because the pins were often used as weapons by the merchant seamen in the defense of their ship and its cargo. This gave Evan a different idea, and he weighted the new knife very carefully.

He finished it using the belaying pin as the handle and carefully bent the protruding tine so that it formed a small hook at the grip end. When it was completed, Evan found that he had made a very serviceable throwing knife. Its balance was perfect. Now he needed accuracy, and over the next week, he practiced throwing the heavy blade.

Day after day he threw the knife against a tiny target drawn in charcoal on the hull of the ship. Within two weeks, he could stick it in the center every time. But he noticed that his distance to the target needed to be exactly correct. A step forward or back resulted in a bad throw.

Then he began to regularly venture out onto the open deck during the evening hours. *I need to know how I can make my plan work,* he thought.

* * * * * * *

"If he works and causes no trouble," the bursar had said to his father on the day Evan left on his voyage to North America. It had been five weeks, and Evan had caused no trouble. In fact, he had done exceedingly well as the ship's blacksmith, and he had stayed out of the way of the merchant seamen who sailed the lumbering vessel across the stormy Atlantic.

But now he was about to do what he needed to do, what he had to do, and what was right for him to do. *I shall avenge you, Catherine!* He thought, and he threw the weighted knife once more. It hit dead center on the tiny target and buried itself deeply into the inside wall of the oaken hull.

CHAPTER 15
...one of my best tricks...

Almost four weeks had passed since Evan had first seen the ex-soldier on the deck of the Hudson Bay Company ship. He had finished the throwing knife, and he could stick it every time into the center of the small target near his forge. Now, every night he spent time on the main upper deck of the ship, and he had familiarized himself with all of the lanyards and rigging ropes that were attached to the deck railings. He felt ready for the final piece of his plan.

He had carefully sketched out that plan in his mind. He was not going to be simply reacting to a situation as he had on the night Catherine was killed. His lack of a plan then had cost Catherine her life, he felt, and he still carried the terrible guilt that she had died because of his lack of planning.

It was a foolish thought. A fourteen year-old boy with a crooked shepherd's staff against three sword-wielding soldiers was no contest. Then, months later he had turned away one night in the alley in Cork and let Catherine's father deal with another of the soldiers who had killed her. This time it would be different. He would control this situation, and he would be the one to avenge Catherine O'Leary. Evan Ryan was now ready.

* * * * * * *

The storm lasted for almost two days. It was finally over, and Evan stood alone on the deck in the late evening looking out onto the ocean. The silver-white foam from the bow coursed past him far below. It looked lovely in the light of the half moon that peeked out occasionally from the clouds of the night sky.

You were so lovely, Catherine! He thought. *Oh, how I still miss ya!*

A noise to his left brought him out of his reverie. Three men were coming out onto the deck. They carried cups in their hands, and it was apparent that they had been drinking.

A daily ration of rum was always provided to British navy seamen, and the practice continued on all of the merchant ships as well. Usually, only one cup was distributed with the evening meal. But the captain occasionally ordered a second and third if the crew had weathered a storm or otherwise distinguished themselves in some way. With the storm now passed, this was evidently the case.

"It's a grand night," said one of the men as the trio stood about five meters away from Evan, who kept his head turned away from them.

"Aye, 'tis! And this rum tastes good. My belly has been bad these last two days," said another. The three laughed.

"Tomorrow we will fire again," said the third. "I've cleaned the cannon, and we need another round of firing. We'll do it in the morning."

Evan was startled. He recognized the voice. He could never forget it. *"Strike the King's men, will ya?"* the big soldier had said as he pinned Evan's arms that night in the O'Leary farmhouse. Then the other soldier had beaten Evan into unconsciousness.

Now, Evan had just heard that voice again. The coldness came over him, and he moved away from the men, silently slipping into the shadow of a longboat that was lashed to the upper deck. The men paid no attention to him. To them, he was just another merchant seaman.

"I need another cup," said one of the men after a few minutes. He turned and started back toward the door of the stairs that led to their quarters one-half deck below.

"I'll join ya, seein' as how the captain has been so generous," added another. Evan peered around the side of the longboat and saw the two going through the doorway. The bigger man, the ex-soldier he remembered from the O'Leary farmhouse, now stood alone.

Evan was wearing britches and a long shirt. He was dirty from all the work he had done at the forge earlier in the day, and his face was smeared with soot. Around his head, he wore a scarf that came down over his forehead almost to his eyes and that was knotted at the back. Tucked into his belt at his back and under his loose shirt was the throwing knife he had made. He approached the soldier.

"It's a good thing that storm has passed," he said, as he came near to the man. The moon was hidden behind the clouds, and it was fairly dark.

"Aye, 'tis. We'll be firing again on the morrow," the big man said, looking out at the water and wanting to immediately establish his prominence as an artilleryman. "Are you a seaman?" he asked.

"Nay, I work below. What are ya drinkin'?" Evan asked, edging closer to the man as if to look down into his cup.

"Rum, of course," he responded.

Then Evan smelled the odor he had remembered so vividly for the past four years. He had never been able to identify the smell, but now he recognized it. The big man reeked of spent gunpowder and of the soap that was used to clean the barrels of the cannon. His clothes were spattered with the dried leavings of the swabbing and polishing that artillerymen were always doing to their guns. That smell, and the odor of the rum he had been drinking, his face and the sound of his voice were all that Evan needed to be certain.

This was him. He raped and helped kill Catherine. The moment has finally come. He thought, and he stepped back away from the man.

"Ya don't remember me, do ya?" he said. He was moving backward, counting the steps and reaching behind and up under his shirt.

"Nay, I don't. Should I?" the man answered, starting to turn toward the lad.

"Aye, ya should. County Tipperary. In Ireland. In a small farmhouse! Ya held me while your friend beat me. Surely, ya remember!" he said. He was back from the man exactly seven paces.

"Then ya raped a girl there on the floor." His voice was getting louder with each word. The coldness was upon him, but he was totally in control of himself and of the situation.

The big man was studying the face of the young man who now stood a bit away from him. The half moon appeared from behind the clouds for a few seconds and cast a soft light on Evan's face.

"Aye, I do remember the night. She was only a colleen and worth bloody nothin'," he answered, using the English slang term for "Irish whore." Then, he dropped his cup in the anticipation of a fight.

"Her name was Catherine, and ya killed her." Evan said the words very slowly so that the man would understand the seriousness of the moment.

It did not seem to unnerve him in the slightest.

"So what are ya going to do about it?" he said with ridicule in his voice. He was now facing Evan very directly.

Evan's hand came up from behind his back without a moment's hesitation. With one fluid motion, he threw the knife straight at the big man whose chest provided a large target. It would have stuck true in the center if the ship had not suddenly lurched slightly the moment Evan let go of the blade.

Although it was not a killing strike because it was off a bit to the right, the heavy knife still went deep into the man's chest. The man howled and grabbed for it, pulling it free and dropped it onto the deck, blood quickly soiling his shirt.

"Irish bastard," he yelled. He paused, trying to stop the flow of blood, and then lunged for Evan.

Evan turned and raced for the opposite side of the ship, the big artilleryman coming slowly after him, still trying to stop the bleeding. The moon came out again, and the deck was suddenly flooded with light. Evan knew precisely where he was going. He saw the ship's edge coming up in front of him, and he saw the lanyard lying loosely on top of the railing, just as he knew it would be.

Tonight would not be as it had been the night Catherine had died, when he had no plan. This time he knew exactly what he would do, and he had every contingency covered. He had gone over the moves again and again in his mind, and had looked over this deck area many times. He was prepared if the knife did not do the killing, as had just happened.

As he neared the edge of the deck, he turned and faced the soldier who was now about half-way across the ship's deck. Evan grabbed the rope that lay on top of the railing with his right hand. It was wrapped securely on two of the wooden naval pegs that were fitted down into their slots in the railing, but loose enough for him to grab onto it tightly. It was the way a saddle cinch would have been on the sides and underbody of a horse.

He reached back with his left hand and unhooked the latch on the deck rail that was immediately behind him. This section of the deck's railing actually served as a gate. It was hinged because it was the spot where the gangplank attached for loading and unloading the cargo.

The big man was almost to him and coming faster. Just as he got to close enough to almost touch Evan, the boy moved to the right and vaulted up and over the railing.

The soldier never expected to see the boy jump overboard, and he lunged forward to grab him. In doing so, he leaned against the unlatched railing. Under his weight and the speed with which he hit it with his body, the gate simply opened, and the man plunged screaming into the dark water below.

Evan was now dangling on the side of the ship holding on to the lanyard. Just as he would have done if it had been the side of a horse, he swung himself up and back onto the side railing of the moving ship. He straddled it like he was riding.

Horse-hopping has always been one of my best tricks! He thought as he peered down into the black ocean water. He loosened his grip on the rope and jumped down onto the deck.

He walked to the other side and, looking around, spotted the cup the man had dropped. He threw it overboard.

"Enjoy your rum, English bastard!" he said under his breath. Then he added, "Erin Go Bragh!"

He looked again at the deserted deck, picked up his knife, took off his head scarf and wiped the blood from the knife with it. He looked at the deck for more blood, and finding none, he went below and burned the scarf in the forge. Then he slept.

* * * * * * *

The next day there was talk among the seamen. An artilleryman was missing. A loading gate was discovered to be only partially latched, and one of the ship's officers presumed that the man had leaned up against it and that it had given way. While foul play was not uncommon on board ships of the sea, everyone seemed to accept this explanation. Evan slept peacefully every night after that.

* * * * * * *

One week later, the ship entered the mouth of the St. Lawrence River. Now, the sailing was much smoother, and with most of the blacksmith work done, Evan spent more time topside. One evening, while the ship was anchored off an island in the river, some of the crew took the opportunity to bathe in the fresh water. It was Evan's first chance at a real bath in almost two months. The water and air were terribly cold. He washed his clothes as best he could, and dried them at the warm forge area. Everyone was looking forward to the final docking in Montreal that was scheduled for later in the week.

Quebec and Montreal were the major ports of entry for the Hudson Bay Company ships that still served the lower part of Canada. They were large cities and the fur trade, while declining, was still an important part of the economy. It had been so since 1608, the year Champlain had planted the French fleur de lis at the settlement he had founded on the site of Quebec.

Montreal was the final destination of this trading vessel, and Evan knew it was going to be his port of entry. The cargo of manufactured goods would be unloaded and then warehoused in preparation for the spring trading season to follow. He was finally in America. And while he felt a bit apprehensive, he was excited about a future that was his to make.

"Make us proud!" he remembered his mother saying as he got ready to leave their little farm in Ireland. *I will, Mother. I will!* He thought, as the ship moved toward the dock. It was a conscious thought. Evan knew he must live up to that expectation.

CHAPTER 16
...some very bad news...

The paddlewheel boat moved toward the shore. The shallow draft of the vessel enabled it to come in almost to the bank. A long gangplank was usually all that was needed to load and unload passengers, cargo and the firewood that was necessary in order to keep the steam engine at a level sufficient to power the somewhat cumbersome craft.

A cannon shot signaled that the soldiers in the fort at the top of the steep embankment high above the river had seen the arrival. Everyone on board was giddy with excitement at the prospect of spending the next night on land, finally off of the river.

Elizabeth Anne Delaney was probably the most excited of all. She would be together at last with Lieutenant John Baker, to whom she was betrothed. She had traveled to Fort Snelling to become his wife, and it was now early in May, and she had reached her destination.

They had met in her home city of Cincinnati, and it had been an almost whirlwind romance. *I can learn to love this handsome officer.* She had thought. Now, almost seven months later, she still thought that way.

She was not the only young woman on board the paddlewheel who was looking for a new life. Ana Hughes was her same age, and the two had become fast friends. They were very different, but they had much in common.

Both had mothers who were skilled in midwifery, as were they; both had found themselves attracted to men they barely knew; both had made rather quick decisions in response to requests from those men; both had needed to move away from the life they had each formerly known, although for entirely different reasons; and both were bright and mannerly, although their educational backgrounds and social positions were vastly different. And, they were both fine-looking young women who always received plenty of attention from men with whom they came in contact.

Elizabeth Anne had arranged for the proper marriage ceremony that had made Ana the wife of Patrick Hughes. He was a big, kind, often bashful Irishman with whom Ana had traveled all the way from their homeland to America. Elizabeth Anne had given up trying to find out how the young couple had managed to purchase their passage and lodging for the past six months. Now they were getting ready to dock at Fort Snelling, and Elizabeth Anne knew that her life would change.

* * * * * * *

Construction on the fort had begun in 1826. While still in the final stages, it provided officers' quarters, a sutler's store, an armory and blockhouse, and housing for the enlisted men. There was also a lovely home for the fort's commander.

Adjacent to the confines of the post were various places of business: a blacksmith shop, a laundry, a cobbler's shop, and a land office where settlers could register their land claims if they had chosen a parcel in the Minnesota Territory. Many settlers lived in the immediate vicinity of the fort as well.

The passengers from the paddlewheel moved slowly up the steep embankment to the fort. The excitement built as they traversed the trail that slanted up the hill. A few Indians and French-Canadian voyageurs carried the packs of goods for the fort and the personal luggage of the passengers who had disembarked. It was a long line of people, and the climb was difficult.

I can't wait to see John. Elizabeth Ann thought as she moved up the hill. *Why isn't he meeting me?* She thought.

They eventually entered the fort complex, and Elizabeth Anne saw that the American troops were lined up in a welcoming review.

But where is John? Why isn't Lieutenant Baker in front of one of these companies? She wondered.

The salute was given as the passengers moved into the center of the fort compound. The new fort commander, Zachary Taylor, gave a short welcoming speech. Suddenly, the troops were dismissed and the somewhat bewildered passengers were left standing in the middle of the parade grounds with their luggage piled around them.

Elizabeth Anne turned to Ana and Patrick and, with a firm look, said, "I am going to the commander's office. John should be here."

She moved away from the Hughes and walked toward the building where she had seen the fort's main officer enter a few minutes earlier. She knocked at the open door.

The voice from inside bade her to enter. She stepped into a small office. Seated behind a desk was Commander Taylor. He was wearing his dress uniform and stood as she came into the room.

"Good day, sir," she said. "I am Elizabeth Anne Delaney, and I have traveled here from Cincinnati to become the wife of Lieutenant John Baker. Can you tell me where he is?"

Taylor rose and took her hand in greeting. He motioned to a chair next to his desk and said, "I've been expecting you. Please, take a seat."

He paused and shuffled papers on his desk waiting for her to sit. Then he spoke.

"I'm afraid, Miss Delaney, that I have some very bad news for you."

Elizabeth Anne's heart almost stopped. *He has been transferred to another post, and he couldn't get word to me in time,* she thought. *He has been hurt and is in the fort's hospital.*

"Yes?" It was all she could say.

"Lieutenant Baker is dead. He was killed about a month ago in a wood-cutting accident. I'm terribly sorry," he said, looking directly at her.

Elizabeth Anne almost did not believe what she had just heard. Her breath caught, and she felt faint, the weight of the news crushing her entire body. Then, willing herself to be calm, she asked,

"Will you take me to his grave?"

The commander was shocked. He had done this before, this telling of the death of a soldier to the man's wife or parents. But never had he seen such strength and composure in a woman.

"Certainly, ma'm. We can go there now, if you like," he said.

Together they walked to the fort cemetery, and he pointed out the new grave. The simple cross at the head was crudely lettered with the words "Lt. John Baker." There were no dates, just his name and rank.

Elizabeth Anne stood for a few minutes looking at the slowly receding mound of dirt. Then she turned, and walked away.

* * * * * * *

Ana and Patrick were silent, not knowing what to do or say when Elizabeth Anne told them her news. They were sitting amid their few bundles of personal belongings. Late afternoon was upon them, and none of them had thought about where they would spend the night. Just then, a corporal approached them and saluted.

"I have been asked to invite you to dine with Commander Taylor this evening. If you will come with me, I shall take you to some quarters that he says you may occupy for a while. They are not yet finished, but you will be inside and out of the weather," he announced.

The three followed the soldier and soon had their belongings laid out in a sparse room amid the carpenter tools and rough-sawn timbers that had been stored there. The soldier returned about an hour later and escorted them to the commander's private home. It was large and looked almost like a mansion.

The dinner was just beginning to be served when the three arrived. Introductions were made. The group included three officers and their wives, and the United States Indian agent for the territory. His name was Lawrence Taliaferro. Neither Taylor nor Taliaferro had a wife present.

The group sat down to a meal consisting of a stew made of venison, wild rice, and root vegetables, obviously from the fort's cellar. Bottles of red wine were uncorked and freely passed around the table to the three guests and the others.

The eating began, and most of the table guests devoured their food with apparent gusto. Elizabeth Ann had eaten venison before and liked it. But she was not hungry and only picked at her food on the plate. She was very quiet, not surprising due to the shocking and sad news she had received only three hours earlier. Everyone at the table was aware of her circumstance, and while they were friendly, nobody tried to engage her in trite conversation.

Ana sat on Elizabeth Anne's right, and Patrick sat next to his wife. *What shall I do now?* She wondered, her thoughts drowning out the table chatter. *Shall I try to go back to Cincinnati? But what is for me there? I cannot stay here with Ana and Patrick. There is nothing here for me either.* She was jolted out of her thoughts by Commander Taylor, who suddenly stood and proposed a toast.

"I wish to toast a young officer who is no longer with us," he said quietly. All of the men stood. The room was silent.

Raising his glass of wine, he said, "To one of the finest engineers I have ever had the pleasure to serve with. To Lieutenant John Baker."

The officers responded aloud with "To Lieutenant John Baker." Then they drank.

With the men still standing, Taylor added, "And another toast: To Elizabeth Anne Delaney, who has come from Cincinnati." He left out the rest, but everyone at the table knew his unspoken thoughts.

The men repeated her name, drank, and then sat down.

The room was quiet for a time, the guests eating and not doing much talking.

During this lull, a sergeant entered the room and excused himself to Commander Taylor. He leaned down to Agent Taliaferro and whispered to him.

Taliaferro nodded and then excused himself with the words,

"It seems that my woman is bringing a new one into the world. I must go to Mendota. Please forgive my hasty retreat," he said.

There was a moment's hesitation as everyone looked at one another. Taylor nodded his assent, and the agent arose. An officer's wife asked, "Is there a midwife at the fort?"

One of the officers answered, "No, but someone will be sent down to the Indian camp and bring a woman to her."

Elizabeth Anne looked up, shocked at what she had just heard.

"Nonsense! I can help her, and so can Ana Hughes here," she said, gesturing toward her friend. "We are both midwives." Her comment was quite bold coming from such a young woman.

But there was a murmur of recognition and approval among the table guests as the two women got up and went out of the door behind Taliaferro. Patrick followed them.

* * * * * * *

Lawrence Taliaferro was from Virginia. He had been appointed as the Indian agent to the Minnesota Territory and was greatly respected by the Indian people of the area. It was well known that he had taken a woman who was a mixture of Indian and white as his wife, although he did not officially marry her. Now the woman was delivering their first child.

Mendota was not too far from the fort, but across the river. They walked quickly with Taliaferro in the lead. Two small boats ferried them across the water and when they arrived at the cabin, they found the woman in the work of childbirth.

* * * * * * *

All night long the agent's wife labored, and by dawn there had still been no birth.

"Something is amiss," said Ana, who had been with Elizabeth Anne and the woman for the entire time. "That baby should have been here by now."

"I don't feel the head down low," said Elizabeth Anne quietly. "I think it is coming backwards."

"Ya may be right," answered Ana. "I only saw that once, and mother seemed to know what to do."

"I have seen it often enough. I think I can help her," said Elizabeth Anne.

It was a good thing that she had something important to take her mind off of her own situation. *Ana and I will deliver this woman. Then I will deal with my future.* She thought as she began massage techniques designed to turn the baby.

But she was not successful, and the birth was as they had expected. The baby was backwards and actually came feet first. Still, she and Ana helped the laboring woman deliver a squalling baby girl in the full breech position. Other than the backward delivery, there had been no other complications, and the mother and daughter were doing well.

"What are your mothers' names?" Taliaferro asked the young midwives. They each answered him.

"Then I shall call her Mary after your mother, Ana, since it was into your arms that she first came," said Taliaferro. "Thank you for your kindness."

Elizabeth Anne and Ana smiled and a short while later, after their work was done, they walked back to the boats with Patrick. They went back across the river to the fort and to their belongings. It was a few hours past dawn, and they were very tired.

But when Commander Taylor sent food over to them with his compliments, they were suddenly wide awake. It was not until the evening of the second night after their arrival at Fort Snelling that the three friends finally slept in the unfinished quarters they had been invited to occupy. Everyone was exhausted.

CHAPTER 17
...you could work on those boats...

The Hudson Bay ship anchored at the docks in Montreal, and the unloading began. French-Canadians, most of whom had been voyageurs in former times, did the work. The ship's crew went immediately into the city to eat, to drink and to visit the many brothels that occupied the area around the docks.

Evan took his small parcel of personal belongings and went ashore. It was that simple. His father had paid a part of his passage, and he had worked long and hard on the journey across the Atlantic for the rest of the fare. He knew that he would not return to the ship and felt certain that no one would come after him.

He walked toward the center of the city. English and French signs and speech were everywhere apparent, and he got his land legs back quickly. With the weather much colder already than it had ever been during the winter months in Ireland, he knew that he needed some different clothes. He went immediately to a clothing shop which appeared to have working men's apparel. The shop was owned by a Scottish trader named McGillivray.

Evan had a little money with him. Rolled up in the parcel he carried was a one pound sterling note which his father had pressed into his hand on that day in Cork when he had left for America.

"How can I help ya?" the clerk said when Evan entered the doorway.

"I need clothing for this land," he replied. "What do ya suggest?" Then both men stared at one another.

"Are ya not Evan Ryan?" the clerk asked. "From County Tipperary?"

"Aye, and do I know ya?" Evan answered, frowning. He knew he had seen this man before, but he could not recall his name. That he was Irish was clearly revealed by his accent.

"I'm not surprised that ya don't know me," the clerk said. "Your father and ya always stayed overnight at my father's farm on your way to and from Cork. The last time I saw ya was when ya came through on the way back with some other men."

"Aye, that was over four years ago," Evan said, remembering the night very well. "O'Toole?"

"Aye, 'tis I," the clerk answered.

"When did ya get here to Montreal?" asked Evan.

"It was just after that time when I saw you four years ago when I left. We were both much younger then, aye?" the clerk laughed.

The two men shook hands and began to speak of Ireland and the many people with whom they were both acquainted. Then the clerk, John O'Toole, laid out some clothing that was correct for the Canadian climate. Woolen trousers, shirt and socks, a pair of tall, leather boots lined with sheep hide, and a wool blanket that had been made into a coat completed Evan's new wardrobe. He put on the clothes at once.

"Aye, now ya look like a regular man of this city," John said smiling. "What do ya do?"

"I can do smithy work. Do ya know of any forges that need another good pair of hands?" Evan replied.

"Go down to the end of the street and turn to the west. Go on a ways until ya come to a forge on the right side. He might hire ya on. Winter is a busy time for smithys here because the York boats won't be leaving for the interior 'til spring. He's a gruff old man, but he'll treat ya fair," offered John.

"What will be the cost of these clothes?" Evan asked.

"I'll take two pounds sterling," the clerk replied.

"Can I owe ya one pound?" said Evan, now suddenly concerned. He knew he only had one pound in his little bag.

"Of course, Ryan! A man from Tipperary, with as good a reputation as your family has, will be good for it. Ya'll not cheat me," he said. Evan paid him what he had, they shook hands again, and Evan left the shop.

My luck is already good. He thought, even though he was now penniless.

* * * * * * *

The smithy was just as O'Toole had described. He was a somewhat grumpy old fellow who moved slowly around the forge. He had done the work for too many years, and Evan's quick motions and skill impressed him. Evan Ryan was hired on for the winter.

Antoine Toussaint was actually a kind man who only appeared irascible on the surface. He had earned his living as a canoeman in the late 1700s and had taken the Voyageur Highway over to Grand Portage on the western shore of Lake Superior many times.

'I could carry two packs with ease, sometimes three," he boasted. Each pack weighed about 90 pounds and voyageurs, as these pack-carrying canoe paddlers were called, were paid according to the number of packs that they were responsible for moving over the portages. They had a reputation for being great braggarts.

There were almost thirty "carrying places" between Montreal and Grand Portage. That trading depot was so-named because of the nine-mile portage up and over the high ridge that formed the western shoreline of the big lake. Although not the longest, it was considered to be the most difficult of all of them.

"But, I could see the fur trade going down," Toussaint said somewhat wistfully one night as they talked in the little cabin attached to the shop.

"So I taught myself how to pound iron. Mon Dieu! Now, I'm lame from that," he laughed aloud.

* * * * * * *

Most of the smithy work was simple and very repetitious. Evan paid his debt to John O'Toole within a few weeks, and as the winter wore on, he found time to visit the city. But unlike many of the young men, he drank very little in the various taverns he visited occasionally. Drunkenness had already taken away his first and only love, Catherine.

The population in Montreal was mainly French, with a large number of people who were a mixture of French and Indian. There were also some Englishmen and Scots, and even a few Irish who had settled in the area as well. Evan enjoyed many evenings talking with O'Toole and other Irishmen who were glad to meet a fellow countryman so recently arrived. In their discussions, he noticed that many of them had lost much of the anti-British feeling that was so common in County Tipperary. The Gaelic phrase, "Erin Go Bragh" got a much less intense reaction in America. Evan found that somewhat strange. He spoke of it to Toussaint one day as they worked together at the forge.

"How can the Irish who come here seem to lose their dislike for the English so quickly?" he asked the old French-Canadian.

"How can the Scots who come here not hate the English? Or us Frenchies for that matter. Mon Dieu! We have fought them for hundreds of years," Toussaint answered.

It was curious. There seemed to be no easy answer. *Could it be that those who come to America are willing to forget the past and think only of the future?* He wondered.

On one particular afternoon Toussaint brought in a musket for repair, and so began Evan's instruction in the repair, cleaning, loading, and firing of these black powder weapons. He had never had any previous shooting experience with them in Ireland, and his employer was surprised at that.

"Every man and woman in Montreal knows how to use one of these," Antoine said. "I can show you how to be an excellent shooter."

They took practice shots almost every day behind the blacksmith shop, and by late winter, Evan had become a reasonably skilled marksman. Toussaint even gifted him with one of the newer styles of muskets that had a rifled barrel. The weapon was very accurate, and Evan could load and fire it twice in a minute. That skill would some day be more important to him than he could ever expect. And that day was coming soon.

* * * * * * *

Marie, Toussaint's wife of over thirty-five years, had likewise grown very fond of the Irish boy, and he took most of his meals with the older couple. He even slept in the shop where it was warm. The three of them usually sat together after supper, and Toussaint often told stories about his past adventures. The tales were fascinating, and Evan always listened intently when the man began to talk about the old times.

You can learn much from the older ones. He often thought.

"So, where in Ireland are you from?" Marie asked one evening.

Evan told them about his family and their little farm in County Tipperary. He spoke proudly of the race horses his father raised.

"We had two boys, but one died on the big lake. Only Pierre is left, and he lives on the other side of the city. We see him and his family fairly often," she responded. "Are you married, Evan?"

"Nay, I have no wife or special girl either," Evan replied. Then he briefly related the story of how he had lost the only girl he had ever loved. He left out the parts about the trip to Cork and his experience with the ex-artilleryman on the voyage to North America.

When he finished, Madame Toussaint was silent for a while. Then she said, "You will find another young woman. Look for one who is fun to be with and strong like Catherine was, but who also has the qualities you admire in your mother and sister as well. You can find such a woman if you look carefully."

"Aye, ya think so?" responded Evan. He had not ever given a thought to finding some other woman. Catherine's memory was still with him, even after four years.

"Oui, I do," the older woman replied. "And she will come to you when you least expect it."

* * * * * * *

He was doing almost all of the work, and his relationship with the older man was becoming very congenial. As the weeks passed, he was increasingly glad to be working at the hot forge. The winter weather had grown very cold.

"Is it always this cold?" he asked one day when the wind was strong and bitter.

"Mais oui! It gets cold here," the man replied, partially in French. "But come spring, the ice will go out, and that's when the boats leave for the western depots."

He was referring to the wooden fur trade boats that were built in Montreal and which were now used exclusively in place of the older birch bark canoes to move the goods to the trading posts some thirteen hundred miles to the west. They were called York boats and were built by Scottish immigrants, many of whom had come from the Orkney Islands off the northern coast of Scotland.

Many of these "Orkney Men," as they were called, also moved these boats up the Ottawa River and across the Manawa River through Lake Nippising and into the Georgian Bay area of Lake Huron. For almost three hundred years of fur trading, the French canoe men had struggled to bring the manufactured goods into the west, and then had returned with bundles of furs. The difficult portages on this route had formerly required the loading and unloading of the birch bark canoes. Now many of these difficult portage paths had been augmented with small-gauge wooden tracks with little rolling platforms onto which the York boats were pushed and pulled. It was still hard work, but it was more efficient than it had been during the days of the fragile birch canoes, and there was seldom any need for repairs to the sturdy wooden boats on the trip into the west.

Once past the rivers north of Montreal, the big lakes of Huron and Superior were crossed on small sailing ships which had been built specifically for this trade. The old route to the western shore of Lake Superior, called the Voyageur Highway, was still used, but the type of vessel had changed dramatically. It was now a much faster journey to Fort William which, since 1803, had been the western terminus of the fur trade out of Montreal.

"I would not like to have you leave me, but I can speak with them that do the hiring, and you could work on those boats if you want," offered Toussaint. He had come to like the young Irishman. It was almost as though Evan had replaced the son who had died years earlier. But he knew that a smithy's life was not what Evan wanted.

"I think I would like that," Evan answered. *I am in America. I am strong. I can do what I need to do. I can make my way in the world by myself and for myself. I will go west.* He thought.

* * * * * * *

The winter seemed to go on and on. But when spring finally did come in late March, Antoine Toussaint was good to his word, and Evan signed on as a boatman. He would leave the next morning and take the Voyageur Highway all the way to Fort William, the British-owned fur trade post on the Kaministiqua River on the far western shore of Lake Superior. It was a journey that would take at least forty-five days, and Evan looked forward to it.

He discovered that John O'Toole was also part of the brigade, and the two young men were eager to begin the adventure.

"Be safe, mon fils!" Toussaint said as Evan prepared to leave for the river dock area. He used the words for "my son." Evan had learned a smattering of French in the five months he had worked for the old blacksmith. Now he simply embraced his friend and then turned to Madame Toussaint.

"Madame Marie, thank you for your kindness. I shall always remember you," he said. Then he kissed her on both cheeks and quickly left the house.

I have been blessed with good fortune. Mother and Father would be glad for me. He thought. He could never have guessed that the relationship between Marie and Antoine Toussaint and his own extended family would continue for generations yet to come.

* * * * * * *

The trip up the Ottawa River was difficult. The York boats were fully loaded with packs of trade goods. Iron, lead, wool and cotton cloth, beads, tobacco, beeswax, flint and steel strikers, vermilion, awls, needles, fishhooks, kegs of rum and brandy, cases of wine from France, and all sorts of other manufactured items were packaged in much the same way they had been for over the nearly three centuries of the fur trade. The boats were heavy, and the men strained at the oars and poles.

At each portage, necessitated by either a falls or a shallow, rocky, river bed, the boats were hauled up by ropes and onto the little dollies that rolled along a series of wooden tracks to the next launching spot. This was the most difficult part of the job, but the men knew that by pushing and pulling together, they could accomplish the work with a minimum of effort. The brigade moved up the river and within two weeks had turned west.

Lake Nippissing was a welcome relief, and they crossed it in two days. Then it was into the French Channel, and at the mouth of that river, which spilled into Lake Huron, the goods were transferred onto sailing vessels that were waiting. From there, the wind would do most of the work. Evan and John were scheduled to cross the big lakes as part of the crew on one of those small ships.

* * * * * * *

The little flotilla arrived at Fort William in the middle of May. It was a huge complex of buildings. Some were living quarters and tradesmen's shops, but the majority were warehouses for the goods that were either going into the western interior of Canada or for the bundles of furs going back to Montreal. The men from the crews slept in separate housing just outside the fort's walls.

"If you stay in the interior, you'll become a Northwester," Evan and John were told. "You can live with friendly Indian groups and trap, or, if you go south, you can find good farm land and lay claim to it." That last idea interested Evan, but not John who left Fort William for the Selkirk colony on the Red River.

"I will work for the Hudson Bay Company there," he said.

Evan wondered what he would do. He only had four options: stay and work at Fort William, return to Montreal with the next eastbound cargo fleet and work again at Toussaint's shop, travel into the Canadian interior as John had done, or go south into the United States and try to find farmland of his own. The last idea intrigued him.

One evening, while sitting with a small group of his crew members, three Indian men approached their fire. They were Ojibwe and were from a band that lived south of the southern shore of the big lake, the one they called Gitchee Gummee. As they sat and smoked, Evan asked if they would take him to their home area.

One of the Ojibwe men, Hole-in-the-Day, was obviously senior to the other two. By speaking in a mix of French and English, and by using sign language, he and Evan struck the deal. Evan would pay them in Hudson Bay Company trade script, and they would transport him to their home area. They would leave in the morning.

CHAPTER 18
...his younger sister...

Evan moved slowly through the thick woods. He knew that the sun would be coming up soon to his left, so he knew he was traveling south. He had been told that there was a large American military post located where two rivers met and that, perhaps, there was farmland in the area that he could acquire.

The thought excited him and helped lessen the weight of the small pack of goods he carried on his back. It contained a warm blanket and a few trade goods he thought might help him buy land. He had purchased the items at Fort William from the small pay he received for the trip across the Voyageur Highway. The rest of his pay had been taken in script which he had given to Hole-in-the-Day in payment for bringing him south.

I will make you proud! He thought as he struggled along a barely perceptible game trail. As he walked, the thoughts of his family in Ireland and of the events that had brought him to America filled his head.

He had been given a map by Hole-in-the-Day who had drawn it with charcoal on a piece of birch bark. "About seven day's travel," he had indicated partially in French and partially in sign language.

Evan carried a fine Northwest trade gun. It was a black powder musket with a rifled barrel and was the one he had used in the backyard of Toussaint's blacksmith shop in Montreal when the older man taught him how to shoot. It had been Antoine's gift to Evan, and he felt capable with the weapon.

In fact, he felt very sure of his many talents. He was a good shot with the musket; he possessed blacksmithing skills; he could row the Orkney boats and carry the heavy packs; and, he was an excellent marksman with a bow and arrow, although he had not used them since leaving Ireland. He had learned to throw a heavy knife with great accuracy, and he was extremely adept in all aspects of horsemanship, even though he had not been with horses since the previous autumn.

"Watch out for the Dakota," Hole-in-the-Day had warned. "They inhabit the lands you are going into, and they are our enemies. Do not trust them."

A sound from up ahead of him caused Evan to stop. He listened and then moved off of the game trail to the right. Crouching down in the thick brush, he waited, peering carefully through the leaves.

Three Indian men and two women came along the trail and began to move past the spot where he was hidden. As they came into closer view, he noticed that they were wearing a combination of leather and cloth clothing. It was a sure indication that they had traded for the cloth, and had already been in contact with white traders. They did not look hostile, but they did not look like the Ojibwe he had known and with whom he had lived for a short time. He decided to not reveal his presence.

After they had passed, he returned to the trail and resumed his journey. It was light now, and the trail was much easier to see. He walked on as the sun climbed into the sky. He came to a river that was on the map and prepared to cross.

"Follow it as the water flows," his Ojibwe friend had told him. "But you will need to cross it before it gets too wide," he had added. The birch bark map gave the same instruction.

*   *   *   *   *   *   *

The river crossing had not been difficult, and Evan waded through the water. It came up almost to his waist, and he was careful to keep his pack and the powder and rifle high above his head. The late spring water was still very cold, and by the time he was on the opposite shore, he was shaking. He built a fire and dried his clothes. Within three hours, he was once again on his way south.

The crude map showed that he needed to leave the bank of the river and move in a more south-westerly direction. He did so, and the thick forest began to thin out somewhat. He had been walking for almost a week now and had eaten only dried cranberries, some pieces of dried squash, dried deer meat and bits of smoked fish, and a few finger dabs of a dark, oily substance called pemmican. It had a strange taste, and he did not like it. Hole-in-the-Day had told him to be sure to eat at least one good glob of the paste each day, and so he had gagged it down every morning.

But he thought about the Ojibwe! *They are very generous. They treated me as a guest, and their kindness is certainly not what the clerks at Fort William said I should expect. How wrong we can often be about people!*

Just as the map had shown, two days later he came to a second river that he needed to cross. It was much larger than the first one, and the water level was very high. Evan could not swim very well, and he was afraid he could not make it all the way across. A large, barkless tree trunk floating near the shore gave him the idea.

He waded out and straddled it with the pack and rifle in front of him. Lying on the wide log with his legs and arms doing the paddling, he moved out into the fast-moving water. He kicked his legs and flailed his arms. Slowly, the makeshift craft began to move into the current. Almost a mile downstream, he reached water on the opposite shore that was shallow enough for him to slip off the log and wade to the bank.

Once again, he built a fire and dried his clothes. It was getting dark now, and he decided to spend the night at this spot. Perhaps he would reach the American soldier fort in a day or so.

He slept. During the night, he dreamed of his younger sister, Ana. He saw her running toward him as she had often done when he came in from the pasture. This dream seemed so real.

CHAPTER 19
...No! It can't be!...

Ana Hughes walked along the outer wall of the fort. Patrick had left early in the morning for the store owned by Jean Faribault. He was doing well as a clerk and had been with the old French trader for almost a month. It was the middle of June, and they still lived in the unfinished warehouse inside the fort walls. The kindness of the fort's commander, Zachary Taylor, had afforded them these quarters. It was his way of thanking Ana and Elizabeth Anne, who had been successful in helping Agent Taliaferro's woman with a difficult birth.

Elizabeth Anne Delaney still shared the unfinished room with them, as she had since their arrival at Fort Snelling. The untimely death of her betrothed, Lieutenant John Baker, had forced her into a very bad situation, and there had been nowhere for her to go. Military regulations did not allow unmarried women to remain in or near a fort. Elizabeth Anne had to either find a suitable husband among the soldiers or civilians at the post, or she would be required to leave. Sixty days was all that a woman was given to make this choice, and the time was running out. It had been her friendship with the Hughes that had sustained Elizabeth Anne during these trying weeks.

The shared quarters had not been difficult for the three friends. Elizabeth Anne's area was on the other side of the room, and a large piece of canvas divided their sleeping space. A cooking area just outside of the rear door gave them a bit of additional privacy from the rest of the fort's activities. Patrick always bought the food, and Elizabeth Anne continued to wonder how this Irish peasant couple could have so much money.

* * * * * * *

Patrick knew that Elizabeth Anne could read, write, and do numbers.

"Would ya teach me those skills?" he asked her one night. "I could use them in my work with Faribault."

If the truth be known, he did not have to work at all. The large sum of money he had received from Little Thomas O'Leary on that night in Cork was still largely intact. He had used a small portion of it to buy their passage on the clipper ship to New York. While in that city, he had cashed in the British pound notes for American currency. He had gone to a number of banks, making the exchanges in small amounts so he would not arouse suspicion.

He and Ana had lived frugally in a modest New York hotel throughout the winter months, and in the spring, they had traveled to Philadelphia and then to Pittsburg where they had taken a boat down the Ohio River. In Cincinnati, they had met Elizabeth Anne, and now they shared a fast friendship, one that had become even closer because of her sad circumstance.

"I will, Patrick," Elizabeth Anne answered easily.

He had been a fast learner. The numbers came much more quickly than did the reading and writing, but he was starting to understand the reading skills. All the while, Patrick was making some modest purchases of land in the area to the north and east of the fort. He still carried the money belt strapped to his waist under his shirt and vest, but he only took out the needed cash for his purchases in the privacy of their warehouse quarters.

Elizabeth Anne always read the sale documents for him and approved the land acquisition documents before he signed. Although Patrick appeared to be only a trade clerk on the surface, he was becoming a very large landowner.

But the sixty day period was nearly up for Elizabeth Anne. Her options were few.

"Patrick is planning to build a home for us over on the high bank of the river just north of the fort," said Ana one afternoon. "Ya would be welcome to live with us for as long as ya need." She was worried about her friend who spent long hours walking in the area near the fort. It was relatively safe there, although she was often bothered by the unwanted attentions of unmarried soldiers who frequently tried to begin conversation with her. It only vexed her, and Ana tried to go with her as often as possible so as to lessen that irritation.

"I can't, Ana," replied Elizabeth Anne. "You deserve your own life, and a boarder is not what I want to be. That is kind of you, though." Then she lapsed into the quiet, melancholy state that was so unlike the bright, animated young woman that Ana had met and grown to love while on the paddlewheel. Ana was very concerned about her friend. It seemed that Elizabeth Anne was floundering in a deep state of depression.

* * * * * * *

Ana walked along the outer wall of the fort on her way to Faribault's trading store. She was taking Patrick his lunch. She saw the man coming toward her. He was a long way off, but she was sure that she recognized his gait. She stopped and set down the small package of food she was carrying. She watched the man carefully.

Her mind began to reel, and she felt faint. *It is not possible!* She thought. *Could it be him? No! It can't be! I must wait 'til he gets closer before I can be sure.*

She was standing in the shadow of the fort and partially behind a wagon-load of wood. She continued to watch as the young man approached to within about forty yards of the wall. He was looking to his right, searching for the fort's entrance and had not seen her behind the wagon. Her stomach was in knots, and the tears were now streaming down her cheeks. She was sure.

"Evan!" she screamed and ran out from behind the wagon. The man turned, and his eyes grew wide in astonishment. *Ana? It can't be ya!* He thought.

"Evan!" Ana screamed his name again as she raced toward her brother.

"Ana," he yelled.

He dropped his rifle and the pack just as the girl leaped into his arms almost knocking him down.

"Ana! Oh my god! Oh my god! Ana!" It was all he could say. They stood there together. He was holding her off the ground and turning around in joyous circles. They were both crying and clinging to one another so tightly that it seemed that neither could breathe. Then, he let her down and looked at her.

"What are ya doing here?" he asked, still not believing that the girl before him was really Ana, his sister.

"What are ya doing here?" she answered.

The dream was real. He thought.

* * * * * * *

Ana and Evan delivered the food to Patrick. He was also stunned by the appearance of Ana's brother, whom he already knew, of course. After the introductions, Faribault sent them all back to the fort, handing them four bottles of French wine so that they could celebrate.

* * * * * * *

The three were sitting together in their warehouse quarters when Elizabeth Anne walked into the room. Ana jumped up and ran to her.

"Elizabeth Anne! It's my brother, Evan," she said, her voice almost a scream as she grabbed her friend by the arm and pulled her over to where Patrick and Evan were sitting. Evan got up off of the floor and looked directly into the young woman's eyes. He knew nothing about her connection to his sister and Patrick.

"I am pleased to meet ya," he said.

Evan was wearing buckskin leggings and a breechclout, and his feet were covered by Indian moccasins. His long-sleeved shirt hung loosely down to mid-thigh and was cinched at the waist by a green, finger-woven, wool sash. His hair was long, and his beard had about a week's growth. Although he was dirty and looked a bit disheveled, he was still a good-looking young man. Elizabeth Anne nodded to him but did not speak.

"He just showed up here today at noontime," Ana said excitedly.

Elizabeth Anne smiled and sat down.

"We've just begun telling one another what has happened to us since we all left Ireland," said Patrick. "Start over. There should be no secrets among us. Evan, I want ya to know that Elizabeth Anne is like a sister to Ana. We can trust her. Ya left home first, so ya should tell first. Start again so Elizabeth Anne can hear it all."

* * * * * * *

Evan began his story once more. He left nothing out. He told how his father had bought his passage across the Atlantic with racehorse money, and how he had worked on the Hudson Bay Company ship as a blacksmith. He related how he had discovered one of Catherine's murderers on board. Only when mentioning Catherine's name did his voice quaver.

Ana's eyes began to tear up as she recalled the terrible event, and Patrick pulled her into his shoulder. Elizabeth Anne noticed the reaction and was puzzled.

When Evan told how he had caused the man's death on the ship, Patrick gave a measured nod and, in a barely audible whisper, he muttered, "Erin Go Bragh." Elizabeth Anne heard the words and was again puzzled, but she said nothing.

Evan spoke fondly about his winter in Montreal and of the kindness shown by Toussaint and his wife. He described his trip to Fort William with John O'Toole, and how he came south with three Ojibwe men. His description of the welcome he had received from the Ojibwe people took the others a bit by surprise.

"Are they not savages?" asked Ana.

"Nay, girl. Quite the contrary. They were most kind to me. Their men are not drunkards like the British, and the women are soft in their speech. They reminded me of ya when they laughed, ya know! How ya look down and put your hand up over your mouth," Evan answered. He mimicked his sister, and the others laughed in recognition and agreement.

Finally, he told how the Ojibwe had provided directions on how to get to Fort Snelling where they thought he might find land. And he spoke of how they had provisioned him with plenty of food for his journey.

"I will make my own life, and Mother and Father will be proud," he said as he finished.

When he said those last words, Elizabeth Anne searched his face carefully. *I like this man!* She thought.

Then it was Ana's turn. She told of her decision to go to England with the landlord.

"Shortly after ya left, Evan, the landlord came for the rent. I thought it would help Mother and Father if I went with him," she said. "He wanted me for an upstairs maid, whatever that is."

Evan and Patrick exchanged knowing glances.

"I couldn't bear to not see her again," Patrick added quickly. Ana blushed and looked down, so Patrick continued their story.

He told of his search for Ana in Cork and how he found her. Then, he told how Little Thomas O'Leary had suddenly appeared that night and robbed the landlord there on the dock.

"Little Thomas gave us the Englishman's money belt," Patrick said. "We are very wealthy now, Evan, and your sister will want for nothing ever again. I give ya my word on that." He looked directly at Evan when he made the promise. Evan nodded his head in understanding and held his brother-in-law's gaze.

If Patrick Hughes says it, it will be true. Evan thought.

So that's how they came to have so much money! Thought Elizabeth Anne. But she could not fault them. *Why can't I have that kind of luck?*

Patrick continued with their story. He told of their crossing to New York and of their stay there throughout the winter. Then it was Ana who told of their trip to Cincinnati almost three months earlier, and how they had met Elizabeth Anne and began traveling west and north on the paddlewheel boat. She smiled when she spoke of how she and Patrick had finally been married by a priest on board the boat. Then, she looked at her friend and waited for her to begin her story.

"Patrick and I know ya, but Evan does not. Tell him about how ya've come to be here," she said.

Elizabeth Anne was quiet for a time. Nobody spoke, each of the listeners giving her plenty of conversational space. She began with the words,

"I don't know what to do." Her voice was soft. It was a simple statement, and they waited for her to continue.

"My story is really very short compared to all of yours. I grew up in Cincinnati, and last autumn I met a young American Army officer there. John Baker was passing through on his way to this fort. He courted me for the two weeks he was stopped there, and I agreed to marry him in the spring. When I got here, Commander Taylor told me that he had been killed. I've been to his grave, so I suppose that it's true. But now I must either marry another soldier, or leave the fort area," she said. "There are no soldiers here that I would give the slightest thought to marrying. And there are no settlers, either."

At that point, Ana interrupted her friend. "I've been wanting to ask ya. Why don't ya go back to Cincinnati?" she inquired.

"Because there is nothing there for me. My brothers have taken over Father's business, and there are no men there I have any interest in marrying," she answered. She did not add that for her to return home would be, in her eyes, an admission of vulnerability and personal failure.

When she had finished, the four were silent for a time. It was Evan who spoke first.

"I'd like to go to the river and bathe." They all laughed, and Patrick said,

"I have clothes that will fit ya. Ya look like an Indian dressed that way. And have ya the fixins for a shave?" he asked.

A short time later the two men left.

* * * * * * *

Ana and Elizabeth Anne began to prepare the evening meal. They were alone now and working at the small fire located outside the rear of the warehouse where they had been staying for almost two months. Elizabeth Anne wanted to know more about Ana's brother.

"Why did your brother's voice change when he spoke of Catherine? Was that her name?" she asked.

Ana's breath caught in her throat. She turned toward her friend and began to speak.

"I was twelve when it happened. Catherine O'Leary was her name. She lived on the place next to ours. I always knew that she and Evan loved each other, even though they were both only two years older than me. Her mother and father were at our house. Missus O'Leary was having her third baby, and Father sent Evan over to the O'Learys' place to tell Catherine and her brother, Little Thomas, what was happening. When he got there, he found that three British soldiers were planning to attack Catherine. He went into the house and tried to defend her but they ... they ...." Ana's voice began to choke out the words.

"They beat ... oh god, they beat Evan almost to death. When father brought him home later that night, he was unconscious, and his face was so bloody and swollen it didn't even look like him." She paused and wiped her nose and eyes.

"And those soldiers raped Catherine and killed her. They crushed her throat." The words came painfully, and Ana had to stop again. Then she continued.

"When we went to the O'Learys two days later, Evan just stood there and looked at Catherine lying in the coffin. He never spoke. Oh, he must have loved her so," she said.

She paused again and then went on. "Everybody in our area knew what he had tried to do, and they all respected him for that. But I know he feels that he failed. He punishes himself every day. He has never looked at another girl since that night. All of my friends wanted to dance with him at the festivals, but he never would. He still loves Catherine, I know it," she said. "And it has been almost five years now."

"Oh my!" said Elizabeth Anne. She hardly knew what else to say, but she was thinking. *We have both lost someone.*

* * * * * * *

When Evan and Patrick returned from the river, Elizabeth Anne was very surprised at the change in Evan's appearance. Patrick's clothes fit him well, and he was clean-shaven.

I can see why they all wanted to dance with him! She thought. *He certainly is a handsome man.*

As the two men walked into the warehouse, Evan once again grabbed and hugged his sister. They were both laughing out loud and jumping around as they had done earlier. Patrick smiled at their show of affection. Then he asked, "So what are we eatin' that will go with this fine French wine?"

With that, everyone began talking at once. The mood of all four had become joyful. Even Elizabeth Anne was smiling and laughing and sharing fully in the conversation. It was a dramatic change in her behavior. Ana noticed it and exchanged looks with Patrick, who nodded at her and smiled.

Evan had already commented to him about the young woman when they were down at the river.

"Patrick. I need to ask ya. Who is this Elizabeth Anne?" he had said.

CHAPTER 20
...I shall make them proud...

Over the next week, the two couples traveled all over the area assessing land purchase possibilities. They kept meeting settlers who were continuing to come in from the northwest. The Selkirk colony on the Red River in Canada had not done well, and many of the Scots were leaving it and coming across the border into the Minnesota Territory, which belonged to the United States.

"Oh, there is money to be made out there," one of the settlers told them. "The herds of buffalo stretch as far as the eye can see, and they are easy to kill. You can sell the hides for a good sum, provided you can get them to the markets."

Patrick and Evan listened to the man with interest.

"Ya are a Scot, aye?" asked Evan.

"Aye. Why do ya ask, laddie?" the man replied.

"By the way ya talk. My mother was a Scot, but from the south of Ireland near Cork. Her name was Patterson," he said.

"That's my name, too. What was her first name?" the settler asked.

"My mother was named Mary, and her mother was Sarah, I think," he answered. "I don't remember her father's first name."

"Well, we are probably related. Some of me father's brothers and sisters went to Ireland many years ago. So, we're probably cousins at least, laddie," the older Scot replied. "Do ya know of land for sale in these parts?"

* * * * * * *

As the week passed, Patrick and Evan began to formulate a plan. If Evan could bring back raw buffalo hides to Patrick, he would sell them to the tanneries down river from Fort Snelling. Patrick was developing a number of solid trade contacts through Faribault, and he was acquiring an increasingly large amount of land in the area. And if some of these Red River settlers would do the transporting on their two-wheeled carts in exchange for some of Patrick's land, Evan would not need to come all the way back to Fort Snelling. He could meet the carts at some spot out on the prairie where the hides would be exchanged for trade goods. They would bypass St. Louis and Chouteau's trade monopoly centered in that city, and they could make a very good living in hides. The plan seemed plausible, and they continued to get more information from the settlers.

Ana and Elizabeth Anne were not part of this planning. It was certain now that Ana was expecting her first child.

"Have you told Patrick yet?" inquired Elizabeth Anne.

"I have not. He has been so busy with Evan, and we have had no time to talk," she answered. Elizabeth Anne nodded in understanding.

*   *   *   *   *   *   *

Evan had been stealing glances at Elizabeth Anne ever since the day he arrived. She was a little shorter than Ana, and, like his sister, she was almost slight of build. Her face was fine-featured, and she was a very pretty young woman. Evan could not keep from looking at her every chance he got.

Strangely, he did not feel that his increasing interest in her was inappropriate. Perhaps it was because he was no longer in Ireland, where the memories of Catherine had been so very strong. He just knew that he was attracted to Ana's friend, and he wondered if she shared a similar interest in him.

"Do ya think I could walk about the fort alone with ya some evening?" he asked her early one afternoon.

"I'd be delighted, Evan," Elizabeth Anne answered. She looked at him directly and waited to see if he would say something else.

"Then tonight after supper, if the good weather holds," he replied. He turned and went out of the doorway to meet Patrick.

* * * * * * *

That evening they walked to the north of the fort. Evan wore a blanket coat called a capote. Elizabeth Anne was wearing her skirt and a blouse over her shift. They strolled together, and Evan pointed out a piece of land that Patrick had recently purchased. It had a small cabin on it.

"Patrick told me it will do until he can build a bigger place for Ana," he said.

"I'm not surprised. He is very kind to her," replied Elizabeth Anne.

As they walked along, the evening breeze suddenly grew sharper. Elizabeth Anne shivered slightly. Evan noticed her discomfort and turned quickly to her.

"Here, put this on," he said, taking off his capote. He reached it around her and pulled it over her shoulders.

She smells like soap and firewood smoke. He thought. *Catherine smelled that way.* The memory of her scent was intense, and he fought the urge to pull this girl into him.

He was standing there with his arms around the young woman as he adjusted the coat on her shoulders. She looked up at him saying nothing.

"Ya look beautiful," he said.

Her eyes softened, and she looked down. Not looking at him she said, "Thank you, Evan." Then, very slowly her hands came up through the front of the capote, and she gently placed them on his arms which were still around her shoulders holding the coat in place. She looked up and her eyes found his. It was as if the world had stopped.

They were staring intently at one another, and it seemed that even the birds were silent. Elizabeth Anne said very quietly, "I would very much like for you to kiss me, Evan, but only if you understand that it is me you are kissing, and no one else. Can you do that?"

Her words brought the world back into motion once again, and Evan was jolted out of his temporary paralysis.

She is right. I am with her and not Catherine. Oh god! Catherine! Will I ever forget you? He thought.

Slowly his arms came from around her shoulders, and he pulled the front of the capote shut just under her chin.

"Such a beautiful lass shall not be cold in my presence," he said. Then, he took her hand, and they started walking back toward the fort. They walked slowly, but neither of them spoke for the entire way.

What have I done now? Thought Elizabeth Anne. *What have I done?* But he kept holding her hand.

* * * * * * *

"I cannot stay here any longer, Patrick. If we are going to have a business together in hides, I must start at once. The prairie is a big place, they say, and I will need to find lodging among the Indians out there for the winter," said Evan.

It was the morning after his walk with Elizabeth Anne, and he was still greatly disturbed by his apparent feelings for the young woman. Now, he was pressing his brother-in-law partly because of the insecurity caused by these new feelings.

"Aye, Evan. Ya should be goin' if we are to get this venture started. I will purchase the horses and trade goods from Faribault, and you can be on your way within a day or two," Patrick answered.

*I must leave. She is too...*Evan thought, unable to put into words even in his mind what he was feeling about Elizabeth Anne.

* * * * * * *

That evening the four sat in their unfinished barracks housing. Ana was quiet. She knew Evan was planning to leave for the western prairies.

"I wish there was some way we could tell Mother and Father that we are here and that we are well," she said quite seriously.

"There may be," said Elizabeth Anne. "I could write a letter for you, and the next boat that comes here will take it to St. Louis, and then up the Ohio River to Pittsburg, and then to New York. In America, we have a Post Office system that gives us the chance to stay in contact with one another. With a bit of luck, a letter might reach your parents in Ireland."

"We'd have to send it to John Burke. He can read and write," said Patrick.

"Let's do it," said Ana excitedly.

"Let me go and ask the commander what he thinks about the chances of it getting there," said Elizabeth Anne. Without waiting for their approval, she left the building.

She returned shortly with writing materials she had borrowed, and over the next hour she wrote the letter for her friends. Early the next morning, she took it to Commander Taylor. He had readily agreed to post it on the next boat. It was not a guarantee that it would ever reach Ireland, but he said that he would put it with his military reports bound for West Point and that it had a good chance of reaching County Tipperary eventually.

She also gave him a second letter which was to go to her parents in Cincinnati.

"This one will be delivered, I'm sure," he said. Then, he reminded her of the fort's rule regarding unattached women.

"I'm afraid that your time here is coming to an end," he said. "Is there no one you would marry?"

Elizabeth Anne thanked him for his kindness, but did not answer his question.

* * * * * * *

Two days later Evan departed Fort Snelling early in the morning. He rode one horse and had two pack animals behind him loaded with bundles of trade goods. The packs contained metal goods in the form of knife blades, tomahawk and axe heads, fishhooks, small saw blades, files and awls. He also had a few iron pots, but they were bulky and took up too much room for him to carry more than he did. He also carried many pounds of beads, a good bit of woolen, linen, and cotton cloth, and various other items known to be prized by the Indians. Of course, he also carried lead and powder.

Faribault had urged him to take plenty of liquor, but he did not. Evan knew of Agent Taliaferro's position on trading liquor to the Indians, and he agreed with him. It was not good for fair trading, and it had a detrimental effect on the trade relationship and on the Indian people themselves. Taliaferro forbade it, and was known to send away those traders who did not obey his rule on this.

It was very hard to bid Ana goodbye. This was the second time they had done so in less than a year, and it seemed much more difficult this time.

"When ya return next summer with the hides, ya'll be an uncle," she said. Patrick smiled at Evan. It was obvious that now he knew the good news.

Then Evan turned to Elizabeth Anne.

"I shall miss looking at ya," he said, as he took her hands in his. "Perhaps ya shall be here, too, when I return. I would like that."

"Perhaps," she answered.

He turned, mounted his horse, and rode off toward the west. *I shall make them proud!* He thought. He looked back once to see if they were still watching him. They were. All three of them.

PART THREE

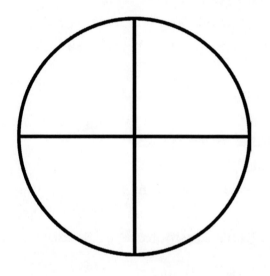

The People: 1828—1856

List of Characters in Part Three

Evan Ryan—from Ireland; buffalo hide trader on the western American prairie

Elizabeth Anne Delaney—his wife; from Cincinnati

Sarah Ana Ryan—their daughter; called Blue Flower

Michael Ryan—their son; called The Red Plume or Wiyaka-ska

Patrick Hughes—from Ireland; businessman in St. Paul

Ana Ryan Hughes—his wife; from Ireland; Evan's sister

Patrick Evan Hughes—their son

Matthew Hughes—their son

Mary Anne Hughes—their daughter

The People

Tsitsistas—the Cheyenne (Northern)

Lakota—the Sioux (Western)

Enemies of the People

Palani—the Pawnee

Crow—the People of the Little Black Eagle

Blackfeet—not to be confused with the Blackfoot Lakota

Patterson—Evan's cousin; from the Selkirk colony

In Ireland:

John Burke—owner of a public house

Michael and Mary Ryan—Evan's parents

Thomas and Elizabeth O'Leary—close neighbors and friends of the Ryans

Little Thomas O'Leary—their son

Patrick and Zoe Hughes—Patrick's parents

Peza—Lakota boyhood friend of Michael Ryan; later called John Grass

Otter (Little Evan)—grandson of Evan and Elizabeth Anne; son of Sarah Ana and Otter, a Cheyenne warrior

General William S. Harney—U.S. Army officer at Fort Laramie

Map for Part Three in Appendix I

CHAPTER 21
...how else will you know...

It was dark. Evan heard the horse coming nearer to the camp he had quickly set up just off the main trail. For the past few hours, he had suspected that someone was following him, and he expected to learn the identity of the person very soon. He was ready for any attempt at foul play. After all, he had three horses, two of them loaded with trade goods. The horses and trade goods were all extremely valuable in the Minnesota Territory of 1828. The coldness that he had discovered in himself back in Ireland five years earlier began to envelop his body once again.

He had left Fort Snelling early that same day. His plan was to travel along the well-marked trail that led from the fort along the Selkirk ox-path to the start of the Red River. Then he planned to turn west and go out onto the prairie. With a bit of luck, he could get to the Mandan villages that he heard were located on a big river, a river he would eventually need to cross. These Indians were acquainted with white traders, and Evan had been told he could stay with them over the winter. The whole journey was very risky. In fact, the entire venture was a huge gamble.

The sounds of the intruder's horse were getting louder now, and Evan set the hammer of his trade rifle at half-cock. His throwing knife lay on the ground, and he put it loosely into his belt at the middle of his back.

Let him come! He thought, as he moved just out of the firelight to stand behind a tree. The hoofbeats of the horse stopped, and he saw a figure moving slowly through the brush toward his fire. The light revealed that the person was small and wore a hooded capote similar to the one he was wearing.

He stepped partially out of the shadows and called out, "Warm yourself if ya like! There is tea there in the pot." His rifle was not raised, but it was at the ready. The person turned and lowered the capote's hood. It was Elizabeth Anne Delaney.

"What are ya doin' here? How did ya get here?" he asked, stepping fully into the firelight, shocked by the young woman's unexpected appearance. The coldness had suddenly been replaced by a warm flush that surged through his body.

"Patrick gave me this horse, and I came with a family that was going back to Pembina. They will camp down the way tonight," she replied, pointing to the west.

"Why did ya come here," Evan asked. He was still in an almost total state of disbelief that she had suddenly shown up at his camp.

"I came here because you never answered me the other night when we were walking together," she said, her voice very steady.

"I didn't?" he asked, not knowing what in the world she was talking about.

"No. You did not! I asked you to kiss me, if you thought you could do it knowing it was me and not anyone else. You didn't kiss me, but you never answered me with a yes or no, either. So, I'm asking now! Can you kiss me because it is me, Evan Ryan?" she said, her voice strong but still gentle.

He was totally taken off guard by this bold question, especially since it came from this very small young woman to whom he was attracted. He paused, and then said,

"Yes, I can do that." He set the rifle back to half-cock and leaned it against the tree. They moved toward one another, and their bodies met in a tight embrace. They kissed, and it seemed to go on and on. When their lips finally parted, they continued to hold one another snugly.

"You came all this way for a kiss?" he asked, smiling down at her.

My god! She is so very pretty. He thought.

She eased her grip on him and pulled back away a little. She, too, was smiling now, and her eyes sparkled in the soft firelight.

"Yes, I did, partly," she said. Then she added, "But you know what has happened to me, and if you let me stay here with you at least tonight, I will tell you the other reasons I have come. You can send me away in the morning if you do not like what you hear."

She gently pushed away from him and when he relaxed his hold on her, she stepped out of their mutual embrace.

"Would ya like some tea?" Evan asked, motioning toward his little fire.

* * * * * * *

The horses had been watered at the nearby stream and picketed for the night. The packs of trade goods were next to them on the ground, and Evan had made a bed between them. They had eaten a light supper and were finishing their tea when Elizabeth Anne began to speak. Their small talk was over, and it was obvious from her tone that she was going to talk about important matters.

"As you know, I was born in Cincinnati and grew up there. I have always been rather independent, and I never found any of the men in our neighborhood to be of the sort I wanted to marry. Oh, plenty came to call, but they were all depending on their own families for a secure future. My brothers have taken over our father's business so when John Baker came through, I found him very eligible. He was making his own way in the world. Maybe that is what impressed me the most about him," she began.

"I am not even sure that I loved him, but I followed him to the fort so I could build a life for myself as well. Maybe it was just the adventure of it all. I guess I'm not entirely sure why I followed him. Anyway, his death has put me into a very bad situation. Over the past few weeks, I have been more lost than I have ever been. Until you arrived, I did not know what I was going to do," she said.

Evan listened, his eyes on the fire waiting for her to continue.

"You are doing the same thing, Evan, trying to make your own place in the world. All of the hardships you have endured and the way you have dealt with whatever life has brought your way, they have just made you stronger. Here you are now, going off to a world you know nothing about to make a place for yourself," she said. "Are you not afraid?"

"I guess I am," he answered. "A bit. But I have skills I can use anywhere, and if my fortune is to come from farming or buffalo instead of sheep, so be it. Do ya think I can herd them like I did the sheep?"

They both laughed, the serious nature of their conversation interrupted momentarily. They both knew the answer, although neither had ever seen buffalo.

"Ana says that you are a good man, and I trust her. I know that she loves you very much, Evan," Elizabeth Anne continued. "She told me how you always helped her by doing her heavy chores, and she said that you are an excellent horseman."

"Aye, I do know some horse tricks," he responded, smiling.

"Evan!" she said, lowering her voice. "Ana told me about Catherine and what happened five years ago. I'm so sorry."

"Aye," he said, not looking up.

They were silent for a time. Then she said,

"I must make a place for myself in this world. I cannot stay at the fort any longer, and I do not want to live with Ana and Patrick. There is nothing back in Cincinnati for me either. But you are here, and I am here, and I think

I can learn to love you, and maybe you can learn to love me."

She paused again and then said, "Evan, look at me!" her voice suddenly becoming very authoritative.

They were each sitting facing one another with their backs against the packs and their legs stretched out in front of them next to each other. He was surprised at her directive, and he looked straight at her face.

"I need for you to tell me about Catherine. I want you to tell me why you loved her and what happened on the night she died. I want you to tell me all of it, Evan, and do not look away," she said.

He held her gaze for a long moment. Then he began to speak, not breaking their eye contact.

"Catherine O'Leary was the same age as me. Our families both worked the land and had small flocks, and our fields were next to one another. We grew up in different houses, but it was almost like we were brother and sister. We always got along, and I just liked her. She was playful and had an independent streak that came out one day when we were fourteen." He began smiling as he thought of that afternoon in the pasture.

"We were both tending the sheep and happened to meet in the field. She asked me if I was going to the festival later in the week, and if I would dance with her. I said I didn't know how to dance, and so she taught me the steps right there in the pasture. And then she kissed me." Evan was still looking directly at Elizabeth Anne. Her expression was one of complete attention.

"I remember it as if it were yesterday. I kissed her back, and then she ran off toward her house. But she called back to me that she loved me. I knew then that I loved her, too, and I yelled it out loud to the whole earth." He paused and was quiet. He was no longer looking at her eyes as she had requested, but she did not press the issue. She knew he was coming to the difficult part and remained silent, waiting for him to continue.

He began to speak again, his voice very low.

"Two days after that, her mother and father stopped at our house. Mother was a midwife, and Elizabeth O'Leary was ready to deliver her baby. Her mother's name was also Elizabeth. Father sent me over to the O'Leary place to tell Catherine and her brother what was happening. When I got there, I found that three, drunken British soldiers were planning to go into the house, and I knew Catherine was in danger. I crept up to the house and went inside. I had only a shepherd's crook in my hand, and I tried to stop the one soldier from hurting her."

His voice was becoming more pained as the events of that night came again into the forefront of his consciousness. He paused.

"What did you do to protect Catherine that night?" asked Elizabeth Anne gently.

"I asked the soldier to leave, and when he drew his sword against me, I tripped him with the crook end of the staff, and I hit him when he went down. But just as I moved toward Catherine to help her run out of the house, another soldier grabbed me and held me. The one on the floor got up and beat me, and that's all I remember," he continued.

"Evan! Look at me!" she said softly. His eyes found hers.

"Did you kill Catherine?" she asked.

His face registered a look of shock.

"No, of course not. They did, those British bastards! They killed Catherine," he half-shouted at her.

"Then, why do you blame yourself?" she asked. He was stopped cold by her question. A perplexed look came over his face, and he struggled for an answer.

"Because, because..." he searched for the words and then blurted out, "I ... didn't ... do enough ... and ... they killed her ... and ... took ...." His voice trailed off. Tears had formed in his eyes, but he still looked at her. The silence around them was interrupted only by the crackling of the fire.

"What else could you have done, Evan?" she asked softly.

The tears were now rolling down his cheeks. His pain was hard for her to watch, but she remained silent, waiting for his answer.

He clenched his fists tightly at his sides and looked wildly from side to side. His frustration peaked, and he looked back at her. The words choked out, and in a strangled, almost pitiful voice, he said,

"I don't know!"

* * * * * * *

For a long time, they sat there by the dying fire. Evan's tears had dried, and their tea was gone. Elizabeth Anne got up and went off toward the horses for a private moment. Evan sat staring straight ahead, and when she returned to her spot against the pack across from him, he looked up.

"Ya asked me to tell ya why I loved Catherine." Evan was remarkably composed now and spoke calmly.

"I really never thought about it until now. I'm not sure why except that I had just always known her, and she was fun to be with. And she was so lovely! She had light red hair and was tall but not big like many of the other girls in our area. But mostly, I guess, she was just easy to be with, and I always felt comfortable around her," he paused, smiling now at his memory of Catherine.

"Ya are right! There was nothing else I could have done that night. I did all that I could have done," he said. He was calm now, and his words came more easily.

"I don't want you to ever forget her, Evan. Catherine will always be with you, and that is the way it should be. But I want to tell you this: I will be your wife if we can learn to love one another. But I will not be Catherine. You must learn to love me, Elizabeth Anne, for who I am, and not because I remind you of her. Do you think you can do that, Evan?" she asked.

He was silent for a time before he answered her.

"Aye, I think I can do that. But I do not want ya for my wife until I am sure that I like ya," he said quite seriously.

"Then, can I go out to the western prairie with you?" Elizabeth Anne asked.

"Why would ya do that?" he answered, his tone clearly revealing that he was shocked by her proposal.

"How else will you know if you like me?" she answered, smiling.

CHAPTER 22
...when you least expect it...

When the Selkirk trail had almost reached the Red River, Evan and Elizabeth Anne turned west and crossed before it got too wide. The land was becoming more and more open, and if it had not been for the many small ponds and lakes, fresh drinking water would have become a major concern. As it was, each day the couple traveled about 35 miles. Horse travel was considerably faster than oxen-drawn wagons. Every evening they bedded down amid the packs, the horses picketed close by. With firewood almost non-existent now, they began using dried buffalo chips for their fires.

"My cousin from Selkirk's place told me to use this for fires. It smells like burning grass," Evan commented the first time he lit the fuel which lay on the prairie in great abundance. Elizabeth Anne just shook her head in disbelief.

Still, they saw no Indians or any other whites for that matter. And they had seen no buffalo either.

"Where are these great herds that are supposed to be out here?" Evan asked aloud one afternoon as they were riding along. At that very moment, they crested a hill and stopped, their eyes growing wide in disbelief. Before them, stretching as far as they could see, was a dark blanket of buffalo. The herd was traveling to the north, the great beasts grazing lazily as they moved slowly along. Red haired calves romped playfully among the big cows, while the younger bulls appeared to stay to the outside of the group.

Evan and Elizabeth Anne dined that evening on fresh buffalo meat, the first that either of them had ever eaten. It was delicious.

They spent the next three days drying strips of meat over their little fire and on pieces of canvas they laid out on the ground in the sunlight. They both knew that fresh meat would not keep and that by drying it they would be able to eat it weeks, even months, later.

* * * * * * *

It was late July, and they were getting close to the Missouri River. They had moved through the big buffalo herd with no problem. The Selkirk settlers he had met while at Fort Snelling had briefed Evan well on the habits of the big animals. Occasionally, Evan was able to kill a small, deer-like creature that was quite plentiful on the prairie. He also shot rabbits and some fat, low-flying birds, all of which provided good eating.

He was finding Elizabeth Anne very likeable, and they laughed a lot. They talked a great deal about their families and their childhoods. But while they slept side by side in a little makeshift tent they made so as to escape the bugs, they had not kissed again since that first time weeks earlier when Elizabeth Anne had first entered his camp just west of Fort Snelling. This was simply because Evan had told her that he wanted to be certain he liked her before she became his wife.

Small, spring-fed ponds and lakes provided their fresh water, and they usually camped on the banks of one each evening or two. They both made a practice of bathing in the cool water in the evening, and Elizabeth Anne always washed her shift and outer clothing every few days when she bathed.

"If you give me your shirt, I shall wash it, too," she offered. He declined.

"I can wash my own shirt and britches, thank ya!" he said.

It was during one such bathing time that she happened to glimpse him as he came out of the water. She was a good distance from him, but she saw him wring out his shirt and spread it over the bushes that partially blocked her view of him.

He is such a handsome man. And he is serious about this new hide business with Patrick. She thought. *We seem to get along very well, and he appears to like me. But will he love me? And will I love him?*

* * * * * * *

There was no question that Evan was an excellent horseman. Patrick had provided each of them with a riding horse, and Evan had two well-loaded pack horses as well. Evan easily controlled the animals and showed Elizabeth Anne how to ride hers so that she would be more comfortable. The riding horses had no saddles, and for a long time she had trouble staying on the animal's back.

"Hold onto this belly rope, and then grip the horse with your knees," Evan advised. It worked, and even in her long skirt, she was able to guide her horse with increasing proficiency.

They had been traveling now for almost four weeks. The weather had been dry for the most part, and the occasional rain had not been a problem. But on this particular afternoon, Evan pointed toward the western sky and said,

"We need to find cover for ourselves and the horses. There is a storm coming, and I fear it will be a bad one."

He whipped his horse, and with his two pack animals trailing and Elizabeth Anne riding along side of him, they rode rapidly toward some tall cottonwoods near another small pond. He was taking off the trade packs when the first raindrops came.

Evan tied the four horses to the heavy packs that he placed on the ground. He left them plenty of rope so that they had some motion. He and Elizabeth Anne huddled next to the bundles. The cottonwood trees were a short distance away from them so they were not actually under them. It was a good thing, because suddenly there came a loud crack and a bolt of lightning struck the tallest tree of the little grove. It shattered, and a large branch came down leaving a long scar on the central trunk.

The loud crash of the lightning caused the horses to panic. Evan stood between them and began speaking softly, his steady voice calming the animals. The rain was coming in great torrents now, and it was icy cold. He was soaked within seconds. The fury of the wind drove the drops into him so hard that they stung his flesh. The horses could barely stand against its strength. They turned so that they faced away from the wind with Evan hunched down between them holding their lines. Elizabeth Anne curled against one of the packs and pulled a piece of canvas over her head.

Suddenly, the rain and wind ceased. The sun came out abruptly, and the ground began to steam from its heat. He noticed little particles of ice all around him.

"Are you all right, Elizabeth Anne?" Evan called out.

She stuck her head out from under the canvas and smiled at him.

"You won't need a bath tonight," she said. They both began laughing.

"You will find another young woman. Look for one who is fun to be with and strong like Catherine was, but who also has the qualities you admire in your mother and sister as well. You can find such a woman if you look carefully." He recalled Marie Toussaint saying. *"And she will come to you when you least expect it."*

* * * * * * *

The sun began to dry them. Evan went off toward the little pond, the water in which appeared quite clean. He stepped into a stand of willows and removed his clothes. He had decided to bathe after all. He washed his clothes in the shallow water and hung them on the willows to dry. Then he slipped into the deeper part of the water. He began paddling quietly toward the spot where Elizabeth Anne had been sitting with the packs. She was nowhere to be seen, and his eyes swept the area. He was immediately concerned for her safety.

Suddenly, her head broke through the water a few feet away in front of him, and she smiled, shaking the water from her face.

"Don't you ever swim under water?" she asked, and then splashed his face, quickly disappearing beneath the surface. He was unable to catch her since she was obviously a much better swimmer than he was. She reappeared behind him and called out to him.

"Come this way. There is a sand bar here, and you can stand," she said.

He moved in her direction, and his feet soon touched the bottom. They were looking at one another now. The water came up to her shoulders and was clear enough so that he could see that she was wearing only her shift.

"Do you swim often with no clothes?" she asked.

"Only to bathe, and I don't really swim," he answered. It was difficult for him to look only at her face.

"Evan, I want to know if you like me," she said.

"What?" he said. He started to laugh. "Well, no. Actually I don't like ya at all. Ya make me laugh too much, and I cannot concentrate on watching the direction of our travel; and ya are much too pretty, and I can't stop looking at ya; and I keep wondering if ya like me, because we need to like one another if we are going to be married, and...."

"I do like you, Evan very, very much, and I know now that I want to be your wife, if you'll have me," she said, interrupting him. She moved toward him, and suddenly he felt her body crushed against him. Her mouth sought his, and they embraced there in the water. It was only the second time they had ever kissed.

"I love you, Evan," she said, breaking the kiss.

"Oh, and I love ya, too, Elizabeth Anne," he answered as he bent toward her.

She met his kiss, but it was quickly ended when he slipped, and they went under the water. Evan released her and came up coughing.

"Let's go up on the bank. I don't want my husband drowning on his wedding night," she said, laughing.

He followed her across the little pond and came out of the water a few yards behind her. As he stepped up onto the bank, he noticed that their blankets had already been spread on the ground.

CHAPTER 23
...they were...intending to attack....

The river was very wide. Evan went down the bank where it was obvious from the horse tracks that others had crossed at the same spot. The water was moving very slowly, and it was so shallow that he moved his horse across quite easily without having to swim at all. On the opposite bank, he looked to the west. The barren hills stretched on and on. He returned to the eastern shore.

"We must go north along this water until we find a river that comes into it. We can follow it north. That should take us to where the Mandan village is. We need a water source," he said.

They led the pack horses down into the water and soon were safely across the Missouri River. Then they turned north and began moving along the western shore right along the water's edge. Often, large piles of driftwood blocked their passage, and they were forced to backtrack and go up onto the higher bank. The travel was slow.

* * * * * * *

He was riding alone on the upper part of the bank when he saw the riders far out on the prairie. They were coming toward them and were a long way off.

"Elizabeth Anne," he called down to her. "Stop and secure the horses. There are Indians coming, and they will be here soon." He checked his rifle and set it at half-cock. Then he began moving slowly toward the group of seven Indian men.

Just over the river bank and out of sight, Elizabeth Anne suddenly felt more fear than she had ever before known. Then she thought. *This is crazy! I am afraid of the unknown.*

With this realization, she calmed. But she set out another powder horn and a bag of lead balls just in case Evan needed more ammunition. She peered up over the embankment and watched her husband ride forward to meet the approaching group.

* * * * * * *

Evan Ryan knew almost nothing about Indian people. His only experience had been with some Ojibwe with whom he had lived for just a few days prior to coming to Fort Snelling. He did not know their languages or their customs, nor did he know sign language—that universally understood language of the Plains Indians which made it possible for speakers of many different tongues to communicate successfully.

Some of the voyageurs at Fort William had said that the "buffalo Indians," as the Plains tribes were commonly called, were excellent horsemen and that they were impressed by courage. Evan suddenly remembered these things as the Indian group stopped, and one of the riders came toward him.

The man reined up about one hundred yards away, and Evan did the same. They sat facing one another, and not knowing what else to do, Evan raised his right hand palm inward with his fingers in a fist except for his index finger, which was extended upwards. He wanted to show the Indian that he was only one man. Then, just as he began to drop his hand back down onto his rifle which lay across the horse in front of him, a large fly buzzed onto his head, and he swiped his hand down the side of his hair to brush it away.

The Indian nodded and then raised both of his hands in a similar gesture, but then crossed them quickly back in forth in front of himself. Evan nodded and began riding toward the man, who also began moving. Evan had no way of knowing that he had just made the sign for "man" and then, with the motion of his hand on his hair, the sign for "woman." The Indian man had responded with the sign for "trade," made by showing the two "man" signs and then the sign for "exchange."

The two riders continued to approach one another until they were about thirty yards apart. Suddenly, from the south and coming up over a low rise in the prairie that had hidden them from view, came about a dozen Indians on horseback. They were clearly intending to attack the group with whom Evan had just made contact.

The man closest to Evan shouted at his friends. They began riding swiftly toward Evan. The attackers were enemies, and their arrows began falling among these riders as they moved closer to Evan and their comrade. He had ridden forward and was now almost next to Evan.

Suddenly, one of the riders in the friendly group was hit, the arrow burying itself in his right shoulder. He sagged and tried to stay on his horse, but another arrow struck the animal in the neck, and it faltered and then stopped. His friends rode on, not having seen his wounding.

Evan kicked his horse and, passing the other riders who still were not aware of their friend's problem, he rode quickly toward the man who had slid off his animal. He was now on the ground, and the attackers were about ninety yards away and coming fast.

Without thinking, Evan dismounted and knelt next to the man. Raising his musket, he waited until he was sure that the attackers were within range. Then he fired. The bullet struck one of the lead animals. It went down, and the charge slowed, the riders milling around the fallen animal and its rider, who had been hurt in the fall. Evan reloaded.

He finished the process quickly and just in time. The attackers mounted a second charge against him and the wounded warrior next to him. The man was now kneeling and trying to notch an arrow to send toward the enemy. Evan fired a second shot. This time the ball struck one of the enemy warriors in the chest, and the charge was halted. With two of the attacking force now down, the odds were becoming much more even.

The wounded man was trying to stand. Evan helped him up and onto his own horse since the wounded man's animal had run off to join the other horses. The man's friends had stopped their retreat and were only a short distance away. They were watching Evan and their wounded friend as they prepared to mount their own attack against their enemies. Evan put the reins of his horse between his teeth so he could reload. He began walking away from the attackers, leading his horse with the wounded man on it. The man's friends responded to his action with cries of salute, raising their bows high above their heads.

Evan copied their motions by raising his gun in the air, and not really knowing what to yell back, he hollered "Erin Go Bragh!"

Suddenly, the wounded man's friends thundered past them as they charged their attackers. At this unexpected action, the enemy turned and raced away from the downed horse, taking their wounded man with them. The warrior Evan had killed was left on the ground.

Evan watched, horrified, as two of the men dismounted and began to hack apart the body of the enemy. Then, he continued leading his horse with the wounded man on it down the embankment to Elizabeth Anne, who was waiting with the other animals. She had watched the entire event.

CHAPTER 24
...They call themselves Tsitsistas...

With the attackers chased off, four of the six remaining Indian men joined Evan and Elizabeth Anne and their wounded companion next to the river. They suddenly found themselves in the midst of unfamiliar faces. Two of the warriors had been left on the higher part of the bank to watch for any return of the enemy group. It was not probable since neither group had firearms. It was clear that Evan's rifle was much feared.

The arrow in the man's shoulder appeared to be not too deeply embedded, and Elizabeth Anne began to work with him immediately. Evan built a small fire and filled a cooking pot with river water. The water looked clear, but he knew that he had to boil it. The Indian men alternated between caring for their horses and going back up onto the higher ridge to watch for the enemy.

The man with whom Evan had first made contact stood close to the white couple. He watched as Elizabeth Anne firmly pulled the arrow out of the wounded man and staunched the bleeding. She gave her patient a drink of water and propped him up against one of the packs that had been removed from the pack animals. Though in pain, he smiled at her.

"Tsitsistas," he said, and pointed to himself and the other Indian men around him.

"Tsitsistas," he said again, and made four slices across his wrist with the index finger of his right hand, moving it slowly since it was the side with the shoulder wound.

"Tsitsistas," repeated Evan, pointing at the wounded man and his friends. The man nodded his head up and down.

"They call themselves, Tsitsistas, I think," Evan said to Elizabeth Anne.

She stood up and moved next to Evan. She raised her right hand with her index finger pointed up and turned it toward Evan. Then she took his hand in hers.

"I want him to understand that I am your wife," she said as they waited for the man's reaction.

The man smiled and nodded. Then, he pointed at them both and moved his hands quickly in front of his chest in a criss-cross motion. He followed it by putting his two index fingers together and pointing at them. It was the sign for "married."

"He understands," said Evan, smiling back at the man.

One of the Indian men came to the fire with a haunch of the small, deer-like animal that Evan had seen often on the prairie and that he knew from past experience made for good eating. He gestured toward the fire and began to prop up the meat for roasting. Elizabeth Anne put her hand out and took the meat from him. He let her have it, and she walked over to the partially open pack and retrieved another black metal pot. She cut up some of the meat, and soon it was simmering over the fire. The Indian men exchanged knowing glances.

Later, as they were eating, Evan and the Indian men talked. They used words in their respective languages and signs made with their hands to help convey the ideas. They were surprisingly successful in this communication, and Evan learned that they were hunters. It was also clear that they would be willing to trade buffalo hides for trade goods like those Evan carried. They were most interested in iron tools and, of course, guns.

In the afternoon, the Indians made it clear that they needed to move from this spot to avoid any further contact with the enemy group, whom they referred to as "Palani." Elizabeth Anne and Evan joined them unhesitatingly, and the group moved up from the protection of the deep river bank and out onto the prairie. They traveled north along the river.

* * * * * * *

They rode for the remainder of the afternoon and stopped where another river came into the larger one from the west. They made camp and turned the horses out onto the prairie to graze. While each of Evan's animals was picketed to an iron stake, he noticed that the Indian's horses only had rawhide cords attached to their legs which prevented them from straying too far away.

Interesting! He thought. *Their leather ropes are much shorter than mine. And yet they work just as well. I can learn much from these men.*

"I will stay awake first and then wake you later in the night to watch the packs," Evan told Elizabeth Anne. "I think these men are honorable, but I don't want to take a chance of being robbed or worse."

"Do what you think is best, Evan," she responded. "I am going now to attend the wounded one. I think kindness always prevails over greed."

* * * * * * *

It took only six days of travel for the hunters to reach their home village. As it came into view, Evan and Elizabeth Anne were amazed at the sight. About eighty tipis stood along the banks of the river they had been following, and off to the west they saw the unmistakable outline of mountains against the sky.

The wounded man had been moved on a drag which his friends had fashioned from two poles which they had cut along the riverbank. The poles crossed just behind one horse's neck, and they had fixed a platform between the poles that extended out behind the horse. A travois was the common way to move bundles or even people, and the man had been transported back to the village on it.

It seemed as though the entire population of the village had come out to greet the hunters. Children ran about everywhere, and there was a good deal of hollering when the group approached the large encampment. Their interest in Elizabeth Anne and Evan, who led their pack animals, was immediately very obvious.

The wounded man was helped from his place on the pony drag and taken to sit in front of one of the tipis. The man with whom Evan had first made contact immediately began talking to the assembled people. He talked excitedly and pointed often at the white couple. The response he got was obviously favorable. The people responded to the man's words with a din of yells and whoops. Evan and Elizabeth Anne understood at once that they were being welcomed.

When the man had finished speaking, an old woman who had been standing next to the wounded man came forward. She placed a tanned buffalo robe around Elizabeth Anne's shoulders and, using her hands to sign her spoken words, said,

"You have been kind to my son. You are now my daughter, and I welcome you."

Even if Elizabeth Anne did not understand either the words the woman spoke or the signs she made with her hands, the look that passed between them was clear. It was the silent language that women throughout the world speak to one another, no matter what their origin or culture, when the message involves their children. Elizabeth Anne smiled and nodded, taking hold of the robe.

We are safe with these people. She thought.

Then she remembered what Evan had said about the Indian people he had met and lived with shortly before coming to Fort Snelling. "Ojibwe" he had called them.

They are not savages after all. I think they are people, just like us! She thought. *He was right.*

The crowd eventually dissipated, and Evan and Elizabeth Anne made their camp next to the tipi of the wounded man. They were too excited to be hungry, and they were tired from the day's travel. They looked forward to a night of peaceful sleep.

When they had first met these Tsitsistas, their concern was that they would be robbed, or worse. That had now been replaced by a guarded trust for the men. Here in the village of the Tsitsistas, they felt relatively safe and rather at home. They arranged their bed between the packs, and Evan picketed their four horses nearby.

Their anticipation of a good night's rest was soon to be interrupted.

CHAPTER 25
...you danced...

As they began to relax against their packs, four men, led by the one Evan had first met on the prairie, approached the couple. Signing to them, he invited them to come with him. He pointed to their packs of trade goods and again crossed his hands rapidly in front of his chest. Then he walked over to the packs and placed his hands on one of them. He made a motion that was easily interpreted as an indication that they were secure. Evan and Elizabeth Anne nodded and followed the men away from their belongings.

The entire camp was arranged in somewhat of a circle. The tipis were made of buffalo hides, and some were beautifully decorated. Near the center of the circle, a large fire was burning, and buffalo ribs were being roasted. A crowd was gathering, and soon some women were passing out the meat to the people. What appeared to be some of the choicest cuts were brought to the white couple.

"I think we are the guests of honor," Elizabeth Anne said, accepting a large piece of roast from a woman. She began eating the succulent meat.

Evan smiled at her and said, "Ya are hungry, aye?" She nodded, the juice running down her chin. He began to eat. It was good.

The crowd continued to grow in size until it seemed that the whole village had gathered. Then a group of men brought a drum into the area, and, kneeling beside it, they began to strike it in a rhythmic pattern. One of the men began singing, and the others joined him, raising their voices in a high-pitched song unlike anything either Elizabeth Anne or Evan had ever heard.

Suddenly, the men from the original group they had met began dancing near the seated singers. Their dance motions were fluid, and it was clear that they were telling the story of their meeting with Evan and of the attack by the Palani. Behind him, a Tsitsistas man tapped Evan on the shoulder and pointed at the dancers.

"He wants you to join them," said Elizabeth Anne. "You should step out there and tell everyone your part of the story."

The man behind Evan nudged him, smiling and pointing at the dancers.

"But ... I don't know how to dance," Evan said. "Certainly not their way."

"Watch them! They are stepping to the beat and using their arms and body movements to tell the story. You can do that," she answered.

Evan took a few steps toward the dancers and then began to mimic their dance movements. He began slowly and got the rhythm of the drum easily, his shyness quickly leaving him.

This is not difficult! He thought. Whoops of encouragement began to erupt from the many people who were now watching him and the other dancers as they moved smoothly across the open ground.

One of the dancers was gesturing at a spot across the dance area. Evan watched him as he made the motions that told the crowd that they were under attack. A second man moved next to him and suddenly dropped down, acting as though an arrow had struck his shoulder. The other men moved away from him and past Evan, who was now dancing easily in place.

As they passed him, one motioned to Evan to dance up to the wounded man. Evan understood at once. This was a reenactment of the battle against the Palani that first day a week earlier. He danced up to the man and made the motions of firing his musket toward the enemy. He pretended that he was reloading, and he fired again. Then he reached down and helped the man up. Together they danced toward the others.

They had gotten about half-way when suddenly one of the other men came dancing toward them, his steps simulating that of a prancing horse. He handed Evan a long rawhide rope and indicated that he should put it between his teeth. Then Evan remembered that he had led his horse away from the attackers by holding the reins in his mouth.

He put the rope into his mouth and began to dance slowly toward the others. As he did, he made the motions of reloading again. Then the other dancers moved past them in a fake attack at the unseen enemy.

As he neared the edge of the dance area, Evan and the other man turned and faced the others. They had wheeled about and were dancing toward them. As they came up in front of Evan and the man, the song ended, and the crowd yelled in salute.

One of the dancers in front of Evan stepped forward and handed Evan a gift. It was a small, circular hoop on which had been stretched a piece of what appeared to be skin. Long black hair hung down. It was the scalp of the slain enemy warrior. The men in the dance group whooped loudly at this presentation. Evan took the hooped scalp and smiled at them. Raising it high in the air above his head, he shouted, "Erin Go Bragh!" and followed the words with a shrill whoop of his own.

****

The dancing continued for the next few hours with various men pantomiming their war exploits. It was obvious to Evan and Elizabeth Anne that these people valued bravery very highly, especially courage in the face of seemingly insurmountable odds.

If you all only knew what I know about my husband's bravery! She thought as she watched the men gather around Evan in small groups, patting him on the back and speaking to one another in their own language.

Evan had his own thoughts. They were of Ireland and the time when he was only fourteen years old.

* * * * * * *

Later in the night, the songs seemed to change, and the women began to move around the outside of the circle in small groups. As they stepped gently to the drumbeat, they talked with one another. Soon Elizabeth Anne had joined them.

At the end of one song, seven women approached Elizabeth Anne. They were the wives or sisters of the men she and Evan had first met on the prairie. They each handed her a small, decorated stick, and one of them gestured toward the area in the camp where the white couple had left their packs. She could not understand their words and was mystified by this little ceremony. The women began pointing and making motions which indicated that she was to follow them.

They left the dance area together and were soon at the place where their packs had been. They were nowhere in sight. Evan's musket was gone, too.

Oh god! Someone has taken Evan's musket! Thought Elizabeth Anne, suddenly alarmed.

Then one of the women pointed at a tipi that had been set up near to the spot where the packs had been. She gestured at three of the women and at herself and pointed to the decorated sticks in Elizabeth Anne's hands. One of the women raised the flap of the tipi door and motioned for Elizabeth Anne to go inside. In a moment, all eight of them were in the semi-dark interior, illuminated only by the soft glow of a buffalo chip fire.

Another woman pointed at what appeared to be mats of willow shoots that had been strung together and hung from little tripods to form a sort of chair. She sat down and leaned back against one to demonstrate its use.

One of the others pointed to a bed in the rear of the tipi. It was raised off of the ground and covered with tanned buffalo robes. She made the sign for "man" and for "woman," and then the sign for sleep. She pointed again at the bed and said something in her language, at which all of the women began laughing softly, their hands up in front of their mouths. Elizabeth Anne understood at once and laughed with them, nodding her head affirmatively.

They are women, just like me. She thought.

Finally, one of the women pointed to the packs of trade goods that had been placed carefully around the tipi's perimeter. They were still tied shut, just as they had been. Then Elizabeth Anne saw that Evan's rifle and shooting bag were propped up next to the backrest on the north side of the tipi.

Using hand gestures and a few words, the first woman made it clear that the tipi and its inside furniture were being given to Elizabeth Anne and that she owned all of it now.

She was stunned. *These people are more generous than the whites. They have given me an entire household. We are now out of the weather. But, how does one set these things up?* She had the fleeting thought.

Elizabeth Anne did not know what to do. *How do I thank them for their kindness?* She waved her hand in a circle and then stepped forward and hugged each of the women gently. They smiled at her act and, one by one, they left the tipi.

She followed them out and together they returned to the dance circle. As they neared the spot where Evan was standing, the older woman pointed at Evan and made the sign for "man." Then she pointed back at the tipi.

She is telling me to take my husband home. Elizabeth Anne thought. *That is exactly what I am going to do.* She led him away from the group.

"Evan, you danced," she said to him as they moved hand in hand toward her tipi. He nodded. *But not with any woman!* He thought.

Then he questioned his own feelings. *I think some day I will dance with ya, my love!*

His wife snuggled into his side as they walked.

"Wait 'til you see this," she said.

CHAPTER 26
...the same as us...yet different...

Early the next morning Elizabeth Anne followed some of the women down to the river which ran near the village. Together they bathed in the shallow water, a thick grove of willows shielding them from the rest of the camp. It was very clear that this was the women's bathroom area, and she was at once comfortable learning this new cultural way.

Returning to the tipi, she untied one of the packs and took out a cast-iron pot. She had noticed that many of the women and girls were filling large bladders with the clear river water a bit upstream from the bathing area. She joined them once again and soon had some of their dried buffalo meat simmering on the fire which Evan had started in front of the tipi. It was still summer, and cooking was obviously being done outside. The interior fire had only been used to keep the night chill from disturbing their sleep.

She thought. *They have it all worked out. I like these people.*

* * * * * * *

It had been a week. The sights and sounds of the Tsitsistas village were becoming less and less foreign to Elizabeth Anne and Evan. She continued her interaction with the women she had met, and he had gone out with one of the small hunting parties. He returned with the meat of a buffalo, and following the custom of the other hunters, he gave away most of it to the families whose tipis were near to theirs.

"Ya should have seen them hunt," he said to Elizabeth Anne. "I can use the bow and arrow myself, but I never expected to see what I saw." She looked at him quizzically.

"They rode right up along side of a running buffalo and shot straight down at their target. Sometimes the arrow went all the way through the beast and stuck in the ground. I couldn't believe it," he said. "I have never seen such bow strength."

"But they point at me and laugh every time I get on or off my horse," he added. "They get on from the other side, ya know, and then slide off on the left. I think I figured out why they do it that way," he went on.

"Why is that?" Elizabeth Anne asked, interested to hear her husband's response.

"By getting up on the right, they can get on their horse shooting the bow; then, by swinging their leg over the horse's neck and sliding off on the left, they can dismount shooting as well. They are perfectly at ease with their horses and with those bows in their hands," he answered. "They can teach me a lot."

Elizabeth Anne smiled and nodded her assent. *And me, too.* She thought.

*   *   *   *   *   *   *

She had seen the woman around the camp a number of times. It was obvious that her baby would come at any time, and Elizabeth Anne was curious about how these women would accomplish this age-old and common occurrence. *Do they have midwives like we do? What do they do if there are complications?* She would soon learn the answers to her questions.

*   *   *   *   *   *   *

Right from the beginning, Evan was able to trade for tanned buffalo hides, and he made it clear that untanned hides would be welcome the next summer. He used sign language to make his wishes known. He found the method fairly easy, and both he and his wife were becoming more proficient with this form of talk. While they were also acquiring a good number of words in the People's language, they both depended on the hand signs to communicate on a daily basis.

"Next spring," he signed, "we will take the hides to the east. I will go with many horses loaded with hides, and when I return, I will bring guns."

There was a good deal of smiling, the Tsitsistas men making the "a-hou, a-hou" words. Evan knew it meant that they agreed enthusiastically with what he had said.

Within four weeks, most of the trade goods had been distributed. Often Evan accepted a decorated stick from a man instead of a buffalo robe. The number of marks on the stick indicated how many buffalo robes would be due in the summer hunt. Since he had already given them the trade goods, Evan was actually extending credit to the men.

"I think I can trust them," he said to his wife. She nodded in agreement.

I'm sure you can! She thought.

Some of their trade items were given as gifts. Both Evan and Elizabeth Anne noticed how important it was to give away things, and they saw the People doing it regularly. Naturally, Elizabeth Anne gave presents to the seven women who had gifted her with the tipi and its furnishings. And Evan gifted the men he had first met on the prairie and with whom he had fought against the Palani. Those men and women were, not surprisingly, very closely related. Having too many things in their tipi was unnecessary. It made the interior much too cluttered.

"We came to trade. Let's get rid of the rest of the goods," said Evan. "We will need the space for fuel and dried meat."

Winter was coming not too far off, and the white couple was actually eager to spend that season with their new friends.

* * * * * * *

It was just at sundown. Elizabeth Anne saw the concern in the eyes of her neighbor as the woman walked hurriedly past her tipi. She caught up with her and signed,

"Is your heart hurting? Can I help you?" Her hands made the gestures, and the woman quickly signed back so fast that Elizabeth Anne had a hard time following her message.

"My sister is trying to have her baby, and things are not going well," she signed.

"I know about those things," Elizabeth Anne said with her hands. "May I come with you?"

Together they moved to a tipi not too far away. Some men were standing outside the door. One of them looked particularly stressed. The Tsitsistas woman called out softly, and a muffled response from inside the tipi indicated that she should enter. Elizabeth Anne followed her into the dimly lit interior.

Two women were already inside with the pregnant woman who was obviously in a good deal of pain. Yet, she made no sound as the contractions peaked and ebbed. Elizabeth Anne sat silently and assessed the woman's labor. She felt somewhat helpless, even though she had attended the births of dozens of babies. She finally signed to one of the women.

"How long has she been like this?"

"Since last night," came the non-vocal response.

"May I look at her up close?" she signed.

The woman nodded and made room for Elizabeth Anne next to the laboring woman.

Women are women. She thought. *Having babies can't be any different in a tipi than it is in a carpenter's bedroom in Cincinnati or in a log cabin at Mendota. Perhaps I can help her.* She felt the woman's protruding stomach, pressing gently.

Her first suspicions were quickly confirmed. The baby had not turned. It would be another dangerous backwards delivery unless Elizabeth Anne could cause the little one to reverse its position. She began to massage the woman's stomach using the special techniques that her mother had taught her. In a short time, she had achieved the desired result. With the baby's head now positioned low in the woman's belly, the chance for a successful delivery was much greater.

Within two hours, the baby came.

* * * * * * *

Evan was eating when his wife entered the tipi.

"I did not know where ya were," he said.

"I was just helping a woman have her baby," she answered, becoming suddenly very quiet as she helped herself to some of the soup that was warming on the small fire.

"Is everything all right?" he asked, sensing that something was wrong.

"It is. The little one is healthy," she responded. "But I saw something that has disturbed me, something very strange. And I do not know why it happened." Her voice revealed that she was terribly confused and bothered. Evan waited for her to continue.

"The little one came out, and an older woman who was in the tipi with us cut the cord. Then she wrapped the child in a soft piece of buckskin and used another to wipe the boy dry. Naturally, the baby started to cry. The woman immediately pinched his little nose shut and covered his mouth so he could not breathe. When he squirmed and began to kick, she let him take a breath. But when he started to cry again, she cut off his air. She did this again and again, and all the while she was softly singing a little song to him," she said.

Evan stopped eating and put down his bowl. He was listening intently to his wife.

"I was busy with the mother, waiting for the last of the birthing process to be over. Still, I kept glancing at the old woman and the way she was treating this little baby. I was about to sign to her to stop, that she was hurting him. But suddenly the baby stopped struggling, and when she released him, he did not start to cry. The woman was singing to him all the while," she went on.

"It did not take very long for the baby to learn that he could not cry and be loud. Every time he would start to cry, she just sang the little song, and he would stop. At first, she would sometimes have to touch his nose a little to remind him, but usually the song was enough. I have never seen anything like it," she said, shaking her head in disbelief. "Why do you suppose she did this?"

"I have noticed how quiet the camp is throughout the night. I think a baby that cries loudly could alert an enemy to the location of the village," answered Evan.

He was correct. For the People, the individual was less important than the survival of the group. It was a lesson that began with birth.

They are the same as us, yet different. She thought.

* * * * * * *

The next day Elizabeth Anne was surprised by a visitor. It was the father of the new little baby boy she had helped to deliver. The man was holding the lead ropes of two horses. Signing to her, he simply said,

"You helped my woman bring my first son into the world. I am grateful. The women are calling you She Helps Them to Be Born."

He smiled and handed her the ropes.

* * * * * * *

The next day the entire village moved. They passed a large butte that stood prominently on the eastern edge of the wooded mountains Evan had seen in the distance off to the west.

"It is a very special place for the People," he was told. "Many of our young men go there to meet the One Above."

Within three days, the People were encamped in the mountains. It was a good place.

CHAPTER 27
...we will trade honorably...

Their first winter with the People was a continual learning experience for both Elizabeth Anne and Evan. They were only eighteen and nineteen years old, and as was the custom for young couples, an old woman moved into their tipi. She helped Elizabeth Anne learn the correct housekeeping ways which their new lifestyle demanded. And she began teaching her how to speak in the language of the People. But she never spoke directly to Evan. It was considered improper.

"He is not my son-in-law," the old woman signed to Elizabeth Anne. "But it is our way, and it is good."

"It's a strange thing," said Evan one evening. "She seems to know when to turn away from us and begin to sleep."

Elizabeth Anne just smiled. *Of course! She was a young woman once, too, you know.*

By the time late spring had come, it was certain that Elizabeth Anne was expecting her first child. She was glad to have the grandmother living with them to help with the tipi tasks that were sure to become increasingly difficult for her. And she would be a companion for her when Evan left to take the first load of hides back to St. Paul in the summer.

* * * * * * *

Transporting the buffalo hides was really not difficult. By piling a number of them on the wooden platform that was dragged behind a horse, one rider could move fairly quickly across the prairie. This would be Evan's first hide shipment, and he knew that he would have to travel all the way to Patrick at Fort Snelling.

The group of thirty Tsitsistas men rode together, each of them pulling their own bundle of hides on a travois and holding the lines to which alternate horses were attached. Some of those horses carried hides as well.

Within four weeks, they were crossing the Red River, and Evan knew that it was only another week's travel to his brother-in-law's place near the fort. But the Cheyenne men were becoming concerned that they were in enemy territory, and they grew more agitated each day. They were not a war party, and they worried about the prospect of an attack by either the Palani or the Dakota that lived in this eastern part of the prairie. The Cheyenne were beginning to establish a peaceful relationship with the western Lakota, but they had little contact with these eastern Dakota and were unsure of what their contact with them might bring.

* * * * * * *

They all heard the creaking and groaning long before they saw the carts. They were two-wheeled affairs and were pulled by oxen, mules, or horses. It was a long caravan of carts passing along the wide and clearly marked trail just east of the Red River.

Signing to his friends to stay back, Evan rode forward to intercept the noisy convoy. Within a short time, he had made a business arrangement with the group of drivers.

* * * * * * *

When he arrived at Fort Snelling with the buffalo hides less than a week later, Patrick and Ana were elated to see him. The reunion with his sister and brother-in-law was a happy one.

"How did you get here? Where is Elizabeth Anne?" Ana asked excitedly.

Evan told them of his trip across the prairie and how he had bartered with the cart drivers. They had agreed to take the hides the rest of the way to the fort. The caravan of carts had been making the return trip from the Selkirk settlement north of Pembina down to Fort Snelling. By piling four or five hides on each already-loaded cart, they were able to take Evan's cargo on the remainder of the journey. Everything had gone smoothly. It had been a very lucky break for Evan. His Cheyenne friends would wait for him to return with the trade goods.

"These hides will bring us a good sum of money," Patrick said, when he saw the number and the quality. "These tanned ones are beautiful and will bring the biggest money. But the raw ones will sell well, too."

Patrick paid the drivers in cash and negotiated with them to make a trip back out to the Red River within the week. The return trip would be led by Evan, and the carts would carry trade goods for the People. Extra men to guard the caravan were also hired.

* * * * * * *

"He is a fine looking boy," Evan said when he held up his new nephew. Patrick beamed with pride.

"We've named him Patrick Evan after the two of us," he said.

"'Tis a good pair of names, aye?" Evan replied.

Ana was very excited to hear that Elizabeth Anne was now expecting. The three of them sat for hours talking about Evan's first winter with the People.

"They are not savages," he said. "They are extremely generous, and they look out for each other the way we did back in Ireland. And ya should see them ride and hunt!"

* * * * * * *

Five days later, a small caravan of fifteen carts loaded with the manufactured goods that were so desired by the Indian people of the plains, left for the west.

"We will trade honorably with the People," Evan had said when Patrick asked him again if he wanted to take liquor along. "I want only goods that the women can use, and knives, tomahawks, rifles and powder for the men. That

is what they want. I shall not be a party to drunkenness."
He knew too well the negative effects of liquor. He had seen
its terrible results as a fourteen-year-old boy in Ireland.

*   *   *   *   *   *   *

And so began one of the most unique American
business ventures in the annals of Native American
experience. Coming some thirty years before the great
buffalo herd slaughter that would begin in the 1860s and
that would decimate the herds within twenty years, the
trading relationship between this one white trader and the
Cheyenne, and later the Lakota, would be based on mutual
trust. It would be respectful and fair.

*I know this is the right thing to do. I shall be honorable
and fair with the People. I shall never be like the English
landlords in Ireland.* Evan thought as he neared the meeting
spot. His Tsitsistas friends were waiting, and he smiled at
their reaction to the trade goods he had brought them.

Evan knew that the next summer, in the Moon When
the Cherries Are Ripe, they would only have to go as far
as the confluence of the Cheyenne and Missouri rivers to
make the exchange. He had made the agreement with his
cousin, the Selkirk settler named Patterson who he had
met at Fort Snelling.

"I know about where that place is," Patterson had
said. "I was there once on a long hunting trip. It is south
of the Mandan villages. The carts can go that far to meet
you."

No pony drags were needed for the return trip since
each Tsitsistas man had two additional horses with him
that now served as pack animals.

This trade will work. Evan thought. He could not
know that he would be more successful with it over the next
twenty-three years than he would have ever imagined.

*   *   *   *   *   *   *

That second winter with the People was cold, but Elizabeth Anne's tipi was warm and comfortable. A windbreak of brush surrounded each of the lodges in the encampment, which was now reduced to about half of the original number. They had again moved the camp closer to the mountains that had been visible to the west. It was a good place. It was protected and had fresh water and plenty of firewood. The saws and axes which Evan had brought back made life much easier for the People.

The baby within her was growing rapidly, and Elizabeth Anne knew that in the early winter she would be a mother. The old woman who lived with them continued to assist her with the daily tasks that had to be done. The baby was born in the Moon of the Popping Trees. She was named Sarah Ana, and she was beautiful.

Elizabeth Anne had turned away as the old woman taught the new arrival the importance of being quiet. Within a few weeks, the little girl was happy and perfectly content within the confines of a cradleboard.

"She sleeps easily in that little portable bed, and I can prop it up anywhere. It is a wonderful invention," Elizabeth Anne said to Evan.

* * * * * * *

One night when they were sitting inside the tipi after an evening meal, the old woman pointed to one of the dogs that shared the tipi with them. She signed as she spoke the words of the People.

"Do you see the way that mother dog is lying?" she asked.

The white couple nodded. The dog was lying on its side with its legs stretched straight out from its body. But the dog's head was looking away from the direction of its legs. It looked very uncomfortable, although the animal was clearly asleep.

"It is the promise of the dogs," signed the old woman.

Evan was watching and following the conversation.

"What is this promise?" he signed. Although the old woman never looked directly at him or spoke directly to him, she saw his signed question from the corner of her eye. As though he had never asked at all, she continued.

"I heard about this promise when I was very young. My grandmother told me," she signed to Elizabeth Anne.

"Grandmother told me that an old woman told her that very long ago, when our People lived in much smaller tipis, there would sometimes be starving times in the winter when it was difficult for the hunters to go out for fresh meat. During one such hungry time, an old woman had a dream," she signed. Her hands made the movements slowly so that Elizabeth Anne could keep up with the story.

"In the dream, an old female dog came to the woman and said this: 'You two-leggeds always are kind to us. You feed us scraps of meat, and in the cold weather you allow us to sleep inside with you. We want to give back to you.'"

The old woman paused in the telling so that Elizabeth Anne could say the words to Evan in their language. It was the pattern of conversation to which the three of them were accustomed. When Elizabeth Anne had finished, she continued.

"The dog told the woman that she knew that her two-legged friends were starving and that it was time for the dogs to pay them back for their kindness. She said to her, 'When you see one of the dogs lying in that position, take your knife and slit its throat. It will die quickly and painlessly. Use the meat to keep you and your children alive. That is our gift to you. As you live, so do we.'" The old woman was quiet, waiting for Elizabeth Anne to say the words to Evan.

He was silent for a moment. Then he said to his wife, "Tell her that the dogs are always welcome here. We will always remember this story and honor the meaning of the dogs' promise."

Elizabeth Anne signed the words. The old woman smiled and put her hand on the sleeping animal, petting it gently in recognition of the dog's symbolic position.

It reminds me of the sacrament of Communion! Elizabeth Anne thought. *We take the wine and bread as a promise of life in one sense, and the dogs have made the same promise of life with their willing sacrifice. How interesting!*

* * * * * * *

Spring came and with it a terrible threat to the People. The cholera came into the camp without warning, and the children and old people began to die.

Elizabeth Anne and Evan had both seen this disease before. Although they did not know what caused it, they knew that dehydration was the real killer.

Elizabeth Anne moved through the camp, telling all of the women to "heat the water in the metal pots until it bubbles and mix this tea into it. Drink as much of the hot water as you can," she signed.

Still, many died.

It is so hard to see the little ones die. She thought as she listened to the wailing throughout the camp. But the sadness did not come to her lodge.

Shortly after, the entire camp moved out onto the prairie. The annual summer hunt was about to begin.

* * * * * * *

"Come with me, Elizabeth Anne. Bring Sarah Ana. We will be gone overnight. I will pack some food," Evan said. He seemed preoccupied and was seldom short with his words like this when speaking to his wife.

They rode toward a large butte that was located on the northeast side of the low mountain range where they had been camping over the winter months. By the middle of the afternoon, they had left the horses picketed at its base and were walking up to the summit. Evan carried their blankets and food supplies while Elizabeth Anne walked with the baby in the cradleboard strapped to her back.

"What are we doing here?" she finally asked when they had reached the top.

"There is something I must do," he replied. "My friends say that this butte is one of their most holy places. From a distance, it looks like a sleeping bear. Tomorrow at dawn, ya will understand." He was very secretive.

They ate and then bedded down for the night. It was windy, but they were able to find a secluded place that afforded them good protection. Evan was awake just before dawn.

"It is time, Elizabeth Anne," he said as he gently awakened her. She picked up their sleeping daughter and held the little girl in her arms as they moved to the summit.

Looking to the east, they watched as the far horizon turned red and then golden as the sun came into view.

"It is so beautiful," Elizabeth Anne said softly.

"Aye, 'tis! And if I could look far enough, I could see Ireland," he said. Then he turned and took his wife in his arms, the baby between them. He looked down at them and then into Elizabeth Anne's eyes.

"We have never been properly married before God. I am going to make that right," he said.

He turned to the east and raised his hands to the sky. Then he shouted out for the whole world to hear,

"One Above! Hear my words! It is I, Evan Ryan. This woman is Elizabeth Anne. She is my wife. I promise to always love her, and there will be no one else but her. Ah-hou! Ah-hou!"

Elizabeth Anne was stunned. She looked at Evan, who continued to stand facing the east.

I thought I knew you, but there are places in your mind that I may never know. She thought.

He turned back to her and smiled. She handed him their daughter and stepped toward the east. She stood there for a few minutes in silence. Everywhere around them the prairie seemed to go on endlessly.

Our love will be endless, too. She thought. Then she crossed herself and turned back to her husband.

"I am glad to finally be married to ya," he said with a grin.

They gathered up their things and went back down the butte to join the People.

* * * * * * *

In the Moon when the Cherries Are Ripe, Evan and about two dozen of his friends left for the East. The early summer hunt had been very successful. But each hunter took only enough buffalo to meet his family's needs, and they did not slaughter the beasts just for the hides. It was his second shipment, and the group carried many pelts.

The Cheyenne group got to the meeting place on the Missouri River two days before the carts arrived.

My second shipment! Evan thought, and he smiled broadly when the bundles of trade goods were loaded onto the pack animals for the return trip to the west. Then he handed a small packet of letters to the cart foreman, Patterson.

"My wife asks that you give these to Patrick and Ana Hughes. And bring back more paper and ink next year," he said.

It was the first such group of letters that came with the hides every year thereafter. At times, there was a return letter from Patrick.

CHAPTER 28
...there is a letter here...from America...

It was a letter addressed to the Michael Ryan family, the Patrick Hughes family, and the Thomas O'Leary family.

"Go to the Ryans, the Hughes, and the O'Learys and invite them here. Tell them that they must all come, that there is a letter for them from America," John Burke instructed his tavern assistant.

The three families arrived at the pub just at the dinner hour. They brought their own food and enough extra for Burke and his family. It was the courteous thing to do.

Burke supplied the ale, and after they had eaten, he took a large envelope from behind the bar. He had not opened it because he wanted to do so in their presence. It was addressed simply:

> *To Michael Ryan, Patrick Hughes, Thomas O'Leary*
> *and Families*
>   *c/o John Burke   County Tipperary   Ireland*

He opened it and began reading.

> *From Fort Snelling, Minnesota Territory, United States of America*
>
> *To Our Dearest Mothers and Fathers,*
>
> *It is with great pleasure that we write to you so that you know that Evan and I and Patrick are well. There is so much to tell, and we do not know where to begin. It has only been eight months since we left, but it seems almost like a lifetime. It must be a shock for you all to hear that we are together. But we are.*

Evan is here with Patrick and me. As you know, he came to America on the trading ship. It landed in Montreal and he worked as a blacksmith over the winter. He met John O'Toole there. Please tell his father that John is well and that he is working in the fur trade.

In the spring, Evan went with John to a large fur trade post, but then decided to go south instead of farther west. He came to this American fort quite by chance and found that Patrick and I were here. Imagine our shock in finding one another here in the middle of America! Evan is fine.

Now let me tell you about Patrick and me. We are married, and I am carrying his child. You may not know that we left Cork last October. I really did not want to go to England and I am sorry if my decision has caused you any hardship. Patrick said that you knew he was going to follow me. We were able to purchase our passage to America and arrived in New York City after a fast crossing. We spent the winter there and in the spring we came on a river boat to Cincinnati.

That is where we met Elizabeth Anne. She is from that city, and the three of us traveled together to this fort. She has become our very dear friend. Patrick is working as a trade clerk and buying up land.

Evan and Patrick are starting a business. Evan will go out onto the American prairies and send buffalo hides back to Patrick, who will sell them. It will be hard, but it should be a profitable venture.

Evan says to tell Thomas O'Leary that he came across another one of the soldiers while on his sea voyage, and that part of the account is now settled.

We miss you all and speak often of you. We send our affection to you and especially to Timothy and Little Thomas.

You may write to us here at Fort Snelling Minnesota Territory, in care of the United States Military Academy at West Point, New York State, America. With luck, this letter will reach you, and we will look forward to your response at some time in the future.

Your loving daughter and sons.

Written this 24th day of June, 1828 at Fort Snelling by

*Elizabeth Anne Delaney for
Ana Ryan Hughes, Patrick Hughes and Evan Ryan*

Burke finished reading and looked up.

"Did it say that my son was buying up land?" asked Patrick Hughes.

Burke nodded affirmatively.

This cannot be! My son is owning his own land! Patrick thought, smiling broadly and shaking his head in disbelief.

"It isn't possible. My children are together in America," added Mary Ryan. She was still trying to believe, to understand all that she had just heard.

"John, read it again," requested Michael. He, too, was in a state of incredulity, if not shock.

Burke read the letter again, this time more slowly. When he finished, the group was silent.

"When was it written?" Michael asked.

Burke answered the question and added, "That was just over two years ago."

"Thank god, my children are safe," said Mary. She crossed herself and then reached for Timothy and hugged him. He was her only child still at home.

"I suppose ya'll be leavin' me some day as well," she said to him. Timothy did not respond. He was balancing between childhood and adulthood.

John Burke stood and said, "I'd like to propose a few toasts." The men stood, and everyone raised their tankards of ale.

"First, to our sons: May they be men always and honor their families, past and present," he said, drinking a sip. Everyone drank.

"Second, to our daughters: May they honor us with the fruits of their loins and teach their little ones how to live rightly," he said and drank again. The others drank, too.

"Third, to America: May your children do well there and make ya proud." He drank another sip. Everyone murmured their agreement and sipped again from their cups.

"And finally, to Evan Ryan, I toast with these words, Erin Go Bragh." He finished his cup as the others repeated the old Gaelic words.

Only Thomas O'Leary did not drink. Instead, he nodded to the others in recognition of the toast, and with his cup raised high above his head, he added, "Aye! To Evan Ryan! A man of honor!" He finished his ale.

* * * * * * *

Throughout the evening, the three families celebrated the good fortune of their children. It was all quite astounding. Patrick was a land-owner; Ana had given the Ryans their first grandchild; Evan was alive and well and in business with Patrick.

They asked Burke to read the letter again and again. While it gave them information, many other questions were left unanswered. How did Evan get to this fort? Where did he meet O'Toole? How did Ana and Patrick come to have enough money to buy passage to America? How did they survive in New York? How did they get to Cincinnati and then to this American fort? Where is the money coming from with which to buy land? Where was this fort? Are they not in danger of being killed by the red savages?

When the questions about money were voiced, Little Thomas O'Leary remained silent, his eyes fixed in the cold, vacant stare for which he was known. But, as the families left Burke's pub, Little Thomas turned to his father and said very softly,

"All three of Catherine's killers have paid for their crimes, Father. I collected part of the debt myself. Erin Go Bragh."

CHAPTER 29
...We must take the children back...

The Lakota tended to be shorter and stockier than the Tsitsistas. A small group of them had come into the Cheyenne village, and it was apparent that the People knew many of these Lakota families and that they were considered allies.

They also spoke an entirely different language than did the People, and almost everyone used sign language to communicate. The camp was now a mixed one of Cheyenne and Lakota. The Lakota word for this type of village was "tiyospaye." It meant a group of loosely related people who came together for the purpose of mutual protection and increased hunting capability. Evan noticed that the Lakota were very interested in all of the rifles the People had.

Evan and Elizabeth Anne had just been starting to become familiar with the Cheyenne language when the Lakota families joined the group. While the two groups appeared to practice very similar cultural patterns, the white couple was faced with new communication demands. But the language challenge brought by the Lakota was foreshadowed by an even greater one.

It came first in 1831 and again in 1833. The white couple recognized it immediately. Smallpox.

"We must warn the People about this," Evan said to his wife when he first saw the red sores on the faces of some of the newly arrived Lakota. They had traded far to the north and east with the Mandans, and Evan suspected they had probably gotten the infection from them. Evan was also sure that the Mandans had been infected by white traders. It was a dangerous disease, and he knew he must act forcefully.

He went immediately to the elders, and signing his warning as strongly as he could, they understood his panicked concern.

"You must leave those with the spotted faces behind. You can do nothing for them. They will die, and if you touch them, you will die also," he said. Within two hours, the criers had gone among the People, and shortly thereafter the camp seemed to just melt away.

"There is nothing else we can do," Evan said to Elizabeth Anne. "In Ireland, we sometimes had to do the same. Then we burned the bodies and their houses as well."

"It is hard to live," she answered. She had learned the words from the old woman who lived with them.

* * * * * * *

The hide trade continued unimpeded. Usually, the carts of trade goods met Evan and the men at the mouth of the Cheyenne River. In mid-summer, the larger river was relatively easy to cross for the horsebacks. Only once were they attacked. It came while they were still about two days travel from the rendezvous spot.

Evan's group that year was made up of about forty men. Naturally, they were well-armed, and many carried the muskets they had traded for in earlier years. The enemy force was slightly larger and was plainly a raiding party. They were recognized as Crow, the People of the Little Black Eagle. Evan and his group immediately switched horses so that they would not be encumbered by the travois loads of hides. It was during the ensuing battle that Evan realized the different way that the People thought of war.

He stayed back and watched. He was amazed to see some of his friends ride forward to do battle with the Crow. Ten of the People approached the larger force which immediately sent out the same number. For almost an hour, these twenty men charged one another and parried each others' spear thrusts. None of the People used their muskets. They seemed to want to touch the Crow warriors in battle instead of trying to kill them.

Eventually, after all of the men had been involved at some point in the battle, it suddenly ceased. The enemy withdrew, and the People continued their journey to the east. Neither side left any dead on the prairie, although the Crow did manage to run off a few of the extra horses, and both groups had some men with flesh wounds. A few packs of hides were lost as well.

* * * * * * *

When Evan returned with the trade goods a few weeks later, he spoke to Elizabeth Anne about what had happened with the Crow. She signed a question to the old woman who lived with them and who was busy showing little Sarah Ana how to put beads on a piece of leather. The little girl was now five and a joy to her parents. The grandmother nodded and began to both sign and speak aloud.

"I remember when I was a little girl, our warriors fought against the Crow, too. One morning all of our people left the village and went to a nearby valley. We sat down on one slope, and soon the hill opposite us began to fill up with other women and children. We recognized them as the enemy. Our men fought against their men most of the afternoon. We women cheered them and taunted the enemy women on the opposite hillside. They did the same. Late in the afternoon, it was over. I don't remember any of our men killed. Some had broken arms, and there were some wounded men on both sides, but nobody died."

The old woman smiled as she added, "Our men were very brave that day."

Elizabeth Anne looked at Evan. He shook his head in disbelief.

* * * * * * *

Sarah Ana was being called Blue Flower by the People. She had just turned six when her brother, Michael, was born. Right away, the People began calling him The Red Plume.

* * * * * * *

The tiyospaye of Cheyenne and Lakota was a wonderful place in which to grow up in the late 1830s. Two languages were vocally spoken, one language was done with the hands, and the Ryan children were fully capable in each of them. Naturally, English was spoken inside the tipi among the family members.

By the time he was six, one of The Red Plume's closest friends was a little boy living in the tipi next to his. Peza was named for his grandfather, and his father was a Lakota warrior of some prominence. Soon the Lakota lad was able to speak English quite handily. Then Elizabeth Anne had an idea.

"What would you think if I taught Peza to read and write English while I am teaching our children?" she asked her husband.

And so it began. Every day the teaching of the three children took place in and around the Ryan tipi. Sarah Ana was growing into a lovely young girl, and Michael was six now. It was 1841, and the family had truly become part of the People.

* * * * * * *

The camp normally moved four or five times during the year. Hunting was the main industry, and the People were careful to not over-hunt an area. Usually, there was plenty to eat. In addition to buffalo, there were deer, antelope, elk, and an abundance of fat, low-flying birds which all provided meat. The variety of naturally growing fruits and tubers rounded out their diet. Nothing was wasted.

The trade was continuing to be successful, and once a year Evan made the trip to the rendezvous spot with an increasing number of warriors who pulled the travois and led pack animals loaded with buffalo hides. He also sent back the little folder of letters from his wife to the Hughes. When the warriors returned from the trading trip, there was always much rejoicing in the tiyospaye as the women looked over the wonderful goods their men had brought back.

But Evan was under increasing pressure from some of the men who had traded with other whites.

"Bring us some of the white man's dark water," they said. It gave them visions very quickly. "Minne wakan" the Lakota called it.

"I shall not," Evan told them. "It is not holy water. It will bring you false visions, and you will never be the same again. I will not bring it into this camp."

Evan spoke with the Council of Forty-Four. It was the group of Cheyenne leaders charged with the responsibility of the People's welfare. They were sometimes called "Peace Chiefs."

"Tell your young men to not drink the traders' whiskey. It will destroy them and all the People," he warned.

* * * * * * *

Evan Ryan was a good hunter. He shot his musket capably, and his horse skills were equal to those of his Cheyenne and Lakota friends. In fact, he often showed off some of the riding tricks he had learned in Ireland, and he enjoyed their trick moves as well. But he still mounted and dismounted from the left side of the animal, and everyone called him He Rides the Horse Differently. One day a challenge came.

"You shoot the magic iron well. But can you shoot a bow as well?" said Peza's father. He was a good friend, and the two men teased one another often.

"Come with me," Evan answered.

The two men rode off together and stopped not far from their village which was located on a stream the whites would some day call Crazy Woman's Creek.

The Lakota handed his bow to Evan.

"Hit that little clump of sage," he said, pointing to the plant about thirty feet away.

Evan thought back to his childhood in Ireland. *Father never had a musket. He told me the British soldiers took all of the firearms from the Irishmen. So he taught me to shoot the bow. I was once very good with the bow. I could even kill small game with it. I shall try to make you proud today, Father.* He raised the weapon and notched an arrow. Then he smoothly released it. It hit the silver-green leaves right in the center.

Later that evening Evan was gifted with the bow and a quiver of arrows.

* * * * * * *

It was an almost comical sight; six little children sitting around a fire made of buffalo chips and blowing through hollowed-out sumac sticks. With each gust of air, the coals burned hotter.

Evan used the blacksmith tongs to move the small, red-hot, glowing piece of iron in and out of the coals. Then he set it on a small anvil and pounded it into shape. He had learned to do this in Ireland at the Murphy forge, and he could do it quickly. By sundown, he had made almost forty arrowheads. He knew they would make a useful gift.

* * * * * * *

One evening Peza's father sat with Evan outside the Ryan tipi. The coming trading trip promised to be successful. There would be a good load of hides, and many were tanned, winter pelts that would bring the highest price. The two friends smoked from one of the long pipes which the Lakota man had brought with him. They leaned against backrests which had wool blankets draped over the top and sides for additional comfort.

"What is the little symbol that your wife wears?" he asked, referring to a crucifix which Elizabeth Anne often wore. He said the words in his language but signed them to Evan as he spoke.

"It represents the way we think of the One Above," answered Evan. He was not sure what else to say.

He called to Elizabeth Anne. She joined them and listened as Evan repeated his friend's question and his answer. Then she said,

"My husband has spoken correctly. Many of our people believe this way. It is very complicated, and often we are confused," she signed. While she was speaking for herself, she was accurate in that Catholics from both Ireland and the United States were often very unknowledgeable about the doctrine and practices of the Church.

"What is the People's belief about the One Above? How do you describe the world?" she asked.

The man was quiet for a time. Then he began to speak aloud and sign at the same time.

"We believe that the Power of the World is a circle, and that everything is round. Everything comes back to the beginning and is never-ending. All of our days begin in the east with the morning sun, and the color of the east is red. The east is the place of understanding, and every day brings us new understanding. The sun then moves to the south, and we use yellow to remind us of that direction. It is the place of the great growing power. That power is woman's power. Then one moves to the west, and black or dark blue are the colors of that direction. The storm clouds are that color and come from the west. The storms have the power to give life and to take life. That is men's power, too. And north is white for the snows that come from there. It is the place of wisdom. Then, the next day the sun does it all over again." He paused and smiled, making a circular motion with his hand.

"Those four colors and directions also represent the four seasons; spring, summer, autumn and winter," said Elizabeth Anne to Evan. "His wife told me that once. She also told me that it also means the four parts of a human being's life; babyhood, childhood, adulthood, and old age. It is amazing, isn't it? It is so simple. And the evidence is all around us."

Their Lakota friend began speaking again.

"This is the great circle of life which Wakantanka, the One Above, has given to all living things. There are many People that are joined together in this circle; the four-legged animals, the little flying and crawling people, the wings of the air, the fins of the water, the grasses that grow everywhere and the standing people that grow by the rivers and mountains, and the two-leggeds. We are just part of the entire universe. We are all related."

"Only the rocks live on and on. Even they have life which we can see when we use them in the sweat-lodge."

Seven creations. Elizabeth Anne thought. *It is similar to what it says in the Bible. Yet different.*

The Lakota man continued.

"But there are two roads of life that we all travel. One starts in the east with the morning sun and goes across this great circle of life to the west where the sun sets. It is a black road of hardship. There is war, hunger, disease, and death along that road. We must all travel it. It is hard to live."

Yes, it is often hard to live. Thought Evan.

"But there is another road which we can follow if we choose to. It is the good, red road of spiritual understanding, and it starts in the south where the growing power lives. It goes across the circle of life to the north, to the place of the white hairs and of wisdom. We must seek to walk this road, and not all human beings choose to do so," he said. He stopped speaking, and Evan sensed that his friend did not want to say any more.

"Pilamaya, kola. Thank you, my friend, for your words," Evan said in Lakota. Evan knew that the proper protocol would have been for him to have given his friend a gift of tobacco or sage. That would be the correct way to request information about so sacred a topic.

When they were alone in the tipi that evening, Elizabeth Anne turned to her husband.

"We must take the children back," she said. "It would be good for them to meet their family and to learn about our people. Don't you agree?"

They know nothing of the Church, even though I have told them about my church in Cincinnati ... or of cities ... or of paddlewheel boats ... or of their other family. We must take them back. She thought.

Evan knew that she was right.

"Aye!" he said.

* * * * * * *

Three weeks later some of the men of the tiyospaye left for the rendezvous place. The entire Ryan family rode with them.

"Keep them safe," Evan had said to Patterson once the exchange of hides for manufactured goods had been accomplished. "I will be here to meet you next summer. Bring them back to me then."

The groaning, creaking carts were soon out of sight. So was his family.

CHAPTER 30
...he had been only eleven...

Little Thomas O'Leary was doing just what he wanted to do. He was killing British soldiers, landlords, land agents, and English government men. Although he never kept count, it was surely in the dozens. He felt no remorse.

Usually, he was able to find a drunken soldier in the port city of Cork or Waterford, one that was separated from his fellows. It was always the same. A quick pistol shot to the head, or a knife to the heart or throat. He was quick, efficient, and because he was so small and did not look his age, he was never suspected. He just appeared to be a young, Irish peasant lad who happened to be in the area and who certainly could not be a ruthless killer.

The docks of Cork were one of his most fruitful killing places. He had been only eleven when he made his first kill there years earlier, and he had returned regularly to repeat the deed. That he was doing wrong never entered his twisted mind, a mind that had been shaped by witnessing the savage rape and murder of his sister, Catherine. The event had never left him. It continued to dominate his every thought and action.

They will die. Every one of them. He thought, as he pulled the sharp blade across the throat of a very drunken British soldier who had been staggering alone on a Cork sidestreet. "Erin Go Bragh!" He said under his breath, as the man fell gasping to his knees, blood pooling rapidly on the rough, cobblestone pavement.

As he walked away from the corpse, he thought about one of his kills in the same neighborhood some twenty years earlier. It had been only a few weeks after that day when he had killed the Ryan landlord there on the docks and then had given Patrick and Ana the man's money belt. It had been one of his most satisfying kills because it had been one of the soldiers who had killed his sister.

He vividly remembered the moment. He had first seen the man from his hiding place behind his parents' bed. The soldier had been the last one to enter the little house, but his actions had been no less responsible for Catherine's death. When he saw the man four years later, the boy had followed him and waited for his chance. The man never expected that a small, eleven year old boy could threaten him in any way. The killing strike had been very fast there in a darkened alley. Little Thomas had simply thrust the long dagger up and into the throat of the soldier, just under his jaw. He remembered saying,

"That's for my sister, Catherine. Erin Go Bragh!"

Little Thomas was now almost thirty years old and a small man. He had gotten away with his murderous spree for over twenty years. What he never suspected was that there were Irish men and women who had eyes and who would, for a price, turn in their own. Being a traitor to Ireland was a thought that had never occurred to him.

He rounded a corner, moving away from the fresh corpse, when suddenly a squad of British soldiers appeared from the shadows.

"Take him," the officer said, as two soldiers tackled him to the ground. Within moments, he was standing up and shackled, his illegal pistol and the still slightly bloody dagger on the ground.

"That's the one who did the killin'." The voice came from behind him, and while he could not see the person, he knew the man was Irish.

* * * * * * *

There was no trial. The British felt no need to go through the pretense of a legal proceeding. They had their man; they were sure. Little Thomas O'Leary was scheduled for execution the very next day.

He had built quite a reputation for himself. "The Killer Ghost," he had come to be called by the English, who could never catch the person who had plagued them for two decades. They would make an example of him.

* * * * * * *

The hastily erected gallows stood in the center of Cork. Little Thomas was moved up the steps. He was really not afraid.

Ya can do nothin' to me except kill me. And when ya do, others will just take my place. He thought. His eyes revealed not a hint of concern or fear.

A silent crowd had gathered around the hanging place. Two soldiers stood on either side of the condemned man.

"This man is a traitor to the King and a murderer," announced the officer in charge. "Watch what happens to those of you who deny the King's authority."

It had not been seen for many years. "Pitch-capping" it was called, and it was a dreaded form of torture that usually did not kill the victim. Instead, the resulting suffering was among the worst examples of inhuman treatment ever devised.

One of the soldiers on the scaffold put the noose of thick rope around Thomas's neck and pulled it up tight, purposely placing the knot so that the condemned man's neck would not break. Then the other soldier began to smear Thomas's hair with pitch. The tar covered his entire scalp.

"How do you like your new hat, ya Irish scum?" asked one of the executioners. "Maybe we ought to make more of an illuminating example of ya." He laughed callously and lit a taper. He applied the flame to the tar on Thomas's head, and it caught fire easily.

"Let it burn a while," he said to the other soldier, whose job it was to kick out the stool on which Thomas stood.

Although the tar on his head blazed fiercely, Thomas never screamed in pain. Nor did he move. Instead, he muttered quite audibly, "Erin Go Bragh." Then he yelled it loudly to the crowd, many of whom were turning away from the awful sight. He turned his head slightly and spit at the soldier next to him.

It angered the man, and he dislodged the stool. Little Thomas O'Leary dropped. Within minutes, he had strangled, and his wide-open eyes took on the fixed, blank stare for which he was known. This time, that stare would last forever.

CHAPTER 31
...shall I join them?...

It had started a few years earlier. The flow of white settlers across the southern portions of their hunting lands had disrupted the game. The People of the Painted Arrow, as the Cheyenne were called, and the Brother People, as the Lakota were known, did not like it. The leaders wrestled with the question of what they should or could do about it.

What concerned them most was that the white man's road cut across the annual migration route of the buffalo herds. That disruption meant a less successful summer hunting season for the People, and they depended on the buffalo for their very lives.

Evan was also worried about the continued success of his hide business. But he worried more about the future of the People, a people whose ways he had come to respect. They were more than just business associates. They had become friends and family.

"I am afraid for the People," he said to Elizabeth Anne. "What will become of them if the buffalo disappear?"

She shared his concern. She, too, had come to love and respect the ways of the People. It made sense to her that all of the children in the tiyospaye were like her own children and that her two were looked after by every other family. It was a caring community, and the responsibilities were shared. Everyone had a part in the well-being of the group. Hunters always shared their kills; certain warriors were charged with the responsibility of defending the women and children; and men who were known to have the fastest horses were even given the specific task of saving the little children if the village was attacked.

Elizabeth Anne was pleased with her own two children. Sarah Ana was now seventeen, and a young Cheyenne warrior had courteously expressed his interest in her. Michael was now eleven and growing tall. He was already getting very muscular like his father. They were good children, and she and Evan were justifiably proud.

* * * * * * *

Four years earlier Elizabeth Anne had taken the children to St. Paul, as the community around Fort Snelling was now starting to be called. It had been an interesting experience for the three of them. Ana and Patrick and their three children had been very kind and supportive, and the Ryans had lived with the Hughes for the entire year.

"I have been putting all of the profit money into a bank for Evan and ya," Patrick said one evening as the three old friends sat in the kitchen. The children were already upstairs in bed.

"Ya have a good sum of money that ya can draw on whenever ya need it," he added. Elizabeth Anne was shocked when he told her the amount. She had never given a thought to the obvious fact that the hide business was making a profit and that half of that profit belonged to her husband. She thanked her brother-in-law, but she wondered.

The People need none of the white man's money. And I doubt that Sarah Ana or Michael will ever need it either. But she did not say the words to Patrick.

Their year's stay with the Hughes had also provided more structured learning. For the past few years, Patrick had arranged for a tutor to teach his three children. Now the man was teaching all five. The Ryan and Hughes cousins already had a good knowledge of reading, writing, and numbers, and the tutor was pleased with everyone's progress.

"They are all doing exceedingly well," he said to the three parents after two months of tutoring the children. Then, addressing Elizabeth Anne, he added, "I notice that neither of your children will look directly at me when they speak, and they are very quiet. Are they always that quiet, or are they just feeling out of place?"

"They are fine. The people we live with are also very reserved and proper in their actions. Children would never think of speaking out of turn or looking directly at their elders. That would be disrespectful. The children are fine. Please don't expect them to be any different," she answered.

The tutor smiled and shrugged.

"All right," he said simply. They were all good children and never a problem. Anyway, Patrick Hughes was paying him handsomely for the tutoring services he was to perform over the next ten months. He was not about to disrupt the contract.

* * * * * * *

"Is something wrong?" Elizabeth Anne asked her daughter. Sarah Ana blushed and looked at her hands.

"Mother, Patrick Evan looks at me all the time. I don't know what to do. It is not proper," she said quietly. Her cousin was one year older and a good-looking young man.

"Well, I will speak to his father. He is your cousin and should not be inappropriate when he is in your presence," she responded.

She had the private discussion the next day with Patrick. He looked at her very seriously and said simply,

"Aye! Ya are right. I've noticed it, too. I'll speak with the boy. He forgets that Sarah Ana is his cousin."

Then he added, "She is very pretty, ya know!"

Oh yes! I know! She is a woman now. Thought Elizabeth Anne. *Evan will be so proud, and we will have a feast in her honor when we return to the People.*

* * * * * * *

The five cousins got to know one another, and they got along well. Mary Anne and Sarah Ana were each named after a grandmother and an aunt. The two young women, now eleven and thirteen, bonded quite closely, and the Hughes girl took her cousin everywhere. She delighted in showing the older girl the sights and sounds of the rapidly growing city. Her father already owned one hotel and was a large landowner of vacant property which would one day bring him a good deal of money. The three Hughes children were well-known everywhere in the growing community.

By 1842, the entire area was becoming populated by people from many different nationalities: Scots, English, French-Canadians, Germans, Norwegians, and many Irish. A few of these new arrivals were well-educated, but most were not. Only one Catholic church had been built in the area, but there were plenty of public houses where ale, high wines, and spirits were sold. Trade on the Mississippi River was growing, and the waterway attracted many unsavory characters that came into the area.

One evening, as the two young girls were walking along the darkened pathway that led from the small business district to the home that Patrick Hughes had just completed, a man came out of the shadows.

It all happened so fast that only later was Mary Anne able to put together all of the pieces of what had occurred. The man was a bit drunk. He was big, and when he struck Mary Anne across the face, she fell to the ground, her head swimming. Then he turned toward the older girl and grabbed Sarah Ana.

"You are a pretty thing," he said as he wrestled her easily onto her back. He did not realize that he was attacking a young woman of the People, and that he was intending to do something that the People considered to be one of the greatest of all offenses. He also did not realize that this girl was Blue Flower, the daughter of Evan and Elizabeth Anne Ryan.

"Leave me alone," Blue Flower hissed at the man. But she did not scream.

"Oh, come now. Just relax," the man replied. Her body went somewhat limp beneath him, and with his right hand he began to pull up the girl's skirt along with the shift that was underneath. Using his left arm across her chest, he pinned her to the ground.

Since she was not struggling, he relaxed his forearm pressure on her chest and concentrated on her skirts. Her clothing was quickly pulled up almost to the tops of her thighs, and he reached down and began to fumble with the front of his pants.

It was at that moment when Blue Flower pulled the knife out of the leather sheath which was strapped on her right thigh. It had been hidden high up under her skirts and was only accessible if her dress was pulled up far enough. She wore it all of the time as did every other young woman of the People. With the single motion that she had been taught from the time she was eight years old, and which she had rehearsed hundreds of times with her Cheyenne and Lakota girlfriends using a blunt stick, she quickly thrust the short-bladed knife twice into the groin of her attacker. He howled in pain and rolled off of her, holding his lower belly, blood rapidly soiling the front of his clothing.

In less than a minute, both girls were running away from the bleeding man.

"He may die. But if he does not, he will always remember this night," Sarah Ana said when they reached the Hughes house. Mary Anne could only nod in astonished agreement.

Of course, they told their parents about what had happened. Ana was shocked, and Patrick was enraged.

"Damned drunkards," he cursed.

"Are you all right?" Elizabeth Anne asked.

"Yes, Mother. I am perfectly fine. I have been taught well," she answered, not looking directly at her mother.

Elizabeth Anne smiled at her daughter and nodded. *Yes, you have been taught well. You can defend yourself if you must. I am proud of you, Blue Flower.* She did not say her thoughts aloud, but her daughter knew her mother's unspoken words.

* * * * * * *

As the carts moved west across the prairie that summer of 1843, Elizabeth Anne and her children were glad to be going home. Their year with the Hughes family had come to an end.

One more day, and we will be at the river, Patterson says. I can't wait to see Evan. She thought. *This has been a wonderful year for the children, but I know they want to go home. I know they miss their friends and our tipi. And Michael keeps asking when he is going to get to be horseback again. He misses the horses so very much. And I miss Evan and the People.*

At that very moment, the arrow struck the side of the cart.

* * * * * * *

The attacking force was not large, but it was a war party and had to be repulsed. Patterson and the other drivers immediately assembled the dozen and a half carts into a crude square with the horses and mules facing in toward the center. They immediately began firing at the two dozen enemies whose tribe they could not readily identify.

Their muskets were too intimidating, and it was over within twenty minutes. Three of the attackers lay dead, and two of the drivers had been wounded. As Elizabeth Anne turned to help one of them, she suddenly realized that little Michael was not in her cart. Then she saw him.

He had jumped down and run into the center of the carts and was holding the reins of about half a dozen horses to keep them calm. It was a very brave thing for an eight year old to do.

"Wastay, lela wastay, Wiyaka-ska! Ah-hou! Ah-hou!" she yelled to her son. It meant "Good, very good, Red Plume. Yes! Yes!" Elizabeth Anne was so proud.

As she turned to her daughter, the young woman put her hand in the air and made the trilling sound. She was proud of her little brother as well.

They are back! My children are back. Their minds are once again with the People. And I am back, too! We will soon be together with Evan and our People once again. She thought.

Then she saw her husband. He was riding furiously toward them.

* * * * * * *

"I heard the gunfire. I could not wait for ya to come to the river, and I wanted to surprise ya out here on the prairie," Evan said, enfolding his wife in his arms.

"Oh Evan, I am so very glad to see you," Elizabeth Anne answered, holding her husband tightly.

"What has happened here?" he asked, releasing his wife, although he really did not want to.

Ya are still so very pretty to me. He thought, looking down at her. *I have missed ya so.*

"We were attacked, and you should have seen your son," she answered.

Evan turned to his daughter and hugged the smiling girl to him.

My little girl is not a little girl any more. He thought. Then he looked around for his son.

There was no sign of the attackers. Three of them lay dead about fifty yards away from the small group of carts, drivers, horses, and mules. The men began reloading their weapons and trying to organize their defenses in readiness for another attack.

Just then Michael ran up to his father.

"I steadied the horses during the fight, Father." It was the first thing he said to his father, whom he had not seen for almost a year.

"Aye son! Come with me then. You will count your first coup today," Evan said. He did not greet his son the same way he had his wife and daughter. This was a special moment, and he knew the boy would never forget it.

Together the father and son walked out onto the prairie and up to the first body. The little boy knew the protocol. He approached the corpse four times, and on the fourth he struck the chest of the dead man with his open hand.

"Ah-hou!" he yelled, and in his boyish voice, he gave a shrill whoop. He had not done the killing, but he had been the first to touch the dead enemy.

Elizabeth Anne and Sarah Ana watched in silent pride.

* * * * * * *

The remainder of the trip to the river and the exchange of goods were uneventful. Within three more weeks, the group was once again back in the village of the People.

That night, Evan distributed the trade goods following the pattern he had begun some fourteen years earlier. There was much joy in the village, and Evan felt fulfilled.

I have traded honorably. He thought. *The lives of the People are once again better.*

The women especially liked the mirrors, awls, beads, and cloth that this year's exchange had brought. Patrick had held up his side of the agreement.

But Evan's greatest satisfaction came when young Michael danced that night in front of the People, recounting his part in the defense of the trade caravan. His dance movements told the story of how he had held the horses quiet while the battle raged, and of how he counted his first coup. The People cheered him loudly as he finished the dance.

* * * * * * *

They had been back for almost a week when four men approached Elizabeth Anne's tipi.

"We wish to speak with you," one said. Evan followed them into a society lodge that was set up in the center of the village. They were gone for the remainder of the afternoon.

* * * * * * *

"It is a very great honor," said Evan to his wife. "I have been asked to join the Dog Soldiers."

Elizabeth Anne was suddenly very quiet. They were sitting on a pair of backrests just outside of her tipi. The weather was warm, and they had finished eating a buffalo stew that she had prepared. She understood at once the importance of what Evan was telling her, and she remained silent.

"I think ya are happy here, are ya not?" he asked.

"I am, Evan. I found that I did not like the city any longer. I wanted to come back here a lot sooner than we did," she went on. "But this is a very important decision for you and for me."

They were silent for a long time.

On the one hand, Evan was being given the greatest honor that could be bestowed on one of the People. The Dog

Soldiers were charged with the defense of the village. If they were called out by the older leaders, they were the ones who were expected to go to the perimeter of the village to defend the women and children. Dog Soldiers were always the first into battle and the last ones to cover the retreat of the People, if that was necessary.

On the other hand, it was expected that they would never leave their defensive positions and that they would die rather than abandon their avowed duty. It was an awesome responsibility.

"Shall I join them?" he asked.

Elizabeth Anne looked directly at her husband. She understood completely what he was asking her. She knew that it was not a question coming from personal vanity. She realized that his unspoken question really was "shall I take on a position of responsibility that most certainly will mean my death if the circumstances are right?"

"Yes, Evan. You should," she answered.

I would be proud of my husband if he were a Dog Man. She thought. But then she had the fleeting thought. *But remember: this is not Ireland. These are your People now.* She sometimes knew her husband's mind better than he did.

* * * * * * *

The next seven years brought great changes to the lives of the People. The tiyospaye continued to be a mixed camp of both Cheyenne and Lakota, although there came to be more of the latter. The hide trade continued unabated and with each shipment of hides went Elizabeth Anne's letters to Patrick and Ana. Sometimes there was a return letter or two from Patrick. Thankfully, there was no other incidence of either cholera or smallpox.

But the great trail that ran along the Platte River farther to the south was continually filled with white emigrants moving to the lands across the great mountain range to the west. The Oregon Trail crossed the Rocky Mountains at South Pass. From there, the travelers could go northwest to the Oregon Territory or southwest to Utah or California. The Indian leaders were becoming increasingly concerned.

It wasn't that the whites were staying in their land that bothered them. It was not even that they left huge amounts of their belongings along the trail so as to lighten their loads. Some of the refuse could be used by the People, especially the metal items.

It was the concern for hunting. The white man's trail disrupted the game.

Now a new fort was being built at a place with which the People were long familiar. Fort Laramie was its name, and the American government quickly staffed it with troops.

It was 1851 when the People were asked to come to that fort to hear the words of the representatives of the Great Father of the whites who lived far to the east.

Thousands of Indians, many of whom were enemies of the People, came to the huge gathering. Even so, peace prevailed for the entire time. Evan and Elizabeth Anne went with their tiyospaye and camped at a place called Horse Creek, but they did not attend any of the proceedings. White Antelope of the Cheyenne and Conquering Bear of the Lakota were two of the leaders who made their marks on the white man's paper. It seemed that there would be a lasting solution to the concerns of the Indian leaders.

* * * * * * *

During all of these years, Evan had never been called upon to fulfill his Dog Soldier vow. Both the Lakota and Cheyenne had fighting men who were so designated, and each group recognized and honored the men of that elite society. Soon, events beyond his control would present him with the moment, and the values and understandings that he had brought with him from Ireland which would dictate his actions. The decisions he would make as a man would be directly related to the experiences and decisions of his youth.

CHAPTER 32
...Honor your commitment...

The word spread quickly through the Lakota and Cheyenne camps. Along with three other Lakota leaders, Conquering Bear was dead. But so were all of the soldiers who had ridden recklessly into his camp and attacked it. That had been in 1854, and now it was autumn of the following year. Still, the peaceful bands of Lakota felt that they had no reason for alarm.

Elizabeth Anne and Evan were camped with a Brule Lakota group much farther to the south than normal. The Lakota called the place "Blue Water."

"So, you have brought me an antelope for dinner?" said Elizabeth Anne, the one the People called She Helps Them to Be Born. Her grandson, Otter, whom she always called Little Evan, smiled as he put the animal down in front of his grandmother. He was staying with his grandparents while his mother, Blue Flower, and Cheyenne father, for whom he was named, hunted farther to the north.

"It will make a tasty dinner," she said. "But I will give some of the meat to our neighbors and tell them what a great hunter my grandson has become."

The boy looked down and smiled, embarrassed by her words and yet proud of his accomplishment. The little, deer-like creatures were not easy to kill.

The next day his life would change dramatically.

* * * * * * *

It was early in the afternoon. Evan Ryan, the one the People called He Rides the Horse Differently, moved among his personal horses that were hobbled near the Lakota encampment. Ash Hollow, which was another name for this Blue Water place, was a good camping spot. It had fresh water and an abundance of game in the surrounding hills. He heard the eagle bone whistles before he heard the sound of the cavalry troopers' horses and gun carriages. He ran into the camp and found it in turmoil.

"Hoka hey," he heard the men yelling in Lakota. He knew that it meant, "Remember the helpless. Today is a good day to die."

It is very much like Erin Go Bragh. He had always thought once the phrase had been explained to him. The old Gaelic words had been his personal battle cry for many years. Even though it literally meant "Ireland Forever," the broader meaning encompassed the same theme as the Lakota words.

Evan Ryan was a member of the most elite fighting group to be found among the Indian people of the plains. He was a Dog Soldier. He had taken the vow. Defend the village at all cost, even if you must die.

He ran toward his tipi, the whistles signaling that his comrades in the society were to go to defensive positions on the edge of the village. Most of the younger fighting men were away hunting, and the older men were expected to defend the women and children. As a Dog Soldier, his course of action was clear.

He could see the large force of American soldiers on the rise across from the village. They were drawn up into attack formation.

Surely, they will send a small group of officers to speak with us! He thought. *We are just a peaceful hunting camp, nothing more.*

Rushing into his tipi, Evan saw Elizabeth Anne standing there. She looked afraid and yet resolute. He grabbed his Dog Soldier staff. It was a long pole with a curved hook at the top. It always reminded him of the shepherd's crook he had used in Ireland. He picked up the long sash that hung near it and turned toward his wife.

She answered his questioning look with the words, "Go! Honor your commitment to the People."

Then she handed him his musket and shooting bag.

Evan stepped up to her and hugged her to him.

"I love ya, Elizabeth Anne," he said. He looked directly into her eyes. "I shall always love ya."

Then he turned and went quickly out of the lodge.

She watched him run in the direction of the American soldiers, and she saw her husband take up his position in a line with a few other Dog Soldiers facing the cavalry.

Oh god! Our young fighting men are all out hunting. We are almost defenseless. She thought. Then she grabbed a small pair of moccasins which were lying on the south side of the tipi near some of her things and stuffed them into a small shoulder bag.

* * * * * * *

Little Evan heard the whistles, too. *I am a hunter, and I can fight for the People if need be.* He thought as he ran for the village. He had been swimming and had no weapons with him. Still, he ran as fast as he could directly toward the danger he knew was coming at the People.

There was a great commotion in the village as he darted between the tipis. Women and children were running everywhere, and the few older men and young boys left in the camp were picking up weapons and racing toward the western part of the tipi circle. He could see that there were about a half-dozen Dog Soldiers already positioned between the tipis and the line of American cavalry. He saw that one of them was his grandfather.

* * * * * * *

Evan took up his position with his comrades. *They will want to talk with us.* He thought again.

The first cannon shot proved him wrong.

He remembered the words that John Burke had spoken to him so many years before in the cave back in County Tipperary. *"You are one of us now. I know it, Evan Ryan. We will defend our homes and families at all cost."* He put the sash over his shoulder and pegged it to the ground with his knife. He would stay at this position and fight.

Following the example of the other Dog Men, Evan waved his Dog Soldier staff in a wide arc above his head. The long staff with the crooked end was covered in otter fur as was the custom.

"Hoka hey," they called out to one another. "Remember the helpless. Ah-hou, ah-hou!"

He waited for the enemy soldiers to charge, his musket loaded and ready in his hands.

A second shell hit and exploded in the center of the tipi village. He looked back to see if he could spot Elizabeth Anne. He could not see her anywhere, but women were running about gathering up the little children and racing for the pony herd that was off to the east of the village.

He turned back toward the soldiers. They were riding toward him now, and it was clear that they were attacking the village.

These are my People. He thought. *Hoka hey!* He said to himself.

*We will defend our...*Then he felt a blow to his chest, as though someone had struck him with a fist. He staggered, and when he looked down, he saw that blood was starting to come out of the small hole in his shirt. He turned again toward the village and saw his wife. He looked directly at her, and their eyes met. He hollered his personal battle cry as loudly as he could. Then his legs buckled, and he dropped to his knees. It seemed as if the world was closing down around him.

In the increasing darkness of his mind, he saw a green hillside a short distance away. A figure appeared on the hill and began walking toward him. It was a pretty young girl with light red hair. She stopped, and smiling, she motioned to him with her hand. *She is telling me to follow her!* He thought. *I must defend her. I will defend her.*

He watched as she turned and ran back over the hill. In his fading mind, he saw that in front of him the earth was suddenly dark with the forms of stampeding buffalo.

As he watched the thundering beasts run past him, one of the cows turned and came straight at him. Just as it seemed that he would be trampled, the animal stopped and changed into a beautiful woman whom he recognized as his Elizabeth Anne.

"I will be with you soon, and we will dance together forever," she said. She turned away from him, and he watched her form disappear into the herd that continued to run past him. Then, it was dark.

CHAPTER 33
...you had no reason to kill us...

Otter raced to his grandfather's side and pulled the old knife out of the ground where it had been pinning the sash into place. He picked up the ancient musket and pulled the shooting bag off of the man's body. The rifle was loaded and primed and was set at half-cock. It had not been fired. The eight-year-old boy could barely lift it, but he did so and fired at the attacking column. Then he ran. He could not see his grandmother anywhere.

* * * * * * *

There were about seventy-five of them, all women and children. Some had been wounded and were being carried in the soldier wagons. Elizabeth Anne was among the captives. Three days later they arrived at Fort Laramie.

She had been there once before with Evan. Now he was gone, and she had been taken prisoner by these American soldiers along with many of her friends and their children.

Little Evan is not among these captives. Did he survive? She wondered.

* * * * * * *

They had been at Laramie for almost a week when two soldiers approached her.

"Come with us, you white whore," the one said as he roughly grabbed her arm and pulled her away from the little child whose wounds she had been dressing.

The interior of the general's quarters was quite elegant. General William S. Harney was seated behind his desk. He was a career military man and had fought in the wars against the Seminoles in Florida and in the Black Hawk War in Illinois. Later, he had battled against the Mexicans in the war of 1847 and 1848. He had been the one who had ordered the attack on the Brule Lakota village at Ash Hollow on the Blue Water in retaliation for the wiping out of Grattan's force a year earlier at Conquering Bear's camp.

"I see that you are a white woman," the white-haired general said. "What is your name?"

Elizabeth Anne was silent.

"Have you been so long with the Indians that you can no longer speak English?" the general asked.

"You had no reason to kill us," she responded. "We had done nothing to you or to any whites."

Harney looked down and thought for a few moments. Then he stood and came out from behind his desk. The other soldiers had moved back onto the porch just outside of the door, so he was alone with the woman. The general stood in front of her.

"How long have you been with the Indians?" he asked.

"My husband and I have lived with the Lakota and Cheyenne for over twenty-five years," she answered. "My husband was a trader, and you and your men killed him."

"Well, I am sorry, madam, for your loss. But that is the chance one takes when one lives with savage, marauding Indians. We must keep the peace out here on the prairie," the general answered.

"We were a peaceful village. Our men were hunters. No war parties ever left our village. You, sir, are a killer. You are just like the British, and you are a bastard!" she said, her voice becoming louder.

If he did not understand the meaning behind the reference to the British, he understood clearly the rest of her words. But General Harney never expected the physical attack that suddenly burst from the small woman standing in front of him.

With those last words, Elizabeth Anne lashed out with her hand. In it, she held a quirt. The strap of the short horse-whip was securely wrapped around her wrist and from the bone handle protruded a piece of rawhide cord. The blow struck the general across the face.

"Bastard! Bastard! You bastard!" she screamed as she counted coup on the commanding officer, striking him across the face again and again and again.

Then her arms were pinned by one of the soldiers who had run back into the room.

"Hoka hey!" she muttered as she was dragged from the building.

CHAPTER 34
...you will see Ireland...

The hunters who returned to the village at the Blue Water were stunned by what they found. Bodies lay everywhere. They moved through the deserted camp, the silence broken only by the frequent wail of grief that filled the late afternoon air as one man after another found a wife or a child. The Red Plume knelt down, stroking the cold cheek of his father. For a long time, he wept.

"I shall not forget you, Father, and I will find Mother and little Otter, also," he said aloud. "And I promise you this: I will not dishonor you or the People. I will try to live my life as you have lived yours."

He buried his father in the tradition of the Lakota. Evan Ryan's body was placed on a scaffold facing east.

"If you look far enough, Father, you will see Ireland. Erin Go Bragh, my Father, Erin Go Bragh!" he said, sobbing again as he covered the body with a buffalo robe.

* * * * * * *

The Red Plume moved west across the prairie toward Fort Laramie. The trail of the soldiers who had attacked the camp at Ash Hollow was easy to follow, and the signs all indicated that they had captives. Perhaps he could discover if his mother and little nephew were alive and prisoners.

He stayed close to the river. It had been over two weeks since the attack on the camp, and he knew precisely where the soldiers were going. He needed the river water and knew he could avoid any contact with whites by keeping just slightly away from the easily discerned Oregon Trail. The well-traveled route passed a strange rock and crossed a low mountain pass at a settlement that was starting to be built at that location. He knew the soldiers would go that way to Fort Laramie.

He smelled the smoke before he heard the sound of the steam engine. A paddlewheel boat came into sight, and he remained hidden on the river bank. Then he saw her. His mother was standing on the foredeck looking in his direction. He stepped out of the brush near the shore.

"Mother!" he shouted.

Elizabeth Anne Ryan heard the voice above the noise of the engine. She turned and saw her son. She raised her hands to reveal the manacles that bound them to leg chains. Then she shook her head from side to side and signed to him with hand motions that were greatly hampered by the irons. Still, he was able to read her words.

"My husband is dead. I am all right. Do not try to help me. Go and find my grandson. Be safe yourself. I love you."

The Red Plume quickly signed back.

"Yes, Mother. I will find him. I love you."

It was all he could say because the boat moved around a small bend in the river and was soon out of sight.

* * * * * * *

He found his nephew ten days later. The boy had escaped the soldiers at the Blue Water along with a number of other younger boys and girls. He had rejoined his mother's Cheyenne camp to the north of the Paha Sapa. Michael Ryan, The Red Plume, reunited with his sister, Sarah Ana, the one called Blue Flower. It was bittersweet.

* * * * * * *

The paddlewheel arrived in St. Louis a few weeks later. Elizabeth Anne had her wrist and leg irons removed.

"You are free to go," said the young soldier quite simply. He was embarrassed at having been assigned to guard this dangerous woman. She had been quiet on the entire journey and actually very mannerly toward him.

Elizabeth Anne left the boat and began searching the dock for another to take her to Cincinnati. She would pay when she arrived. Her plan was simple. She would go to her parents' home and then north to Ana and Patrick. Then she would go back out to the People. She would look for her children.

I must find them. I will find them. She thought.

* * * * * * *

"Mother," said Elizabeth Anne. Mollie O'Rourke Delaney nearly fainted at the sight of her only daughter. She had been gone for twenty-seven years.

It was the autumn of 1855, and Cincinnati was much different than when Elizabeth Anne had left it for Fort Snelling in the spring of 1828. She had gone there to wed Lt. John Baker. If it had not been for the letter that had come that same summer, Mollie would have never known if the girl had arrived at the fort. Then, for the next twenty-seven years, there had been a letter every year or so.

* * * * * * *

Over that winter, the daughter lived with her mother. Robert Delaney had passed away nine years earlier, but the Delaney business had become the most successful furniture factory in the city. Elizabeth Anne's three brothers were now in partnership, and she enjoyed meeting their families. Many of her nieces and nephews were adults now with little children of their own.

Mollie Delaney had been an O'Rourke, and she took a great deal of pride in reintroducing her daughter "who came back from the buffalo Indians" to her side of the family.

Everyone was gracious and kind. But Elizabeth Anne felt a strong need to go to Ana and Patrick Hughes. It had been with them that she had begun her life as an adult, even though she had been barely seventeen when she first met them. They had shared the adventure of going to new places, of meeting new people, and of making a success of their lives. They were connected, not so much by blood, but by the common experiences they had shared. She needed to leave Cincinnati.

"Please, don't go," her mother implored. "You have only just gotten here."

"It's been almost nine months, Mother. And there are people I must see," she said.

When mid-summer came, she was once again on a paddlewheel boat moving up the Mississippi River toward Fort Snelling and the old trade camp at Mendota.

I hear that there is a growing city there called St. Paul. I wonder what I will find? Are Ana and Patrick still alive? Are their children still there? She thought. *I must go now and then go back to the People. I must find my children.*

CHAPTER 35
...I needed to come here...

It was the late summer of 1856. Ana Hughes sat in the parlor of her large home. She was alone now that her three children, Patrick Evan, Mary Anne, and Matthew were grown. Her husband, Patrick, a very wealthy and successful businessman, was at his office. It was late in the afternoon, and she knew it was time to begin cooking supper. She was thinking about her brother Evan. It had been so long with no word from him.

Where is Evan? Is he all right? Why have there been no hides coming here for the past two years?

A soft knock interrupted her thoughts. She moved to the front hall and opened the door. The little woman standing before her smiled and said, "Hello, Ana." It was Elizabeth Anne Ryan. Ana's hand went to her mouth, and her eyes grew wide in astonishment.

"Oh!" Ana cried out, her voice cracking. The two women embraced one another fondly, both weeping. For a long time, they just held each other there on the front porch and cried. Then Ana backed away, pulling her sister-in-law into the house.

They stood in the parlor studying each other in silence. It had been thirteen years. Elizabeth Anne was simply dressed but looked haggard and drawn. Her hair had turned gray and was quite long. Her skin was deeply tanned, and her face lined with the creases that usually come to those who have lived outdoors in the elements for long periods of time.

Ana looked a good deal less aged. Her years with Patrick in St. Paul and the good life he had provided for her had prevented much of the aging process from taking its toll. She was still a lovely woman.

Neither had spoken since their initial greeting. They sat down together on a small couch, and Ana asked,

"Where is Evan?"

Elizabeth Anne's eyes flooded with tears, and she turned away from Ana.

"He's gone. He was killed last autumn," she answered.

Ana buried her face in her hands and bent low, almost touching the tops of her legs.

"Oh no! Not Evan! Not Evan!" she sobbed.

* * * * * * *

They were sitting together in silence when Patrick came into the house a few minutes later. He was shocked by both the presence and appearance of Elizabeth Anne. He hugged her warmly.

"So, where is Evan?" he immediately inquired, looking around the room as if to spot his old friend and business partner.

"Evan is dead, Patrick," Ana answered, her voice full of pain.

"What?" Patrick could not believe what he had just heard. He looked at Elizabeth Anne, his face quizzical as he slumped into a chair.

"Evan was killed last autumn by American soldiers," continued Ana.

"They attacked the village where we were living," added Elizabeth Anne.

Her voice grew louder, and she looked directly at Patrick when she said, "They had no reason to make war on us. Our village had done nothing." Then she added in a voice so full of anger that Patrick could only stare at her,

"A general named Harney ordered the attack. It was in retribution for a soldier attack the previous year against another camp of the People. Those soldiers were all killed. So last fall he picked our village to suffer the penalty. Many were killed that day, and not only men. The People are already calling him The Butcher. He is a bastard."

Patrick's face registered not only his shock but silent anger. *It is Ireland all over again.* He thought.

Ana asked, "Where are the children, Sarah Ana and Michael?"

"Sarah Ana is married and has two children. She has a Cheyenne husband who is very kind to her. Her family was not in our camp when the soldiers came that day, except for her son, Little Evan. Our grandson was visiting with us. He's eight years old and got away safely, I think. At least, I did not see him among the dead, and I know he wasn't captured by the soldiers," said Elizabeth Anne.

"Oh god! Elizabeth Anne," cried out Ana. She was starting to lose her composure once again at this news.

"And Michael?" asked Patrick. He was no longer the bashful Irish peasant boy Elizabeth Anne had first met years before. He had become a businessman and was now somewhat direct with people.

"He was out hunting when the soldiers came. I saw him on the riverbank when I was being taken on a paddlewheel to St. Louis. He knows that I was not killed. We spoke briefly. But I don't know where he is," she said. "He is not married yet." Then she looked down at her hands.

"Where have ya been? How did ya get here?" asked Patrick.

"I have been in Cincinnati this past winter. But I needed to come here to tell you all that has happened," she answered.

"Of course, ya will stay with us?" said Ana.

"I would like that. Then I must go back to the People. I need to find my children," Elizabeth Anne answered.

* * * * * * *

They sat eating supper in the kitchen of the Hughes house. It was clear to Ana and Patrick that Elizabeth Anne had changed considerably from the woman they first met on the paddlewheel boat almost thirty years earlier. And she was even different from the woman who had visited them almost a decade and a half ago when she had come all the way to St. Paul with her young children. She was much more quiet and reserved.

They talked mainly about Ana and Patrick's children and about the hotel and land sale businesses in which Patrick was now involved. It was apparent to Elizabeth Anne that they were wealthy by any standards. The reading and writing lessons she had given Patrick so many years before had benefited him enormously. He was a very successful businessman and employed his two sons and his son-in-law.

Patrick needed to know more about Evan's death, but he was hesitant to pursue the subject. Ana provided the idea that he knew would yield that information.

"Elizabeth Anne. There are some family members ya have never met who are now living in the city," she said. "My younger brother, Timothy, and his wife and sons are here from Ireland. And Mary Anne is recently married to a wonderful man. May I invite them all for dinner tomorrow?" Ana asked.

"I would rather wait until the weekend, if you don't mind. I am very tired," she answered.

The plan was set. The Hughes and Ryans would gather in two days.

PART FOUR

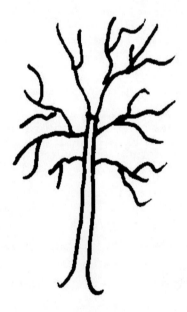

Family: 1856—1891

List of Characters in Part Four

Elizabeth Anne (Delaney) Ryan—wife of Evan Ryan

Michael Ryan (The Red Plume or Wiyaka-ska)—son of
Evan and Elizabeth Anne
    Lorena Corinna Obregon—his wife; from Mexico
        Michael Evan Ryan—their infant son

Patrick Hughes—St. Paul businessman; from Ireland
    Ana Ryan Hughes—his wife; from Ireland
        Patrick Evan Ryan—their son
            Marie Toussaint—his wife; from Montreal
                John Michael Hughes—son of Patrick Evan
                and Marie
                    Bridget O'Maher—his wife; from Ireland
            Matthew Charles Hughes—their son
            Mary Anne Hughes Connolly—their daughter
                Daniel Connolly—her husband; family attorney
                in St. Paul

Timothy Ryan—third child of Michael and Mary Ryan;
from Ireland
    Catherine O'Leary Ryan—his wife; from Ireland;
      second daughter of Thomas and Elizabeth O'Leary
        Michael Thomas Ryan—their son; from Ireland
            Harriet Anderson—his wife
                James Daniel Ryan—son of Michael Thomas
                and Harriet
                    Maureen Flynn—his wife; from Ireland
            Timothy Evan Ryan—their son; from Ireland
            Charles Thomas Ryan—their infant son

Father William Corby—Catholic chaplain assigned to the
Irish Brigade

General William Hancock— a Senior Union officer at
Gettysburg

Brigadier General Cadmus Wilcox–Confederate officer;
Alabama Infantry

Lieutenant William Colville—officer in charge of the First
Minnesota Infantry at Gettysburg

Otter (Little Evan)—son of Otter and Blue Flower (Sarah
Ana Ryan) and grandson of Evan and Elizabeth Anne
        Feather Woman—his wife; Minneconjou Lakota
        woman

Private Robert O'Rourke—U.S. Army soldier assigned to
the Pine Ridge Agency

Family Trees for Part Four in Appendix II

CHAPTER 36
...And now, here you stand...Catherine...

The knock at the door brought Ana to her feet. The family had arrived.

"Elizabeth Anne," she called up the stairs to her sister-in-law. "They are here. Come down."

How do I look? Elizabeth Anne thought, gazing at her reflection in the mirror. *What will they think of me?*

She was dressed quite nicely in clothing supplied by Ana. She had parted her hair in the middle and braided it on both sides of her head so that the two drops hung down on either side. She had used red ribbon to tie off the ends, and she had left the bottom ribbon lengths long so that they danced loosely at her waistline. It was the style to which she had become accustomed. Her belt was a finger-woven sash made of wool yarn. Its basic color was green, and it complimented her full-skirted, dark brown dress that fit snugly through the bodice and down the long sleeves.

Suddenly, she recognized the sash. It was the same one Evan had been wearing when she first met him at Fort Snelling twenty-eight years earlier. *Ana must have saved it all these years. Amazing!* She ran her hand over it gently. *I miss you so, Evan.* She thought.

She began walking toward the door, but stopped after a few steps.

These shoes are much too tight. She thought, and she quickly exchanged them for the moccasins she had been wearing when she had arrived at the Hughes house two days earlier. She looked again at herself in the tall, full-length mirror that stood next to the dresser.

There! That feels better. I guess if I look like one of the People, then so be it. That is what I have become. She smiled and left the bedroom.

* * * * * * *

When Elizabeth Anne stepped into the parlor, it was full of people who were talking quietly. The conversation stopped, and the men stood. Ana arose and quickly went over to her.

"This is Elizabeth Anne Ryan, Evan's wife," she said to the assembled group. Then she quickly added, "And this is my younger brother, Timothy Ryan."

The man moved toward Elizabeth Anne, stopping about two feet away from her. No one in the room spoke. Ana stepped away from them slightly, but remained within an arm's reach of her sister-in-law.

I'm right here, Elizabeth Anne, if ya need me! Ana thought.

Timothy Ryan studied the little woman in front of him. She returned his gaze and held it. Then she spoke.

"You resemble Evan quite a lot," she said. "How much older was he?"

"We were about eight years apart," he answered. "I learned a lot from him, more than I ever realized until I was much older."

"And how old are you?" Elizabeth Anne asked. She knew that Evan had been a year older than she was. She asked anyway and seemed at ease.

A bit of the old Elizabeth Anne was emerging, and Ana breathed a soft sigh of relief. Across the room, Patrick smiled at his wife and nodded.

"I'm almost forty," he said, still looking directly at her.

"And who are these others?" Elizabeth Anne asked, smiling and gesturing at the people who were sitting and standing silently in the parlor.

"This is our eldest son, Michael. And this is our second son, Timothy," he answered, moving slightly toward each of the young men as he spoke. Each of the boys nodded courteously at their aunt.

"And this is my wife, Catherine," he said, moving next to a woman sitting on a small couch. She arose and came toward Elizabeth Anne. For a long moment, the two women stood looking intently at one another. Catherine nodded and broke the silence.

"I am pleased to meet ya, and I am so very honored to meet the wife of Evan Ryan," she said.

Her voice was soft, and the last words were spoken with such deep sincerity that Elizabeth Anne was humbled. But, more than being humbled by the reference to her husband, she was confused by the name she had just heard.

"Your name is ... Catherine?" she asked, as though she had not heard her name correctly. "I thought Catherine ..." she said, looking at Ana and then back at the woman in front of her.

"Aye. It is," Catherine answered.

Elizabeth Anne looked back at her and frowned just a little as she waited for her to continue.

"I was named for my older sister who was killed on the night I was born," Catherine said. "Everyone has always said that I look exactly like her, like an identical twin," she added smiling, not intending anything more than just to give the woman additional information.

Elizabeth Anne had never known this part of the family history. In all their years together, Evan had never mentioned anything about the baby born in 1823. Not if it had been a boy, or girl, not a name, nothing. And neither had Ana ever spoken to her about this second Catherine.

She studied the woman before her. She was a bit taller than she, but not big. Her hair was a soft, light-red that was pulled back in a twist at the rear of her head. She had bright, green eyes, and her teeth were straight and very white. The woman was simply beautiful.

Unbelievable. I had no idea. Then she thought. *You say that you look just like your older sister? Oh my! It is no wonder that Evan was attracted to Catherine. And now, here you stand before me, even though you are another Catherine. I can't believe it.*

She reached out with both hands, and Catherine did the same. They stood for a moment, clasping each other's hands. Then they embraced.

When they released each other, Timothy was right there to greet his brother's widow with a hug. Ana and her daughter were wiping their eyes and smiling.

* * * * * * *

More embraces and a good deal of chatter followed as the Hughes and Ryan families reestablished their connectedness. Both of the Hughes sons, Patrick Evan and Matthew stepped forward. They had met their aunt many years before and felt comfortable giving her a brief hug and kiss on the cheek.

The Hughes daughter, Mary Anne, came forward and hugged her aunt warmly. Then she introduced her husband, Daniel Connolly. He was a tall, dark-haired man and very handsome. He stepped forward and, taking Elizabeth Anne's hand in his, said,

"Mary speaks of you all the time. I am so happy to make your acquaintance."

He was the last to be introduced, and when he had stepped back a little, Mary Anne blurted out,

"Aunt Elizabeth, we all know that Uncle Evan is dead, and we are so sad." Her voice choked. "But where are my cousins?"

The room hushed as everyone looked at the little woman from the western prairie.

"I don't know," her aunt replied. "I want to find them."

* * * * * * *

Dinner was served in the large dining room for the eleven family members. Ana and Patrick had hired two cooks and two maids for the day. It was quite unusual, but "the occasion demands something special," Patrick had said when the plans were being made.

It had been a sumptuous feast with four courses. The two maids had served the group quite capably, and the table was rapidly cleared. They retired to the kitchen to help with the clean-up while the Hughes and Ryan families remained sitting at the table. It was dark now, and the candelabras dressed the room with light.

"Tell us what has happened, Aunt Elizabeth," said Mary. She was the youngest of the Hughes children and, at twenty years of age, physically resembled her mother a great deal. But unlike Ana, she had always been very precocious so her question was neither unexpected nor out of place. In fact, everyone wanted to know the same thing.

"I would like to very much, Mary Anne, and I would especially like to tell you about your Uncle Evan. I know you want to hear about him as well," Elizabeth Anne said.

"Aye, please, Elizabeth Anne," interjected Timothy. "Tell us about my brother." Everyone knew that Evan had been killed by soldiers, and they wanted to know the circumstances.

The family members leaned in and looked directly at her, waiting for her to begin.

"Before I talk about Evan and our life on the prairie, I want to make a simple request. The Lakota and Cheyenne, with whom we have lived for the past thirty years, have a custom that I would like you to all follow. It is this. When someone was speaking about something very personal, that person was never looked at directly. Rather, the others looked at the fire or down at the ground in front of them. It was a mark of respect," she said.

"Ana, you have always done this yourself, but you certainly never knew that it was an Indian custom. It was just what you have always done. But I learned from the People that this is an appropriate way to give the speaker their personal, private moment while speaking, and it gives the listeners their privacy to have their own thoughts as they hear the words." She paused.

"I would ask that you do the same when I or any other speaker gets to a part that is difficult for them to speak about. You will sense when that time is. Just pick a spot on the table and look there, not at me or at one another. I will do the same. That way we will all be able to have our own privacy," she said. "Can you do this for me? It really makes it easier for both the speaker and the listener."

She looked at her extended family around the table. One by one they nodded, and Elizabeth Anne began to speak.

"When Evan and I first came to live with the Cheyenne people, we could not speak their language. We quickly learned some of their words, and we learned to speak a language that was spoken with our hands. It was very easy, and once we understood what they were doing with their hands and what the signs meant, we were able to converse with them quite easily and quickly. They are a kind people, and the security and well-being of the entire group is the first consideration in all of their actions with one another. Evan often said that was the way it had been back in Ireland. Everybody helped each other as best they could," she said.

Everyone was watching her and listening with great interest. "Would you agree with that, Patrick?" she asked.

The group turned their attention at Patrick. Thus far, it had been a very normal conversation.

"Aye, 'tis true. We always shared what we had and helped each other out as best we could. None of us ever had much else except one another, that's certain," he answered.

Elizabeth Anne went on.

"I learned right away that their children were taught from birth to never be loud, even the babies, because they always feared attack by enemies. Babies crying or loud talking, especially at night, could give away the location of the village," she continued.

"I was shocked when I first saw the way they trained their babies to not cry or be loud. They started it right from birth. I taught our children to be the same. You may have found them very quiet," she said, directing her eyes at the two Hughes boys and at Mary Anne.

They nodded in agreement as Elizabeth Anne continued.

"Their women are much like us. They are the centers of their households, and the men respect and appreciate them very much. Sometimes a man who was an important leader had two, sometimes three, wives. They needed more adult women in their tipis, that's what they called their tent-like houses, to prepare the food and all of the gifts that were given out at the many feasts that the leaders were expected to put on."

She looked around at the family. She knew what they wanted to know next.

"Evan was an important man in our group, but he only had one wife," she added, emphasizing the last few words, and smiling broadly. Everyone laughed.

"But we did have an old woman who lived with us almost from the first. That was customary. She had no husband or sons alive. I was always so thankful for her presence. She taught me their ways early on and was a wonderful help when our daughter and then our son came along," she said.

"So, we lived only with the Tsitsistas, that's what the People call themselves, for the first three or four years. Then later, some Lakota joined our group."

"Evan was good with horses, and he learned a few more horse tricks from the People. All of them, men, women and children, are excellent horsemen."

"But, he could never break himself of mounting on the left side of the animal. They get up on the right side so that they can use a bow and be ready to shoot. And they slide off on the left side for the same reason. The people laughed at Evan for this, and they called him He Rides the Horse Differently. We laughed about this name often. Actually, it was a strong name because it spoke of the relationship he had with his horses. They depend on their horses for hunting and for defense."

She paused, and when she continued, her voice was much softer, and she directed her eyes at the candle in front of her. It was a cue to the others that they should look away, and they did.

"Almost from the first, I was able to use my midwife skills. The women have babies, too, of course, and I often attended them. The name I came to be called was She Helps Them to Be Born. Evan was very proud that I was given that name. He said his mother would have been named the same, and now, with Catherine here with me, I know that it's true," she said.

Catherine's hand went to her mouth, and she stifled a little gasp. It was almost too much, all of these small bits of the family's past that were so intertwined. She was delivered by the woman who would become her mother-in-law, named for an older sister who died on the very night she was born, and then had married the brother of the boy who had tried to defend her sister. Now, she was sitting with the wife of that same man. And the woman was a midwife, too. It was astonishing, all of these connections.

Her eyes were fixed on the flower arrangement in front of her. No one at the table looked at her. They were following Elizabeth Anne's request.

"They are very careful about having children too close together. The grandmother who lived with us told me that a woman should only have one child that she would have to carry in her arms if the People had to suddenly flee from an enemy attack. It was their custom, and it made sense to me. As some of you know, Evan and I had Sarah Ana first, and about six years later, our son came along. We call him Michael, after Evan's father. The People call him The Red Plume. He is a handsome young man, and I wish I knew where he was now. I don't know where Sarah Ana is either," she said, her voice dropping as she looked down at the table.

"She is married to a Tsitsistas man, and they have a son, my grandson, Little Evan. The People call our grandson Otter, after his father. And Sarah Ana is called Blue Flower."

Some of the candles began to sputter out, and Elizabeth Anne paused again.

"I think we should have some new light. Can we stop for a few minutes?" she asked.

The family group looked up, and Ana quickly answered, "That's a good idea. Will ya tell us more in a bit?"

* * * * * * *

The interlude had been a welcome break in the conversation. The Hughes sons, both older than the Ryan boys, went onto the front porch where they smoked. They were abnormally quiet. They remembered the year-long visit of Uncle Evan's wife and children, that time when their cousins from the plains had lived in their house and were tutored along with themselves. It seemed so long ago. Now, they had heard that the whereabouts of these cousins was unknown. It was not happy news.

When everyone had reconvened at the table, Elizabeth Anne continued her story.

"Our life with the People was really very good. Food was usually plentiful, and we depended on buffalo for just about everything. We lived in our own tipi made from the hides; we ate the meat at just about every meal, and the dressed hides made wonderful, warm clothing. We used deer and antelope hides for our summer clothing when we did not have enough of the cloth that Evan received from his annual trips to meet your men, Patrick," she said, looking at him.

"It was a good trading business, as you know, Patrick," she said, directing her remark at her brother-in-law seated to her right. He nodded in agreement.

"Our village always had many more iron pots and guns and other trade goods than most of the other Indian groups in our area. We had a good life and not as hard as you might think," she said.

"But were there any hard times, Aunt Elizabeth Anne?" asked Mary. Elizabeth Anne looked up at her.

"Well, I don't know what you mean by that. Yes, there were times when I longed for books. And we always spoke English to one another in our tipi, but I sometimes wished that I could hear everyone in the village speaking it. So, those things were hard for me from time to time."

"But the hardest thing was watching the disease come into our village and to some of the other villages that our friends visited and would then bring back to our village. We saw smallpox hurt the People twice that I remember, and cholera took many of the children a few times as well. Evan and I had seen both of those diseases before, so we did not let ourselves or our children get them. We moved away from the place of the sickness and were very careful about who we touched. But it was hard to watch our friends and neighbors die from them. We did what we could to help, but there is only so much that one can do. Those were the worst times," she said.

Elizabeth Anne looked down again. She did not want to pursue that topic any more. It was too painful.

"But, we never starved, even in the winter when snows made hunting almost impossible. Evan once told me that the hungry time in Ireland was in the summer, before the crops were harvested. He said he was often hungry because the previous year's food had been pretty much used up," she continued.

Timothy moved uncomfortably in his chair and looked at his two sons. How well he knew of the hungry times. Too well! Elizabeth Anne went on.

"Our village was never attacked by the People of the Little Black Eagle. The whites call them the Crow. They were our biggest threat, along with the Blackfoot. Oh, they raided our horse herds, and our men did the same to theirs. But there were seldom any fatalities. They fight differently than the American soldiers. Evan said that the white soldiers reminded him of the British soldiers in Ireland. He ended up hating them almost as much as he hated the British. You can probably understand that, Patrick. And perhaps, you too, Timothy! Am I right about the British?" she added.

"Aye, I saw too many things as a boy in Ireland, and I do understand what ya mean," answered Patrick. He was looking at the spot in front of him. None of the other family members looked up. They, too, were trying to practice the conversational custom that Elizabeth Anne had requested of them, and they all knew that any talk about the English occupation of Ireland would be difficult for the speaker and for some of the listeners. Elizabeth Anne nodded in response to his comment.

"As some of you remember, I brought the children here to this house when they were young. I wanted them to be able to read and write and to know something about the society that Evan and I came from. Evan stayed with the People, of course, to keep the hide business going. Then, I went back out with our children a year later. When was that, Ana?" she asked.

"Ya came here in 1842. That was the year Patrick and I moved into this house." Then Ana added, "Think of it. We moved here fourteen years ago, and we had already been living in this area for fourteen years. We missed all the bad times in Ireland."

"That's true. Evan and ya and Patrick left Ireland way before the bad times started," Timothy said. "Catherine and I and the boys here are the lucky ones. We came to America just eight years ago. We are lucky to even be alive."

"Would you tell me about those times, Timothy? I want to know about Evan's parents and about Catherine's people," Elizabeth Anne said.

Without looking up at anyone, Patrick responded for his sister-in-law.

"Aye! You must hear about Evan's parents and what has gone on in our homeland. But it is very late. Let's meet again tomorrow and continue. Ana and I will have dinner again for us, and we can hear more. Let's start early so that we can hear it all," he suggested.

"And Timothy, ya have something from Ireland that Elizabeth Anne should see. Please bring it with ya," he added.

"Is that all right, Elizabeth Anne? Tomorrow again?" asked Ana, suddenly becoming the proper hostess.

"I will look forward to being with all of you again. Yes. And what is this thing you have to show me, Timothy?" she said.

"It is something ya will want to see, I know it. Let me surprise ya tomorrow," Timothy answered.

CHAPTER 37
...life just got harder...

The two cooks and the two serving maids that Patrick and Ana had hired for the next day began their work in the early morning. It would be another good day of pay for them, and they were glad to return to the Hughes house.

"They are a strange bunch," said Rebecca, one of the serving maids who had worked the night before.

"I don't think so," said Marie. She was the other server and was of French-Canadian descent. She was a pretty, dark-haired girl just a bit younger than Mary Anne Hughes. She was still single and had been in the area for only two years with her family, the Toussaints.

"This is a family that tells stories, just like my grandpa did. I like them," she said. She did not add that the eldest Hughes son, Patrick Evan, a very wealthy and eligible bachelor in the St. Paul area, had been looking at her all throughout the previous evening as she brought in the various dishes and then cleared the table after each course.

* * * * * * *

The family assembled just after noon. They were all eager for Elizabeth Anne to continue with her story. They sat in the parlor, with the younger Ryan boys on the floor. A small table in the center of the room was decorated with a bouquet of flowers that Ana had picked earlier in the morning. At Patrick's request, Elizabeth Anne began speaking.

"After the children and I returned to the prairie, it seemed that things began to change. More and more white settlers were passing through the People's land, not to stay, but on their way to the land across the big mountains. Many of the Indian leaders did not like this. But as long as the whites stayed close to the river that they followed, there were seldom any problems. None of our People wanted to fight them," Elizabeth Anne began.

"Anyway, as I said yesterday, Indian men fight differently. Our men fight basically to do brave things. They will kill if they have to, of course, to protect their homes or families or themselves. But when going on a horse-raiding trip against an enemy group, the object is always to get the horses, not kill as many of the enemy as possible or wipe out the village," she continued.

"Even when our village was the target of a horse-raid, it was the same. Our men defended the herd and our tipis, but no one was killed very often. The two things that our fighting men try to do are touch an armed enemy in battle and get away to tell about it, or rescue one of their friends in the midst of a battle," Elizabeth Anne paused.

"That's amazing," said Patrick. He was about to add something when Ana touched his arm and interrupted.

"There is tea. Please help yourselves," she said. The two maids entered the room and placed the service on the sideboard.

*   *   *   *   *   *   *

One by one the family members served themselves and then settled back into their places, eager to hear more. Patrick opened the conversation.

"Timothy. Would you tell Elizabeth Anne about your parents and the others back in Ireland? Let's give her a rest," he said.

"Yes. I'd like that," added Elizabeth Anne.

Timothy began.

"Our life in Ireland was always hard. After Evan and Ana left, our land was taken over by another man. He was an agent for our landlord's family and came twice a year from Cork. We never saw the English landlord again. Over the years, the agent kept dividin' up the parcels until we had just a little piece of land on which to grow our food. We ate mainly potatoes. Sometimes turnips and cabbage and onions, but mainly potatoes. They stopped lettin' us raise sheep or goats because they said it took away land that could be planted in crops for the owners. All of the flax and wheat we grew and harvested belonged to the landlord. We owned nothin' and we still had to pay rent. The agent even stopped father from raisin' racehorses. Life just got harder and harder," Timothy said.

"I married Catherine when she was seventeen. Michael here came along that first year, and two years later Timothy was born. He was about a year old when we heard about Catherine's older brother, Thomas," he said.

"We don't know everything," said Catherine, picking up the story. "We do know that Thomas, my brother, was never quite right after my sister's death. He had been in the room and had seen what Evan tried to do to help her. He saw her killed, and it tainted him for the rest of his life. The British executed him in Cork the year Timothy turned one."

She knew more of the story, but did not want to tell it in front of her sons. They could hear the full truth about their Uncle Thomas when they got older.

Timothy began to speak again.

"Somethin' happened about a year after we heard about Catherine's brother. The potatoes all went bad. We had never seen nothing' like it. The plants turned black, and when we dug them up in the autumn, they all turned to mush within a few days. Everyone was hungry, and it got worse when the potatoes failed again the next year. The British did nothin' to help us. In fact, they raised our rent, and when we couldn't pay it, we was all evicted. Catherine's parents and my parents lost their little pieces of land, and the houses was knocked down. I had three little boys countin' our new baby, Charles, and we had no place to go," he said. He was becoming agitated as he recounted the past times. Most of the family members were now looking away from him. They already knew the story.

Catherine began to speak again. She knew that her husband was coming to a difficult part. It was a difficult part for her, too, but she knew she could get through the telling.

"Timothy took us up into the hills. He knew of a cave where we would be out of the weather. There was no others livin' around us because so many had either died or gone to the coastal cities. We had this very tiny garden hidden there in the hills near the cave, and so we did not starve as quickly as the others did who was evicted. No potatoes, mind ya, just cabbage and onions, and I got some corn to grow. We also had four sheep, at least to start with. Once they was gone, we was hungry a lot. Every now and then Timothy's father would come up to the cave and check on us. He would bring us a little food if he had it, or we would try to give him some of ours," Catherine said.

"Usually, he wouldn't take it, though. He told us to give it to the children. I could tell he was starvin' himself, and I knew Timothy's mother must have been starvin' as well," she added.

"After almost two years there in the cave, Timothy said that we had to get out of Ireland. The potatoes was still not growing, and we was startin' to starve, too. I tried prayin' to St. Bridget, but it didn't do no good. We knew if we stayed, we'd die," Catherine continued.

"We began walking toward Cork, and that's when we found out about our parents. We hadn't heard from them for a few months because they was all dead. My parents had died of the cholera, and the Ryans just died. They starved, I know it," she said, her voice starting to crack. "We couldn't even find where they was buried."

And the landlords did nothing to help you? Where is the sharing like that which the Tsitsistas and Lakota practice? And the People are not Catholics. Or Protestants, either. Elizabeth Anne thought. But she was silent. She looked at the floor in front of her. The others did the same. Timothy continued.

"We got to Cork and boarded a ship that was goin' to Canada. Most of the other ships in the harbor were trade ships. And they was full of wheat and corn and barley. They was selling all that food that could have stayed in Ireland and stopped the starving," he said, his voice revealing his anger.

Bastards! English bastards! That's what Evan used to say. Thought Elizabeth Anne. *He was right.*

Timothy continued.

"They promised us money when we arrived in Canada, but that turned out to be a lie. We was packed into the hold of the ship and barely had enough room to lie down. We had the two boys plus the baby, Charles. He was named for my grandfather."

"The crossin' took almost six weeks. Everyone was sick, and they fed us very little. Even the water was foul. Rainwater was the freshest we ever got. They treated us like we was animals. People was sick and dyin' all around us," Timothy said. "That's when we lost our little baby, Charles."

Catherine began to speak again. She needed to tell this part herself to Elizabeth Anne. It was something that should be told by a woman to a woman, by a mother to a mother. But her voice betrayed her intense pain. She was already shaking, and tears were running down her cheeks and dripping off her chin. The words came out haltingly.

"I ... held ... my baby ... in my arms ... day after day ... and watched his little eyes ... looking up at me .... I had no milk for him any more ... and ... I tried ... to feed him our food ... with my finger ... but ... he just withered away in my arms ...." Her sobbing grew stronger.

"I could do nothin' .... We had nothin'... No mother should ever ... ever ...have to watch ... her child starve to death ... and then ... and then ... have to throw him ... over the side of a ship." She sobbed out the words. Timothy reached for her hand and held it. Catherine sobbed unabashedly. The loss of her little child eight years before was still painfully a part of her.

Elizabeth Anne looked at the flowers in the center of the room. She could sense that the others were doing the same, or looking down. The room was perfectly silent except for Catherine's soft crying.

Oh Catherine. I have seen it, too. Little ones dying as we sit helpless to do anything. Yes! I have seen it. She thought.

Ana and Patrick and their children already knew these things. Still, it was hard for them to hear it all again.

I will be a mother some day. Thought Mary Anne. *I will remember this story always, Aunt Catherine, and when I have children, they shall never starve, I promise you. My children shall never starve.*

Catherine began to regain her composure, and everyone waited for someone to begin speaking. Ana stood and motioned toward the sideboard.

"I am going to check on dinner. I shall be back soon. Help yourselves to more tea," she said softly, and then left the room. The others took it as a signal to take a break. Some served themselves, and the younger boys went out onto the front porch.

These women are strong women. They remind me of my Cheyenne and Lakota friends. I know what I am going to do. Thought Elizabeth Anne. Then she left the room.

CHAPTER 38
...defending the helpless...

When Elizabeth Anne returned to the parlor, she carried a small shoulder pouch with her. The family group slowly reassembled and grew quiet. Everyone was composed, now that the hard times in Ireland had been described to the woman from the western American prairie. Elizabeth Anne stood and reached into the pouch, leaving her hand inside it.

"I want to give Catherine a gift. I was able to bring very few things with me from my life on the prairie. But I did save these," she said. She brought out a tiny pair of moccasins.

"I made these for our grandson, Little Evan. They are Cheyenne because his father is of those People. The women of our tiyospaye, our hunting group, taught me how to put on the beads. Little Evan wore them when he was a very small boy. I want you to have them, Catherine. I want to give you these in memory of your little son, Charles. You must always remember that you did all that you could for him and that he will never be forgotten as long as we say his name when the family gathers."

She went over to Catherine and handed the little shoes to her. Catherine took them and rubbed her hands over the beadwork that decorated the outside of the tiny footwear. Her eyes were full of tears again.

"I shall treasure them, and they will remain in our family always," she said. "Thank you." She stood and the two women embraced warmly.

Elizabeth Anne returned to her chair. The room was quiet, but everyone was looking at the little shoes in Catherine's hands. The meaning that they now had had not been lost on any of them. It had been a wonderful moment, one that would never be forgotten.

Suddenly, Timothy got up and left the room. He returned quickly and carried something in his hand. It was a wooden stick not quite six feet long, and it had a curved hook at the top. He stood just inside the doorway and waited for everyone's attention. When everyone had turned in his direction, he moved toward Elizabeth Anne.

"Elizabeth Anne. This is a shepherd's herdin' stick. It is all that I could bring with us from Ireland. It has been in Catherine's family for two generations," he said. "Ana and Patrick have seen this before, and so have all our children." He paused and moved in front of his brother's widow.

"This is the crook that Evan grabbed from the sheep pen when he went in to help Catherine's sister. He held it in his hands and tried to defend her on the night she was killed. People still talk about him in County Tipperary. This staff has always been in either the O'Leary or Ryan family, and now I want to give it to ya." He extended the curved stick out in front of him.

Elizabeth Anne stood and took the staff.

"This is very special. Thank you. I accept this gift in honor of my husband, Evan Ryan," she said very quietly. "Thank you."

She remained standing with the stick in her hands, running her fingers over the hooked end. The room was still. The story of Evan's courage that night in 1823 had been repeated often by Ana and Patrick to their children, and by Catherine and Timothy to theirs. Elizabeth Anne looked at her extended family and smiled.

"Oh my!" she said, shaking her head from side to side. "Oh my!"

She looked down at the shepherd's crook and said, "I think now is the time to tell you about Evan and how he died."

She fixed her eyes on the flowers in the center of the room and began speaking without waiting for their reaction. She was still standing, and her voice was steady and strong. Timothy backed away and returned to his place next to Catherine.

"I have told you that the Cheyenne and the Lakota, another group of the People who also joined our village, respect bravery. And I have told you they put personal honor as an important value. But the greatest and most honorable thing that a man can do is to defend the people. They always refer to the women and children and the old people as the helpless ones. They have a special group of men, it's like a men's club, who have taken an oath that they will die in the defense of the helpless. My husband was one of those men."

"It was a great honor to be invited into this society, and when he was asked to join, Evan asked me if I thought he should accept the position. It was not a difficult decision for me. I told him yes, join them. I wanted my husband to be part of this elite group. They are called Dog Soldiers, and they carry long, decorated sticks to designate their membership in this group to everyone, to their own people as well as to the enemy. These long sticks are the symbol that they are the toughest fighting men of all."

She held the stick up in front of her and said, "If this shepherd's stick was longer, and if it was covered with otter hide, it would look exactly like Evan's Dog Soldier staff. They even have the curved crooks at the top. They are identical in shape."

"Oh my!" she repeated quietly. "Yes, they are the same."

"Evan joined the Dog Soldier Society. He kept his crook'd staff in our tipi. He never carried it away from the village because his duty was to defend the people there," she said.

Elizabeth Anne looked at the stick in her hand. Everyone in the room was looking at her, waiting for her to continue. She sat back down and resumed her story.

"About two years ago, one of the Lakota villages was attacked by white soldiers. They wanted the return of a cow that had wandered away from a wagon train of whites. The Lakota leader, one of our old friends, Conquering Bear, tried to pay the white man back for the loss of his cow. But he refused to take horses as payment. The cow had already been butchered for food, so it could not be given back."

"The soldiers came to Conquering Bear's camp. I was not there, but I heard this from some of my Lakota friends," Elizabeth Anne continued, her eyes back on the small table in the middle of the room. She was no longer mindful of where anyone was looking.

"Conquering Bear told his fighting men that he would go and talk with the soldier leader. He did, but the American officer would not take any payment except the cow. That was impossible. It was an unreasonable demand. I don't think the officer understood the signs Conquering Bear used, and my friends said that the half-breed interpreter was drunk. When Conquering Bear went back to his warriors at the outskirts of the village, the soldiers opened fire on them."

"My friends said that Conquering Bear called out to his warriors and told them not to return fire. They followed his command, but the second volley from the soldiers killed him and some others. That's when his warriors retaliated, and all of the American soldiers were killed."

She paused, and her voice dropped. She was coming to a difficult part of her story, and she hoped that everyone was not looking at her.

"Then last year, last autumn, Evan and I were camped with the People near a little creek. Another group of American soldiers came into our vicinity, and our leaders called for the Dog Soldiers to go out, really more for show than anything. They expected the soldiers to send a small group toward the village to talk. That's what they usually did." She paused and concentrated on the center of the room.

"I remember the day very clearly. Evan came running into our tipi and grabbed his Dog Soldier staff. He turned to me, a questioning look on his face. I was the one who handed him his rifle. 'Go,' I said. 'Honor your commitment to the People.' He took the rifle from my hands and kissed me quickly. He told me that he loved me. Then he went out of our tipi."

"I watched him go to the edge of our village. Suddenly, the American soldiers were moving into an attack formation. They weren't going to talk; they were out to avenge the soldiers killed at Conquering Bear's camp the previous year."

"There were six other Dog Soldiers standing in a line facing the soldiers. Evan joined them. They started waving their crook'd staffs high in the air, like this, to get the attention of the soldiers." She stood and waved the shepherd's staff slowly back and forth above her head, the curved top drawing a half-moon arc through the air above her.

"We women were gathering up the little children and preparing to run away. That's when the first shell hit the ground in the middle of our camp. I looked back at Evan. He had taken his sash and pinned it to the ground. The Dog Soldiers have this custom of putting a long cloth or buckskin sash over their shoulder and staking the other end to the ground. That way, they were tethered to their position. It was an announcement that said the man would fight there until he was killed. Evan used the knife he had made on the ship to pin his sash to the ground. He always carried that knife. All of the others were doing the same thing with their dog ropes."

The group was totally focused on Elizabeth Anne, who was still standing. While she was not looking at them, they were now looking directly at her, unable to look away.

"When the second volley of soldier fire came, I ducked back into the tipi. I grabbed this little pouch and put the moccasins into it. I remember thinking that if I must run with the other women, I wanted to save something from my home. I looked for our grandson, but I couldn't see him anywhere," she continued.

But now her voice was beginning to reveal the pain these memories brought. The women in the room began to cry softly, each of them identifying with Elizabeth Anne's experience.

I would have done the same thing. Thought Ana. *I would have saved something from my home, too.*

Elizabeth Anne continued speaking.

"I looked again at Evan. He was waving his Dog Soldier staff high in the air and yelling at the soldiers, and to his comrades who were there in front of the village. Maybe they thought the soldiers would fight them in the old, Indian way ... trying to touch them for personal honor. I don't think anyone expected them to try to kill an entire village."

"That's when the third volley of fire came. A bullet struck Evan, and he staggered, clutching his chest. He turned toward the village and looked in my direction. I know he saw me, and he yelled out to me as he fell. I had heard the words many times before. It was his personal battle cry. He yelled 'Erin Go Bragh'. Then I saw him fall to his knees and then to the ground." Elizabeth Anne stopped speaking.

Her last words had had a visible affect on both Patrick and Timothy. They each had their hands in front of their faces and were weeping audibly, the great sobs racking their bodies and their shoulders shaking with the intensity of their grief.

"Mother of God!" Patrick sobbed out. "Oh! Erin Go ...!" He could not finish the phrase.

Ana, Catherine, and Mary Anne sat with their hands over their mouths, their tears running just as hard and their bodies shaking with their sobbing. Mary Anne shook her head slowly from side to side, and her husband, Daniel, crossed himself in silent tribute.

The Hughes and Ryan sons sat frozen. They were not only disturbed and saddened by their aunt's story, but also by the fact that they had never before seen their fathers cry.

Elizabeth Anne remained standing. She paused in her telling and then, in a louder voice that was firm with conviction, she finished with the words,

"Evan died as a Dog Soldier should die, defending the helpless. I am proud of him. Ah-hou!" she said in a voice that did not have a trace of sadness or self-pity.

She sat back down.

For a long time nothing was said as everyone's crying began to subside. Then Catherine spoke. Her voice was very quiet as she said,

"Oh dear God! Evan did for ya and the People what he had tried to do for my sister."

* * * * * * *

The supper was good. It was not as grandiose as the one the night before, but still somewhat elegant for the Hughes and Ryans. The table talk was sparse, and the two serving maids noticed a distinctly different atmosphere in the room.

"They are certainly a quiet bunch tonight," said Rebecca.

"They are," replied Maria. *He is not even looking at me like he did last night.* She thought.

* * * * * * *

The meal ended, and the family still sat at the table.

"I am so glad to know all that ya told us, Elizabeth Anne," said Patrick, when it appeared that everyone had finished eating. "I've been thinking that Evan was a hero, dying the way he did."

"I suppose you could think of it that way, Patrick," Elizabeth Anne said. "Or, you could think of it as an act of foolishness. Dog Soldiers have no chance against the American troops. They do not fight in the old style ... all that touching in battle for personal honor, and the like. I have a feeling that the People will some day learn how to fight in the white soldiers' style. Then it won't be so one-sided. Those Dog Men are tough. They are much better man for man than the soldiers."

"I don't think Uncle Evan was a hero," said Timothy. He was the youngest of the Ryan sons, and a creative, thoughtful boy. It was an almost disrespectful thing for him to say, this challenge to the views of an adult.

"Timothy!" exclaimed his mother, Catherine. She was embarrassed by her son's statement.

"Why not, Timothy?" asked Patrick, interested to hear the young boy's thinking.

"Because, I think that a hero is someone who does something that they are not expected to do. Like a stranger who runs into a burning house and tries to help people get out. But Uncle Evan was a Dog Soldier, and he was expected to fight for the People. They were all his family, too. And it was even expected that he might die doing so. He was doing his job. It was an honorable job, but still his job."

The boy paused and then added, "I think my Grandfather Michael was a hero. He gave us his food so we could stay alive. That wasn't his job, but he did it anyway because we were his family, and he died because he did," the boy said, and then looked down.

"If I may be so bold."

The voice belonged to Daniel Connolly, Mary Anne's husband. He and his father were attorneys and worked almost exclusively for the Hughes Company. Everyone looked at him.

"As I see it, both Uncle Evan and Grandfather Michael were heroes. They both did what they felt was their responsibility to do," he said. "That is a big word, responsibility. The older you get, the more you will understand how big a word it is, Timothy."

"What I believe is most important is that none of us ever forget the story of what Uncle Evan did in Ireland and what he did here in America. And what Grandfather Michael did for his family in Ireland. And the same for all the others including you, Timothy, and you, Catherine, and both of you, Patrick and Ana," he said, turning to his in-laws.

"Some day far in the future, I hope our grandchildren and great-grandchildren will tell these stories. And when they do, I hope they will smile and shake their heads in wonderment, and then be proud that they are Ryans and Hughes, and Connollys."

What Daniel Connolly would some day discover was that the name of Evan Ryan and the story of what he had done as a boy in 1823 had not been forgotten in Ireland either.

* * * * * * *

When Matthew Hughes left his parents' home that evening, he was still thinking about his Uncle Evan. *There is an expanded expectation which comes when one accepts the symbol of responsibility.* He thought. That realization would guide his choices and actions for the rest of his life.

* * * * * * *

The winter of 1856-57 was one of the coldest on record. Elizabeth Anne stayed with Ana and Patrick through the autumn, intending to return to the Plains in the late spring. The coughing sickness came to her in early January.

The tipi was warmer. She thought, as she lay in the upstairs bedroom of the Hughes house. It was not that Ana and Patrick were not doing all that they could to make her feel at home and comfortable. It was just that Elizabeth Anne Delaney Ryan, the one whom the People had called She Helps Them to Be Born, was no longer used to stuffy houses and the uneven heat of wood stoves. *My lodge was snug and warm always.* She thought. *Where are my children? Is Sarah Ana all right? And where is Michael? Where is my little grandson? I must go back in the spring. I will go back.*

But she grew weaker, her breath rattling in her lungs as she fought to breathe. In the early morning hours of mid-February 1857, her heart finally gave out. It had already been broken by the loss of her husband, Evan, and by the unknown whereabouts of her two children.

She was buried wearing Evan's old voyageur sash. Matthew Hughes had the honor of carrying the crook'd staff in the funeral procession.

The Hughes and Ryan families mourned for weeks. Ana and Patrick personally grieved for months.

CHAPTER 39
...good times and bad times...

It was a wonderful wedding, and the feast that was to follow promised to be extravagant. The festivities would be held at one of the large hotels owned by Patrick Hughes.

His eldest son, Patrick Evan Hughes, had finally married Marie Toussaint. They had often been seen together in the months following the two nights when she had worked as a serving maid for the dinners which his parents had given in honor of the arrival of Aunt Elizabeth Anne. On those nights, he had been almost unable to take his eyes off of the pretty young girl. His younger brother, Matthew, had noticed his brother's interest, and he had encouraged him to pursue her when they had smoked together on the front porch that first evening.

The courtship actually took five years, and everyone was relieved and happy once the announcement of marriage was made. Patrick Evan had been very busy managing one of the hotels his father owned, and often he let two or more weeks go by without seeing her. But he really could not keep himself from falling in love with Marie. She was dark-eyed and dark-haired, and she reminded him of his Aunt Elizabeth Anne in the way that she was able to capably handle anything that needed to be done.

Marie was twelve years younger than Patrick and felt fortunate that so wealthy a man would choose her for his wife.

I am a simple French-Canadian girl from Montreal. I hope I can meet his expectations. She thought after she had accepted his proposal.

Even if the reception was to be large, the group invited to the ceremony had been small and private. The priest said the words as the couple knelt in the tiny church that had been established at Mendota. After the blessing, they arose and faced their families. Marie took the bouquet from her younger sister and split the flowers into two bundles. She handed one to Patrick Evan. Then she addressed the two family groups.

"I want the first act of my married life to be a prayer to our Holy Mother. My prayer will be in honor of my grandpere and grandmere, Marie and Antoine Toussaint. May they rest in peace." She crossed herself and then continued.

"I also pray for my new husband's family who are gone from us. They are Evan and Elizabeth Anne Ryan and little Charles Ryan. In my family, they will not be forgotten." She crossed herself again.

Three pairs of eyes began to fill with tears. The eyes belonged to Ana Hughes, Mary Anne Connolly, and Catherine Ryan.

Patrick Evan then spoke.

"I want the first act of my married life to be a prayer to St. Michael, the Archangel. May he protect my cousins Sarah Ana and Michael Ryan wherever they may be, and may he give strength to my brother, Matthew, and his men as they go forward into battle. May the family be saved, and may the Union be brought back together." He crossed himself also.

The couple turned and walked away from each other to the two sides of the altar. They placed their bouquets on the small offering platforms that stood in front of the two statues. Then they knelt and prayed.

Pierre Toussaint and his wife looked across the aisle at Patrick and Ana Hughes. The four parents smiled and nodded proudly at one another. Then they knelt in reverence. One by one, each of the other family members did the same.

This unique ceremony had never been seen before at any wedding any of them had ever attended. It would be repeated in the Ryan and Hughes families for generations to come with the list of names growing longer.

The reception which followed the ceremony was large and filled with festive joy.

During the dinner, Ana spoke with Pierre Toussaint, who was sitting next to her. A few months earlier the two families had discovered the connection between Evan Ryan and Pierre's father, Antoine. It had happened quite by chance during a conversation over tea one afternoon, and both families marveled at the surprising revelation.

"Evan would be so happy to know of Marie's choice of a husband," she said. "I remember that he held Patrick Evan when he was a baby and that he told Patrick that his son had two good names because of who the names came from. He said it laughing but I know now that he was right. My son loves your daughter very much, and I believe that he is a good man."

Pierre nodded and said, "He is a good man. I am happy for Marie, too. We may be poor people, but we have big dreams for our children."

Ana looked directly at Pierre.

"We come from poor people as well. We have been lucky," she said.

* * * * * * *

Matthew Charles Hughes was a Catholic; he was of 100% Irish descent, but he was also an American. In 1862, he enlisted and became an officer in the First Minnesota Infantry. The Civil War was raging, and he knew he must join the cause.

I am traveling on the Mississippi River just like my parents did many years ago. Only I am going south on this paddlewheel boat, and they went north. He thought. It was the spring of 1863.

At St. Louis, his group of new recruits transferred onto one of the Union ships that moved unheeded on the inland waterways and headed up the Ohio River. The First Minnesota had already distinguished itself in the brutal campaigns and major battles of the first two years of the war, and these replacement officers and enlisted men were being sent east to join McClellan's Army of the Potomac.

* * * * * * *

It was a few months later when Father William Corby, a Catholic chaplain, stood on the boulder at the south end of the long Union line that resembled a fishhook. Three hundred Union soldiers knelt before him as he gave the absolution.

"Go now," he said. "Make us proud, lads!"

The Irish Brigade stood and moved forward, obeying the commands of their officers. Facing a huge force of Mississippians, the brigade moved off into the Wheatfield, their green flag flying above them. It was July 2, 1863, and the place was Gettysburg.

* * * * * * *

Farther up the Union line to the north on that same day, the First Minnesota Infantry of two hundred sixty-two men found itself facing Confederate Brigadier General Cadmus Wilcox's Alabama Regiment of fifteen hundred battle-hardened troops.

Union General William Hancock rode up to the small group of Minnesotans. One aide accompanied him.

"Are there no more troops in this area?" he shouted at Lt. William Colville, the ranking officer in charge. Hancock was clearly panicked.

"We are all, sir," Colville responded. "We have been ordered to guard this gun battery."

Hancock pointed across the field.

"Do you see those colors?" he shouted, pointing at the red battle flags of Wilcox's Regiment less than a quarter of a mile away.

Colville nodded.

"Take them," he said.

It was an order clearly made out of desperation. Hancock knew that if the Confederates breached the Union line at this spot, they would divide the Northern forces and carry the day, if not the entire battle. He wheeled his horse and galloped away to find more troops to fill this critical gap.

Colville looked at his men and officers. He knew many of them personally from before the war. He understood exactly what Hancock wanted. He wanted time. The First Minnesota would buy time for the Union, and they would have to pay for that time in blood.

"Fix your bayonets, men," he shouted. "Get into formation and be ready to follow me. Fire on my command. We will fire once, and then we will charge with steel. We will not reload. Do you understand me?"

The Minnesotans scrambled into formation. The sound of their bayonets clanked as they were locked into position on the rifle barrels. The noise was clearly audible above the roar of the battle that raged in the orchard and wheatfield farther to their left.

Matthew Hughes turned to the men closest to him and nodded resolutely to them. *We will make them proud.* He thought.

Matthew wore the stripes of a Union officer. On that day ten months earlier, when he received them at Fort Snelling, he remembered thinking of how his uncle, Evan Ryan, had lived his life and how he had died. He recalled the story of the crook'd staff that his uncle had used in Ireland as a boy, and the other long staff with the curved top that he had carried when he died in the defense of his village on the western plains of America just eight years before.

The crook'd staff was a symbol of responsibility for him. He thought. *These stripes are the symbol of my responsibility. Our flag is no different than Uncle Evan's crook'd staff.* Now, on this field outside the little town of Gettysburg in Pennsylvania, he looked at again those stripes and then up at the First Minnesota flag.

Lt. Colville began moving forward. The First Minnesota colors were next to him, carried by a young soldier of not more than sixteen years of age. Colville's rifle was at the ready, and his sword was hanging on his left side. The flag bearer was unarmed.

"Forward Minnesota," he shouted. The junior officers behind him echoed his command, and the force moved toward the Confederate lines. Through the haze of the cannon smoke, Matthew could barely see the grey-clad enemy. They had moved about one hundred yards into the open when Colville dropped to his knees and, turning, hollered back to his men,

"Halt and fire at will."

The terrific noise of rifle fire that burst from the muzzles was followed by the roar of attack from the throats of the men from Minnesota. Then the entire force of two hundred sixty-two men began racing madly across the open field toward the Confederate lines.

* * * * * * *

Brigadier General Wilcox could not believe his eyes. *This is crazy.* He thought. *This is a suicidal charge. They are dropping, and still they come. I have never witnessed such reckless bravery.*

He knew his own regiment's formation had been disrupted by this wild Union charge, and that he could not order a counter-attack which would be effective.

This attack will play itself out. He thought.

* * * * * * *

Matthew saw the flag bearer fall. He raced forward and grabbed the long flagpole out of the boy's hands. He knew that if their colors were in the midst of the enemy, the

Minnesotans would fight that much harder to keep their flag from being captured.

I am carrying our staff just like my Uncle Evan carried one of his own. It was the symbol of his responsibility. I will not abandon my responsibility. It was a conscious thought as he ran with the flag in one hand and his rifle in the other. Suddenly he was among the Southerners, who were in complete disarray. The wild bayonet charge appeared to be successful.

"With me, Minnesota," he yelled. The screams of the wounded and dying men around him, and the sound of the rifle shots that continued to dominate the horrible din of battle, almost drowned out his voice. All around him surged the dark blue coats of his men.

Suddenly he felt a sharp, searing pain in his upper abdomen. His breath was knocked out of him, and he fell to the ground onto his back. Still, he held the wooden pole so that the flag stood straight.

Lying there, he knew he had been struck by a Minnie ball. He was not in any great pain, but he felt himself growing weak and very cold. He looked up at the fabric fluttering above him and the pole to which it was attached. It was the last thing he saw as the life left his body.

* * * * * * *

Late that same afternoon Father Corby walked north along the long Union line. He had done what he could for the wounded and dying in the Wheatfield. The day's fighting was over and the burial and ambulance details from both armies were moving through the areas where the battles had raged. It had been a terrible slaughter for both sides, and the priest had hardly been able to touch the ground with his feet as he had tried to walk through the Wheatfield. The bodies lay so thick that they formed a virtual carpet of death.

Still he thought, *Good Irish lads. I trust the nation will remember what they did.*

"Father!" The voice came from a Union soldier who was sitting propped up against a cannon. "Can you help us?"

The priest moved toward the man.

"What do you need, son?" he replied.

"I'm from St. Paul in Minnesota. Some of my friends are lying out there. Could you go? Many of us are Catholic, Father." The man pointed toward the Confederate lines and the small field that stood between it and the Union battery.

"How many of you are there?" the priest asked.

"Only forty-seven of us answered roll call a few minutes ago," he answered. "The rest have fallen."

The priest walked across the field. Nothing moved. He stepped into the area that had been the scene of the fiercest fighting. There was still no movement from any of the bodies that lay in the grotesque positions of violent death.

As he looked around, his eyes caught the glint of a silver medal that lay on the chest of one of the dead Union soldiers. The soldier was an officer. He knelt beside the man and looked at it closely.

The medal was a crucifix attached to the center of a shepherd's crook. He recognized it immediately as the staff carried by Saint Patrick, the patron saint of Ireland.

"Ah, Irish, are ya! Bless you, my son. May God have mercy on your soul," he said making the sign of the Cross over the fallen officer. Then he noticed that the dead man's eyes were still open and that he was smiling.

* * * * * * *

Blue Flower was the name she was called by the People. Her parents had named her Sarah Ana Ryan. She was the firstborn child of Evan and Elizabeth Anne.

The little girl had been born in the early winter of 1829. She had green eyes like her mother, but was tall like her father and had his darker hair. She had grown into a soft-spoken, strong, young woman and possessed the graceful movements for which the Cheyenne women were known. While she knew a great deal about the culture of the People, she also was acquainted with some of the customs and the language of her parents.

She had been thirteen when she spent a year with her cousins in the big city to the east. She was fifteen when Otter made known his interest in having her for his wife. He courted her and her family for almost two years. Then they were married.

* * * * * * *

Her first baby came less than a year later. The baby was delivered by her mother, and the little boy was named Otter after his father. He was called "Little Evan" by his grandparents.

The boy had been just eight when he saw his grandfather killed by soldiers at Ash Hollow on the Blue Water. But the last nine years had been relatively peaceful for the People. There was trading, and the hunting had not been too badly disrupted.

Now tensions had developed, and many of the Southern and Northern Cheyenne bands were moving to new camps, some near to soldier forts where they believed they would have protection.

Otter and Blue Flower also had a daughter. She was almost nine and carried herself with the same graceful demeanor as did her mother. Mollie was her English name, and she was known as Yellow Calf by her father's people.

Their village was located on the banks of Sand Creek in eastern Colorado. It was a day's travel to Bent's Fort and the nearby Fort Lyon. They had been with Black Kettle and his band of Southern Cheyenne now for almost half a year. There was nothing to fear, her husband had told her.

The attack came the next day.

* * * * * * *

It was easy for The Red Plume to blend into the citizenry of Denver. The news of the attack had traveled quickly through the Lakota and Tsitsistas camps, and he had left for the big white man's town immediately. He knew his sister and family had been with the Southern Cheyenne chief.

The years since his father's death in 1855 had been moderately quiet for the People. The Red Plume continued living with the tiyospaye that was always a mixture of Cheyenne and Lakota. He was not married and lived in one of the warrior society lodges. He took great pride in providing food for the families of men who had been hurt or killed in the horse-raids that seemed to happen with regularity. But this news was disturbing, and it was time to find out about his sister's family.

Michael had cut his hair and dressed in a shirt and trousers. Leaving his horse just outside the city, he walked along the unpaved streets until he reached the opera house. He slipped inside. It was full of people, many of whom were clearly drunk.

He watched as a man on the stage reported on "the great and glorious victory over the heathen savages." The crowd cheered and applauded when the trophies of war were proudly displayed. They seemed delighted to see the display of scalps and severed arms, hands, and breasts which the soldiers called the "Hundred Dazers" had brought back from Sand Creek.

The Red Plume left the back of the room, sickened by what he had seen.

I must know. He thought as he rode east.

* * * * * * *

Two days later his worst fears were confirmed. The remains of Black Kettle's camp were strewn all over the prairie. He found the mutilated body of his brother-in-law, Otter. In the burned-out remains of a nearby tipi, he discovered the corpses of a woman and young girl. Although badly burned, he knew they were his sister and her daughter. He could not find the body of his nephew, Little Evan.

He rode north toward the Paha Sapa. His rage was insurmountable.

Bastards. You will pay. He thought.

* * * * * * *

He found his nephew fairly easily. The young man had survived the Sand Creek massacre and had been living north of the Paha Sapa in a tiyospaye of both Lakota and Cheyenne. After the two men had reconnected, Otter had quickly decided to join his uncle and fight with the Lakota and Cheyenne against the soldiers in the hated forts. It was an easy decision.

Over the next four years, The Red Plume and Otter fought alongside their friends against the soldiers who occupied the military establishments along the Bozeman Trail. By 1868, the U.S. Army had had enough and signed the Great Sioux Treaty. The forts were abandoned. William S. Harney had been one of the peace commissioners. The Red Plume did not know of the retired general's presence at the proceedings.

* * * * * * *

"I am going far to the south. I cannot stay here any longer," The Red Plume said to his nephew, Otter.

"I understand. I shall stay here with the People," Otter said.

The one had been born of two white parents while the other had one Cheyenne and one white parent. They each understood the decision of the other.

"Do you want your father's gun or knife?" Otter asked, as the older man began loading his horse.

"You should keep them," he answered. "Just always remember what you saw when my father died. Remember that he honored his vow to the People."

The last two remaining members of the Evan Ryan family stood looking at one another for a long moment. Then Michael mounted his horse and said,

"You are a man of honor, Otter. My father and your father are proud. They would tell you Erin Go Bragh and Hoka Hey, and I tell you ..." He paused, and then said, "Live well and continue to make them proud, my nephew. Ah-hou!" With those emphatic words he turned and rode away.

There have been good times and bad times with the People. He thought as he rode south. *Now I will make a new life for myself.*

He did not expect that this new life would bring him the greatest gift, the greatest surprise, and the greatest sadness of his entire life.

CHAPTER 40
...Mother, I need you...

Michael Ryan, The Red Plume, had ridden south in 1869. He had skirted Denver but stayed close to the mountains where he knew he could find fresh water. He had arrived in the New Mexico Territory in the spring and stopped at a fort. He had cut off his braids and now wore a white man's style coat and shirt. And while he still wore the leggings, breechclout, and moccasins of a Northern Plains Indian man, he blended in quite easily with the other whites in the area.

"Looking for work?" a man asked as Michael rode past one of the sutlers' tents.

"What kind of work are you offering?" he replied.

"We need skinners. There is a big group of buffalo hunters gettin' ready to leave in a week, and we need men to take the hides off."

Michael Ryan lasted in the job for only one day. The indiscriminate slaughter had been awful. Hundreds died the first day, and it sickened him.

They kill the buffalo, strip off the hides, cut out the tongues, and leave the rest to rot. They have no respect. Do they not understand that we are all related and must honor one another? He thought.

He slipped away that same night and rode farther south.

* * * * * *

He had been in Tucson for almost a year when he saw her. She was little, black-haired, and very pretty. He was thirty-five years old now and had never been married. He understood the customs of the People when it came to courting a young woman, but he knew nothing about how to go about it in this new situation.

Michael had been working as a clerk for one of the largest traders in the area. His ability to read and write English, skills learned from his mother and honed by the tutor in St. Paul when he was a boy, got him the job.

"You are a God-send," his boss often told him.

"May I ask you a question?" Michael inquired of the man one day.

"Certainly, ask away," the man replied.

"How do I approach a young woman in this part of the country?" he asked.

"Which one?" the man answered.

"The little, dark-haired one that comes in sometimes with the older woman," he said.

"Oh, the lovely Lorena." He was quick to identify the young woman Michael had described. "She is Mexican, and the other woman is her mother. You should speak with the mother and ask if you can walk with her daughter. Take the mother a gift when you do. But good luck, my friend. Many others have tried to talk with the girl, but the mother sends them away. These upper-class Mexicans are very protective of their daughters."

So were the People. He thought. *The Tsitsistas families expected their daughters to be chaste, and a courtship sometimes lasted for years. I think I know how to do this.*

He remembered his life with the People and how the young men would court the girls. They would bring gifts to the family of the girl in which they were interested. Then they would sometimes stand outside the tipi, with the girl standing with her feet in the doorway, and wrap a blanket around them both to give their hushed conversation a degree of privacy.

Michael selected a lovely piece of silk cloth from the trader's post. He took it to the villa where he knew the girl lived. He found the mother and daughter sitting on the veranda.

Removing his hat, he spoke to the older woman.

"Me llama Miguel." His Spanish was not good, but he continued as best he could.

"I would like to present you with this small gift and request your permission to speak with your daughter in your presence," he said haltingly, putting the Spanish words together somewhat incorrectly.

The woman smiled. *Finally, an American with manners.* She thought. She took the piece of cloth.

"Si," she answered quite simply and motioned toward her daughter.

Michael nodded, and then he turned to the girl.

"Me llama Miguel," he said again.

"I know. I heard you the first time," she said in almost perfect English. "My name is Lorena Corinna Obregon. What is your full name?"

My God! She is spirited just like my mother was. He thought.

"I am Michael Ryan," he answered.

"You are Irish?" she immediately asked.

"Aye. Yes. Both my parents were Irish. Father was a trader among the Cheyenne and Lakota Indians far to the north. I grew up with them," he said.'

"You don't act like a savage Indian," she said. Her eyes sparkled, and he saw that she was making a joke. Then he noticed that her eyes were not dark brown. Instead, they were a soft beige color with flecks of blue and grey. The color variance made them look almost green. He stared at them.

"Why do you look at my eyes so?" she asked, noticing his interest.

"I have never seen eyes that color," he said.

"I must have gotten them from my father. He was from Ireland. Our last name, Obregon, is Spanish for O'Brian," she said.

Michael smiled broadly and said,

"Really? You are half Irish? That is a surprise." Then he added, "I would like to call on you again. May I?"

"If my mother approves," Lorena answered.

And so began Michael's courtship of Lorena Obregon. She was twelve years younger than he, and she was an only child. They liked one another right from the start.

* * * * * * *

One evening as they sat together on the veranda, Lorena asked Michael to tell her about his parents and their life on the northern prairie. Her mother sat about fifteen feet away as she always did. While she did not watch them directly, she was always conscious of the distance between the couple. Since she could not speak English, their conversation was very private.

For over two hours, Michael related as much about his parents as he knew. He spoke with great pride about his father's experiences in Ireland as a boy. He talked about his own life with the People and about his sister's death six years earlier. When he got to the part about his father's death, he simply said,

"Father died defending our village when it was attacked by soldiers."

"Do you know where your mother is?" Lorena asked.

"No, I do not. The last time I saw her was when she was on a paddlewheel boat. The soldiers captured her, and I'm sure she was taken to St. Louis. I don't know what has happened to her," he said.

The following week they spoke again.

"Will you tell me about your father?" Michael asked. "You never speak about him. He was Irish, you said?"

"Yes. I never knew him. He was killed before I was born. Mother has never remarried," she said.

"How was he killed?" Michael asked.

Lorena looked away.

"I don't think I should tell you. You may think badly of him and me," she said quite softly.

"I would like you to tell me about him. Please," he answered. He wanted to know as much about this young woman as he could.

There is nothing you can say that will turn me away from you. He thought. He knew he was losing his heart to this Mexican-Irish woman.

"All right. I will tell you," she said. Then she began.

"My mother has always told me that my father came from Ireland to America. He joined the American Army and was with those forces when they attacked Mexico. Mother said he told her that he did not like the idea of fighting against Catholics. He said that his company was made up of mainly Irish soldiers, and the American officers did not let them have mass or a priest or anything. So one night a whole group of them left the American side and came over to fight for the Mexicans," she said quietly. She seemed embarrassed about the last part.

"He eventually met my mother, and they were married by a priest. Then he returned to the fighting. Those Irish soldiers were very brave and always inspired the Mexican troops. But he was captured by the Americans," she continued.

"What happened to him? You said he was killed," Michael asked.

"The Americans treated all the Irish they captured as deserters. He was hanged along with about forty-five others. I can't remember the name of the American officer who was in charge of his execution," she said.

Lorena turned to her mother and spoke to her in Spanish. The older woman looked up and said something back to her daughter. Michael did not understand any of her words except the last one. The woman spit after she said it, as though to clear her mouth of the foulness of the name.

He looked at Lorena, his eyes wide with disbelief.

"Mother says that the American officer was named Harney and that he was very cruel to those Irish soldiers," she continued.

Michael's eyes narrowed. He could not believe what he had just heard. He stood and walked over to Lorena's mother.

"Please tell your mother the words I am going to say," he said, not looking at Lorena. His voice was not harsh, but his words were clearly more than a request.

She got up and moved next to her mother, waiting for him to continue.

"Lorena says that her father was killed by an American officer named Harney," he began. Lorena said the words in Spanish and then looked back at him. He was looking directly at her mother.

The woman nodded, not breaking eye contact with him.

"Si. Est verdad," she said.

"Fifteen years ago, a General Harney ordered his troops to attack an Indian village where my mother and father and I were living. Many women and little children were killed in this attack," he continued.

Lorena translated the words. As she did so, her mother's eyes grew wider as she continued looking directly at Michael.

"My father was one of the men killed that day trying to defend the village. I found his body a few days later," he said.

Lorena gave this information to her mother. The woman's eyes filled with tears, and she crossed herself.

Lorena did the same and then looked at Michael. He continued.

"That general captured my mother and sent her away in chains. I still do not know what happened to her," he said.

"It seems that we are related already, Miguel," Lorena said. Then she translated his words for her mother.

* * * * * * *

One week later they were married. It was the first time Michael had ever been inside a Catholic church. It was almost one hundred years old and was named St. Xavier del Bac.

I have heard that name before. Thought Michael. But he could not remember where.

* * * * * * *

It was a happy marriage. Nothing ever seemed to mar their relationship. Michael continued to work for the trader, and Lorena assisted. She was bilingual, and the owner eagerly accepted her as part of the small staff. Her mother returned to Mexico to live with her wealthy sister, and the couple built their own adobe house near the trading post. The area was filling with people. It was a profitable time for Tucson.

At Lorena's insistence, they attended mass every week. The church of St. Xavier del Bac was beautifully adorned with painted art and statuary. The priests were always kind, and many local Indians and Mexicans were part of the congregation. But Michael found the rituals very confusing.

The beliefs of the People were much easier to understand. He thought. Still, he went with his wife because he knew it was important to her.

But for ten years there were no children, and Lorena began to attend mass a second time each week, hoping to be granted motherhood. Her devotion was finally rewarded, or so it seemed.

"You are going to be a father, Miguel," she announced one evening. He could not have been happier.

* * * * * * *

By the spring of 1881, Lorena knew it was time for the arrival of their child.

"You know many people here. Perhaps you can find a midwife to help me with this?" she asked. "It is getting difficult for me to walk."

Michael searched the Tucson area, and two local women agreed to attend Lorena. Her time was very near.

* * * * * * *

It was dark. She had been in labor since the early morning, and the baby had not been born.

"I don't like the looks of this," said one of the midwives to Michael. She had assisted many women over the years in this work of childbirth and knew a problem situation when she saw it.

Lorena was wearing out physically. Although she was in a great deal of pain, she had remained almost completely silent each time the contractions peaked.

Then there was a pause in the labor. For almost an hour it appeared that there would be no birth at all.

Suddenly, as though her body needed to expel the little one as quickly as possible, Lorena was thrown into a violent series of contractions that came in quick succession.

It was clear that she was now suffering the worst pain of all. The midwives were powerless to help, and they now feared for the young woman's life.

Michael ran out of their little house and stood facing the east, the direction he saw his mother traveling on that day twenty-four years earlier.

"Mother, I need you. You would know what to do. Help me," he cried out to the clear night sky. But his plaintive cry went unanswered.

The little boy was stillborn, and within the hour Lorena Corinna Obregon Ryan was hemorrhaging.

"Oh, Miguel," she said, a solitary tear rolling down her cheek. "I'm so sorry."

They were her last words.

When she was still, Michael stumbled out of the little house and dropped onto his knees. He wept uncontrollably. It was almost as if he was finally letting out all of the sorrow that had been pent up inside of him for so many years. He wept for his father and mother, and for his sister and her husband and their daughter, and he wept for Lorena and their baby. He said her name over and over.

"Mother, I need you," he cried out again. "What am I to do?"

* * * * * * *

Later, he sent one of the midwives to the mission church. When she returned with a priest, they found him sitting with his wife in his arms and the baby in hers. The little boy was christened Michael Evan Ryan.

The next morning he placed the infant in the arms of his beloved Lorena. They were buried together in the little church cemetery.

The Red Plume had never known such sorrow and such intense anguish.

CHAPTER 41
...of Ireland and America...

Catherine O'Leary Ryan was sixty-seven years old. She had been born in Ireland and had lived the life of a poor, peasant, farm girl. She had survived two years of the Great Potato Famine and then the ocean crossing to America on a coffin ship. Somehow, and she could hardly remember all of the details any more, she and Timothy and their two sons had managed to get to Fort Snelling in the Minnesota Territory where he remembered his sister, Ana, and her husband had been living.

They were still there in 1848 when the Ryans arrived quite unexpectedly. Patrick Hughes had given them jobs, and over the last forty years they had done well. Their two sons now had grown families of their own.

I am truly one of the fortunate ones. She thought as she arranged the dishes on the table. The hotel banquet room was festooned with the trappings of the Christmas season, and the dinner which was being prepared for all of the Ryan and Hughes families promised to be a grand one. The past year, 1890, had been momentous for them all, and the family looked forward to spending time together during the holidays as they always did.

Catherine smiled. *It has been a good year.* She started to laugh a little as she remembered the excitement caused by the telegram from Boston that came to the offices of Patrick Hughes earlier in the summer. It was from her grandson and Ana's grandson.

"Get the church ready. We are coming home." That was all it said. The two boys were such jesters that nobody knew what to expect next from them. This time, as it turned out, they were not joking, something that even they had never suspected when they sent the telegram.

* * * * * * *

Once their business meetings in New York City were successfully accomplished, the two young bachelors made a short side trip to Boston. They wanted to see this birthplace of the American Revolution.

"Lots of Irish girls there, too" James had said, partially in jest to his cousin.

They met them quite by chance. The girls, Bridget O'Maher and Maureen Flynn, were friends and had only recently arrived in the United States where they hoped to get jobs as domestics. They had sailed together from Dublin but were from County Tipperary and County Cork respectively. They were attractive young women, and their meeting with the two men from St. Paul was totally unexpected. What would soon become a pair of courtships began as an honest offer of reputable employment.

"There are too many here in Boston trying to do what you are wanting to do," John said as the two couples sat having supper one evening. They were eating at one of the oldest restaurants in the city, one known for its oysters. The girls were very impressed, not only with the fine eating establishment, but by the courteous way these two Irish-American men treated them.

"You don't want to work as a seamstress. The conditions in those factories are unsafe. If you come to St. Paul, you can both work at one of the hotels my grandfather owns. They are always hiring, and the fact that you are Irish will help. My grandfather hates the way it used to be when the job notices said "No Irish Need Apply." You'll both have jobs there at once. I guarantee it. James and I have railroad passes, and we will buy your tickets."

It was not a difficult decision for the two girls.

*   *   *   *   *   *   *

John Michael Hughes was the son of Patrick Evan and Marie Toussaint Hughes. From the time he was a young boy, he had been taught by his father to have a profound respect for women, an attitude which was somewhat out of the mainstream for men of the period. While many of his contemporaries often visited brothels and taverns in St. Paul, he had remained quite removed from those scenes.

His father had often remarked how Grandpa Hughes once had to take him aside to caution him about the proper way to behave in the presence of females.

"Many years ago, as a young boy, I made the mistake of looking disrespectfully at my cousin, Sarah Ana. We were the same age, and she was very pretty. The fact that she was my cousin did not make a difference to me," he had told his sons. "See that you are always correct in your actions with the ladies. Always make me proud of you."

My father set me straight about that. He remembered. The lesson had stuck. Anyway, as an educated and wealthy bachelor, John was wary of the flirtatious looks and comments from the unmarried women in St. Paul.

I'm not going to marry just anyone. He often thought.

The same lesson had come to James Daniel Ryan from his grandmother, Catherine. She often told him about the terrible way that the British occupiers of Ireland treated the Irish girls. It had even cost the life of her older sister.

"No grandson of mine will be like them. I'll not have it," she always said.

He loved his grandmother and knew he must never disappoint her. He, too, was educated and well-employed by the Hughes business dynasty.

But it was the story of their great uncle, Evan Ryan, that formed the basis of their commitment to their family. Both young men clearly understood the expectations of their parents and grandparents.

I must never dishonor the family. I must always make them proud. My successes in life are expected. There are many who are watching me. They each thought. It was part of a legacy they both shared, and it made the cousins good friends to one another.

In St. Paul, the two young men began courting the young women from Ireland. The girls were hard-working, honest, kind, fun to be with, and their values seemed to match theirs. And, they were attractive. But the cousins needed something more. It would come in an unexpected way.

* * * * * * *

The first time Catherine Ryan met Bridget O'Maher and Maureen Flynn was in the laundry room of the hotel. The eighteen year old girls had been in St. Paul for about two months, and true to John's promise, they were immediately employed. It was hard work, but they were grateful for the opportunity to be in America. It was an old story, one that was shared by almost every immigrant who had ever reached the North American shores.

Catherine made the trip downtown specifically to meet the two Irish girls who were constantly spoken of by her grandson.

"I'm pleased to meet ya," she said when they introduced themselves. She still spoke with a heavy Irish accent, and the two younger women smiled warmly the moment they heard her speak.

Actually, the three of them were really quite similar. They were each intelligent but uneducated; they had each lived a hard, peasant life in Ireland but had become stronger from the experience; they each understood the meaning and value of hard work, and they were not afraid to take on any chore; and, they each had an abiding sense of family responsibility which they celebrated in many different ways.

"We never thought we would make this much money," said Maureen as the three sat together amid the buckets and wash tubs in the laundry room of the largest Hughes' hotel.

"What are ya doin' with it all?" asked Catherine.

"We both are sendin' back what we can. It helps them out greatly back in Ireland, ya know," answered Bridget. "Ya got to share what ya got or it's no good, aye? A new dress don't mean nothin' if your people are hungry."

Maureen nodded in agreement with her friend's comment. Catherine was impressed. The words triggered a memory of the words of Elizabeth Anne Ryan, her husband's brother's widow. She remembered meeting the little woman some thirty-four years earlier.

She always spoke of how the Indians shared everything they had. She called them the People, too. And Ana's daughter, Mary Anne, has set up this bakery to help feed the poor here in the city. These girls have the right idea. She thought.

"Where in the old country are ya from?" she asked.

"I'm from County Tipperary, and Maureen is from County Cork," Bridget answered.

"We are from there, too. Do you know any Ryans or Hughes or O'Learys or O'Tooles from that area?" Catherine inquired.

"Oh, I've met some O'Tooles. That's an old family name. And seems to me that I know of Ryan. Let me think about it," she answered.

"Isn't Ryan the name in that story they always tell? Ya know, the one about the boy who fought the soldiers with a shepherd's crook?" said Maureen.

Catherine's hand went to her mouth, and she looked rapidly back and forth at the two girls.

"Aye! That was the name. I knew I heard it before," said Bridget.

"Tell me that story, please will ya. I need to hear it," said Catherine. She wondered if she was going to hear what she hoped it would be.

"Aye! Oh, let's see now. The old people like to tell about a boy somewhere in Tipperary who fought three British soldiers. He was trying to defend a young neighbor girl. He only had a crook'd sheep staff against their swords. But he and the girl were both kilt," she said. "The story is pretty well-known and gets told all the time in the pubs. The men always drink to the boy and say 'Erin Go Bragh' to salute him. His last name was Ryan as I recall. I don't remember his first name though."

Catherine looked at the girls and began to speak very softly. Her voice was steady and her tone was almost reverent.

"His first name was Evan," she said, "and he was not killed that night. Let me tell ya what really happened. I am that girl's sister. I was born on the night she died."

Bridget and Maureen were taken aback at the older woman's response, and for the next hour they listened with rapt attention as Catherine told the story. Then she spoke of Ireland and America. The two younger women were respectfully silent. They had known many older people who had survived the Great Famine and understood how to act in their presence.

But while they had heard the story of the Ryan boy often enough back in Ireland, they had never met anyone who could corroborate it. Now they were here in America, and speaking with someone who was intimately connected to the story and to their homeland.

When Catherine had finished, she asked, "Would ya like to meet the sister of Evan Ryan?"

* * * * * * *

The next day she returned with Ana.

"I am Ana Ryan Hughes," the woman said. "I understand that ya've heard of my brother, Evan!"

* * * * * * *

Mary Anne Hughes Connolly was a prolific reader, especially now that she had the time. Her children were long gone from the house, and she enjoyed her grandchildren immensely. A grandmother could not ask for a better family.

She found that she could not put the book down. It was entitled <u>Ramona</u> and had been written by Helen Hunt Jackson. Although a fiction story, it was based on a true event in California, and she believed what she had just read. Then she bought Jackson's other book, <u>A Century of Dishonor,</u> and devoured it. She was outraged by the scathing expose.

They are killing the Indian people with the same indifference that my Irish ancestors experienced at the hands of the English. She thought.

She was the activist in the family. She was the one who had persuaded her father to supply the local poor with bread.

"Father. Every day you sweep up from the floor and then throw away more flour than it would take to provide bread for those here who cannot afford it," she had said to him.

The bakery was started one week later, and the loaves were never denied to any family that did not have the modest amount of money which was posted.

St. Bridget is one of the patron saints of Ireland. She fed the poor. Thought Mary Anne. *I should do no less.*

* * * * * * *

Their courtship of the two young Irish girls was destined to happen.

"What do you think of her, Grandmother?" asked James.

"I think what ya think of her is what is important," Catherine Ryan answered.

"But, do you like her?" he asked. He was serious about his feelings for Maureen and needed to have his grandmother's approval.

"Ya are young, James. And the decisions ya make when ya are young will be with ya all your life," she answered. Then she added, "Aye! I do like her."

The same conversation had already taken place between John and his grandmother, Ana Hughes.

Two weeks later John proposed to Bridget in the parlor of the Hughes house. His request was answered simply with the quiet words, "Aye. I would be honored to become your wife."

James proposed to Maureen the next day. His question was answered by a teary nod and then a smile.

* * * * * * *

In November, the double wedding of John Michael Hughes, a grandson of Ana and Patrick Hughes, to Bridget O'Maher, and of James Daniel Ryan, the grandson of Timothy and Catherine Ryan, to Maureen Flynn, occurred five months after their return from Boston. It was beautiful.

Between the two grandmothers, Ana and Catherine, and the two mothers of the grooms, Marie and Harriet, the brides were made to understand the importance of that special part of the ceremony which had begun many years earlier at the wedding of Marie and Patrick Evan.

The list of spoken names was growing longer, and since they could not read, the girls worked hard memorizing it.

* * * * * * *

The great family holiday gathering later that year was to take place three days after Christmas. Catherine had just finished adjusting the table settings when her husband, Timothy, entered the room. Ana and Patrick followed.

"It looks lovely," said Ana. "The children will be arriving any time now. I am so looking forward to this day. It is good that things are so peaceful this time of year. The little ones are always so excited."

Within the half-hour, the families had assembled.

* * * * * * *

The dinner was wonderful, and everyone waited for the annual address of the eldest member of the family. Patrick Hughes was eighty-three and still in reasonably good health. He went daily to his office and continued to oversee all of his business ventures.

Since his arrival at Fort Snelling, he had prospered. He had bought land and then sold it for a profit. He had been able to successfully stay out of the political intrigues that were common in the area, as traders dishonestly cheated the Dakota and Ojibwe out of their lands, often with the full concurrence of the government agents. It had not been easy, and he occasionally made mistakes without realizing it.

"I shall not be like the English landlords," he had often told Ana. "Evan is right. We must be honorable."

Patrick had also participated in a buffalo hide trade with his brother-in-law, Evan Ryan, and it had done exceedingly well. In fact, Evan's share of the profit, which would have passed to Elizabeth Anne, had been reinvested right after her untimely death. That modest amount had grown, and Patrick had used it to purchase one of the first flour mills that was built at St. Anthony's Falls.

Then, seeing another profitable venture, he had become a silent investor in James J. Hill's purchase of a railroad. He enthusiastically supported Hill's plans for a transcontinental northern route, and he recruited laborers for the track building and settlers to farm the lands opened up by the new line. Many of the workers and settlers were, of course, Irish.

The railroad is better than the old ox-carts we used to use. He often thought.

He rose, and the room quieted.

"I wish to welcome ya to this annual family gathering. I shall be brief in what I want to say to ya," he began.

"We have all come to this place and to each other from different and yet similar experiences. For most of us, it has not been easy, and we have suffered greatly. But we persevered."

Timothy Ryan took Catherine's hand. She nodded.

"We have done what we thought was right, and sometimes we had to be reminded of what that was." He looked directly at his daughter, Mary Anne, as he said the words. She smiled at her father in acknowledgment. Then she looked down, suddenly humbled.

"We have tried to help those who needed help, just as we were helped by others. And we have not forgotten them. Tonight, I want to remind ya of two people who have not been with us for a very long time. I want ya to remember them." He paused.

"Evan Ryan was my brother-in-law. He heeded the words of his father as a boy in Ireland, and he lived up to his responsibilities there and here in America. I charge all of ya men, ya Ryans and Hughes and Connollys with this: Remember Evan Ryan's legacy. And this is the symbol of that legacy."

He held up the crook'd staff that Timothy and Catherine had brought from Ireland in 1848. The room was silent. Every man crossed himself in tribute. A few of the women did as well.

The two new brides, who had recently come from Ireland, stared at the old shepherd's crook being held aloft. They had heard about this crook'd staff in Ireland. Now it was before them, and it was real.

"The other person I want us all to remember tonight is his wife, Elizabeth Anne Delaney Ryan. Ana and I still miss her after all these years."

He paused again, looking down at his wife who sat next to him. Her eyes were filled with tears, and she nodded almost imperceptibly.

"When Elizabeth Anne came to our house many years ago, she taught us a little about the ways of the People. She called them the People because they had become her People, as much as we were all her people. She said that the women of the People were the centers of their families, much more so than the men. I believed her then, and I believe that now."

He paused again.

"And so I charge all of ya Ryan and Hughes and Connolly women, whether ya be of those families by blood or by marriage, with her legacy. Teach your little ones to listen and to be respectful of the words of the elders. And remind them that the decisions they make when they are young will be with them all of their lives. Tell them that the harder it will be for them to choose what to do, the greater will be the impact on them."

He held up the little pair of beaded moccasins which he had borrowed from Catherine for this occasion. She had been the recipient of them thirty-four years earlier.

"These little shoes, which Elizabeth Anne made for her grandson, are the symbol of your role as the center of your family," he said.

Every woman in the room nodded in understanding and then made the sign of the Cross over her heart.

The volume of the old patriarch's voice rose as he finished his speech.

"Tell the stories of our families. Say the names of those who have gone on before. And be proud that ya are Irish. Say 'Erin Go Bragh' with pride. But when ya say it, understand all that it means. And be proud that ya are also Americans and that this is now your country. Live well here in America and work to make it better. Make us old ones proud."

He sat down. The room was quiet for a few more moments as everyone pondered his words. Then the applause began as the family members rose to their feet.

"Ya spoke wonderfully, Patrick," Ana said over the clapping. She reached for his hand. "I'm so proud to be your wife."

I have loved ya for sixty-three years. She thought. *From that day on the dock in Cork, all across the Atlantic, in New York, on the paddlewheel when we were finally married, and all these years here in St. Paul. Our family is strong. We have made our parents proud. Our little ones are safe.*

Then she was struck with the thought. *But where are all the little ones? Where are Evan and Elizabeth Anne's children ... and grandchildren? Are there even grandchildren? All these years! We have heard nothing.*

She had no way of knowing that the only remaining grandson of her brother and his wife was, at that very moment, encamped with his young family on the banks of a little creek in South Dakota.

CHAPTER 42
...hoka hey...

They had been traveling for almost a week. It was the time of year when the whites celebrated the miraculous birth of their main god. Their places of worship were often festooned with the words "Peace on Earth, Good Will to All Men."

It was terribly cold, and the snow on the prairie was drifted in places, making it difficult for the people to walk. Even in 1890, there were many still alive who remembered the old way of march when the People moved their camps; women, children, and older people in the middle; warrior society men on the sides; Dog Soldiers at the rear; and the leaders in front with scouts far out in front of them. Now they tried to keep that tradition as they moved along. They had learned it from watching the movements of their brothers, the buffalo, so it could not be wrong.

They had been camping that winter along the Cheyenne River. But the panic that came from the murder of one of their greatest leaders, Tatanka Iyotanka, the man the whites called Sitting Bull, spread alarm throughout all of Lakota country. The leader of this band of Minneconjou Lakota, Big Foot, said they could find their relatives farther south at the Red Cloud Agency near the Pine Ridge.

"We have been invited to come there," he told the People.

And so the little band moved slowly along, following the river and stream beds as often as they could, staying out of the biting wind. Most were women and children, and many were ill from the coughing sickness, including Big Foot.

Otter was one of the men who was helping to move the people along. His father had been Cheyenne, close allies of the Lakota, and after many years of bachelorhood, he had chosen a Lakota girl from this Minneconjou band for his wife. Intermarriage was not uncommon.

His wife rode her own horse with two of their children trying to snuggle against her for warmth. He carried most of their belongings on his horse and on the two pack horses that were behind him. Those horses also dragged the family tipi poles.

They had passed through the strange lands east of the Paha Sapa and were only a day away from the Red Cloud Agency at Pine Ridge. Red Cloud had promised them protection, food, shelter and horses.

In the mid-afternoon, soldiers appeared in front of them. Big Foot immediately raised a white cloth high on a long pole. Perhaps everything will be fine after all.

The soldiers escorted them into the flat bottom-land of a little, dried creek the Lakota People knew as Cankpe Opi Wakpala. They were told that they would stay there for the night. Those with tipis and tents quickly pitched them and they settled in for the bitterly cold night that would soon be upon them.

"I do not like this," Otter said to his wife that evening. "I do not trust these soldiers. I think their hearts are bad. Tomorrow, be ready to run if there is shooting." He had been taught how to read many years earlier by his grandmother, and he had seen the number "7" on the troopers' little flag. He also spoke English, in addition to Lakota and the language of his father's people, the Tsitsistas.

Feather Woman looked at her husband and nodded. *If there is trouble, he can protect me, I know.* She thought.

* * * * * * *

All throughout the night, the soldiers continued to move about the Lakota camp, interrogating the men through interpreters. Many of the soldiers were drinking, and most of the People did not get much sleep, if any at all. The morning of December 29, 1890, dawned clear and cold.

The band of about three hundred and fifty Minneconjou began to stir from their hastily erected lodgings.

Loud shouting brought Otter to his feet. Emerging from the tipi, he saw that the troopers had set up lines on the high ground on two sides of the Indian encampment. Hotchkiss guns were pointed down at the village.

Dismounted cavalrymen were moving through the camp and were disarming the men. Some were even going into the tipis and tents searching for more firearms. Suddenly, as he stood in front of his lodge, Otter had his trade gun wrenched from his hands by a passing soldier. It was a very old muzzle-loading rifle that he had kept ever since the day his grandfather, Evan Ryan, had been killed by American soldiers down at Ash Hollow. That had been thirty-five years before, and he had never forgotten the day.

He had been only a boy of eight. He had seen his grandfather stake himself out in the tradition of the Dog Soldier society to which he had belonged. And he had seen his grandfather die at this position, defending the helpless.

Then he had managed to grab the rifle and a knife from his grandfather's body and had run away with some other boys and younger girls. They had eluded the soldiers and had made their way north. They entered the southern end of the hills called the Paha Sapa and joined up with some Cheyenne hunters. Eventually, he found the camp of his mother and father.

Otter also remembered that it had been nine years after that when his entire family had been killed at Sand Creek. Once again, he had been one of the few to survive.

Will they ever stop killing the People? He thought. *Grandfather was right. They are just like the soldiers were in his home country.*

* * * * * * *

The argument from just two tents away from him was getting louder.

"Black Coyote is deaf. He can't understand you," he yelled in English at the soldier who was engaging in a tug of war with his Lakota friend. The man did not want to give up his gun and kept saying the Lakota word for "hunt." Suddenly, the gun went off, firing harmlessly up into the air. It was almost as if it were a signal. The troopers on the surrounding ridges opened fire on the camp.

"Run," he called into the tipi to his wife. Then he turned toward the guns facing him about one hundred yards away. He reached under his coat and brought out the knife he had carried for over thirty-five years. It was a strange, heavy knife with a rounded handle. It was hand-forged, and he knew his grandfather had made it many, many years before.

A series of shots from one of the Hotchkiss guns raked the ground in front of him, partially shredding the side of his tipi. A spent carbine bullet bounced off the frozen ground and struck him in the left thigh.

"Run," he called out to his wife again.

"I cannot. I am hit," she weakly replied. He turned and dove inside the tipi, his eyes adjusting to the darkness in time to see his young Minneconjou wife drop to her knees, blood soaking the front of her dress and coat. He gently laid her down flat, and she looked up at him.

"The little ones have gone," she said in a voice so soft that he almost did not hear her. He glanced around the tipi interior and saw that it was empty. The two children had already slipped out through a knife slit made in the rear of the lodge.

"Go now. Run, my husband," she gasped, the blood starting to gurgle in her throat.

"No! I will not leave you, Feather Woman" he said. *If I must die, I will die with honor.* He thought.

Grabbing a small hand axe that lay next to the little pile of firewood, he moved back out of the tipi. Shells were now exploding all around him as the gunners on the two ridges walked their fire pattern along the Indian encampment.

So, this is the place! This is where I will die! He thought. *I will die defending my home and family. I will make them proud, and my name will be remembered by all the People.* He was repeating to himself the phrases he had heard his grandfather, Evan, and his father's people, the Tsitsistas, say many times.

Otter had neither the crook'd staff of the Dog Soldiers nor the sash that tethered those elite fighting men to their position. But he had a small hand axe and his grandfather's old knife. He reached down and shoved the point of the knife through the triangular flap of his woolen legging. It refused to go into the solidly frozen earth. He pounded it with the little axe. It stuck.

Pinned to the spot, just as he had seen his grandfather pegged to his Dog sash many years before in front of the village at Ash Hollow, Otter stood in front of his tipi and faced the soldiers. They were now moving into the camp in large numbers.

The bullet wound in his leg was not bleeding much, but he was in considerable pain. Dismounted cavalrymen were coming closer to his tipi, and he waited until one came within range.

"Hoka hey," he yelled at the soldier in Lakota as he threw the hand axe at the bluecoat.

The little axe missed its target. The bluecoat turned and took aim. He did not hesitate and fired only once.

Otter, the son of a Cheyenne warrior and of Blue Flower, the daughter of Elizabeth Anne and Evan Ryan, the man who had once been called Little Evan after his grandfather, died in front of his tipi. Not one of his Minneconjou Lakota family survived the day.

* * * * * * *

Three days later, a burial party arrived at the site of the Big Foot camp. Bodies lay scattered up and down the creek bed.

"What do they call this creek?" asked one of the civilians.

"Wounded Knee, I think," said a soldier. He had not been present two days earlier when the killings had taken place.

"My god! This is terrible," he added. His name was Robert O'Rourke, and he was from Cincinnati, Ohio, where his family had lived for one hundred years.

Some of the men moved through the destroyed camp collecting the frozen bodies and piling them in a row on one of the ridges. Another group began hacking into the frozen ground, preparing a mass grave.

None of the Indian tents or tipis were standing. Private O'Rourke got off his horse and walked over to one flattened tipi.

"There is a body under this canvas," he hollered. He dragged out an Indian woman and laid her body in front of the downed lodge next to that of an Indian man. Then he noticed something very strange.

"Hey Mac! Look at this!" he yelled to his friend, who immediately rode over and dismounted. He pointed to the male corpse on the ground.

"He's got a damned knife stuck through his pants leg into the ground. What in the hell is that for?" the civilian said.

"I don't know. But, I'm going to keep that knife," O'Rourke said, and then pulled the heavy weapon out of the ground. "Strange looking thing," he said.

* * * * * * *

It was late January of 1891. Mary Anne Connolly sat at her kitchen table with her husband. The festive holidays were now behind her, and she could relax. It had been a wonderful Christmas. She had so many blessings to count. Her two surviving children, a son and a daughter, were both properly married, and the extended Hughes and Ryan families had enjoyed a wonderful four days of celebrating there in late December.

Her mother and father, Ana and Patrick Hughes, now lived with her and Daniel, and they were resting in the parlor. They were eighty and eighty-three, but their minds were still very alert.

"Did you read this article about that Seventh Cavalry battle with the Sioux and the editorial reprinted from the <u>Aberdeen Saturday Pioneer</u>?" asked Daniel.

"No," Mary Anne answered. "Should I?"

"You're not going to like it," he responded, handing her the paper.

She took the paper from her husband and began reading. The article reported on the "terrific battle between the Sioux Indians and Custer's Boys" at a place called Wounded Knee, a place near the Black Hills in South Dakota. It glowingly recounted the brave actions of the troopers and announced that almost thirty Medals of Honor would be given. It was followed by a guest editorial which had already been printed in the Aberdeen newspaper.

She finished the first article and began reading the reprinted editorial.

"The proud spirit of the original owners of these vast prairies inherited through centuries of fierce and bloody wars for their possession, lingered last in the bosom of Sitting Bull. With his fall the nobility of the Redskin is extinguished, and what few are left are a pack of whining curs who lick the hand that smites them. The Whites, by law of conquest, by justice of civilization, are masters of the American continent,

and the best safety of the frontier settlements will be secured by the total annihilation of the few remaining Indians."

"What?" she said aloud, her voice revealing a clear disbelief at what she had just read. She continued reading, her anger rising with each callous word.

"Why not annihilation? Their glory has fled, their spirit broken, their manhood effaced; better that they die than live the miserable wretches that they are."

Her breath caught, and her eyes skipped through the rest of the commentary.

"We cannot honestly regret their extermination..."

It was enough. She could read no more.

"Bastard," she said to Daniel. "The bastard! This is just wrong. Who wrote this?" She scanned the paper and answered her own question.

"L. Frank Baum," she said. "Well, you are a bastard, Mr. Baum. You are as bad as the English who let my grandparents starve while they shipped grain out of Ireland."

She stopped talking and looked up at her husband. He was accustomed to her outbursts.

"I wonder if any of my cousins' children or grandchildren were with those Sioux?" she said. Her hand went to her mouth, and she became absorbed with her concern for this distinct, albeit distant, possibility.

CHAPTER 43
...she recognized his gait...

After Lorena's death in 1881, Michael Ryan went every week to the grave, placing a bouquet of whatever flowers he could find at the head of the small rectangle of stones that marked the final resting place of his little family. He had followed this practice for ten years.

You are all that I have ever had. He thought. *It is so hard to live.*

It happened one spring afternoon in 1891 as he was leaving the cemetery. A hawk appeared in the sky and continued to circle him as he walked back to his little house. The old beliefs of the People, with whom he had grown up and lived for over half of his life, suddenly flooded into his consciousness.

The old men of the People always said to always be aware of the four-leggeds and the wings of the air, that they often bring us messages. What are you trying to tell me? He thought, watching the bird. It seemed that the bird spoke to him.

Your people here are gone from you. But you have others who are your people. Go to them. Stay here no longer. The bird flew away.

The hawk is right. There are others. He thought.

As he walked on, he took stock of his situation. He was fifty-six years old. He spoke two of the languages of the People, the People with whom he had fought alongside in the defense of their lands and way of life. They were his extended family. *Yes! They are my People.*

And many years before, when he had come south, he had left the one remaining blood relative among the People that he knew he had. It was the son of his sister.

I need to find Otter if he is still alive. And the People.
He thought.

Then he stopped walking, frozen by the memory of
other people he had not thought about for many years. *I
have another whole group of relatives among the whites.
Ah-hou! Yes! They are my family, too. I must find them.* He
thought.

* * * * * * *

It was the spring of 1891 when The Red Plume rode
north and east. His employer was sad to lose him and
supplied him with plenty of provisions and some cash.

"Good luck, my friend," he had said to Michael as
the two men shook hands. "You deserve a better future."

Michael rode north and stopped at the soon-to-
be-abandoned military establishment at Santa Fe in the
New Mexico Territory. At Fort Marcy he was able to get
the information he needed. He learned that some of the
Cheyenne were confined to a reservation near the Canadian
River in Indian Territory. He would go there to Fort Reno
and to the other place called Cantonement.

*Perhaps the People will know of Otter. Maybe he is
there.* He thought.

* * * * * * *

Within a month, he was once again with the People.
He greeted them in the language he had not spoken for
almost two dozen years. Some of the older people recognized
him even though they were from the southern bands. But
Otter was not among them.

When he asked about the northern People, he was
told the story of how Dull Knife and Little Wolf, both of
whom he had known, had led the Northerners back to their
homeland in the north. He was told about their valiant
battles with the soldiers that had taken place thirteen years
earlier as the People raced for their home country.

He learned that some of Dull Knife's people had been captured and taken to Fort Robinson at the southern end of the Paha Sapa, and that they had to break out of their prison quarters in the terrible cold of January, 1879. He heard the stories of the Dog Soldiers that led the breakout and nodded his head in recognition and appreciation of their sacrifice. But he was saddened by the words and by the downcast eyes he observed and remained silent.

Nothing has changed. The soldiers are still killing the People. He thought. He did not know how true his thoughts were. None of the Cheyenne had any information about Otter. In fact, word of the Wounded Knee killings had not yet reached the south.

The reservation was poor, and The Red Plume knew he should not stay. There was too little food even for them. Yet they had made him welcome.

Even in the midst of this hunger, they still share what they have. He thought. He knew he must leave.

I can look for Otter later. He thought. *What will I find if I go to my parents' people?*

And so Wiyaka-ska, The Red Plume, left his extended Tsitsistas family and again rode north and east. He had been to the big settlement once when he was the boy they called Michael Ryan. He could find the place again, and when he did, perhaps he would find his other family.

* * * * * * *

It was June of 1891. Warm weather had finally arrived and Ana Ryan Hughes sat on the front porch of her daughter's house in St. Paul. She was comfortable there in the rocker. Her thoughts swirled in her memory. It had been sixty-three years since she had arrived at Fort Snelling with her husband, Patrick. And it had been thirty-four years since her brother's wife and her dear friend, Elizabeth Anne Delaney Ryan, had died there in her home.

Elizabeth Anne never found out what happened to Sarah Ana or to Michael. And we know nothing either. She thought. *Perhaps it is just as well. Sarah Ana and Michael have just vanished.*

Ana's own life had not been free of sadness. Her son, Matthew, had died during the Civil War, and her daughter, Mary Anne, had lost two infant children and one grandchild. Now her own husband, Patrick, was ailing.

Sometimes life is hard. She thought.

But there had been happiness and much success, too. Her eldest, Patrick Evan, had married a good Catholic girl, and Mary Anne had married well also. Daniel Connolly was a kind, supportive man. As the family attorney, he still represented the large business interests and landholdings of the extended Hughes and Ryan families.

Her younger brother, Timothy, still lived in the area with his wife, Catherine. And their sons and grandsons were also part of the community. They were all doing well.

Aye. We have made the Ryan name a proud one.

Then she smiled.

And think of it! Two of our grandsons have married young women recently come from Ireland. Think of it! Real Irish girls. Aye! 'Tis good.

Father always said that Evan should make everyone proud. I know he expected the same from me. I think we have. Aye, we have made them proud. She smiled as she looked across at the large oaks that lined the street.

Then she saw the man. It was almost as it had been that day at Fort Snelling so many years before. She recognized his gait.

"Mary Anne," she called out to her daughter. "Come out here quickly."

Her daughter rapidly stepped onto the porch.

"Are you all right, Mother?" she asked, moving hurriedly to her mother's chair.

"Aye, girl, I'm just fine," she said, her voice cracking just a little.

"Then why did you call me?" asked Mary Anne.

"Oh, he's come at last," the old woman said almost in a whisper, pointing at the man who was walking along the edge of the street about half-way down the block from their house.

"Who is he?" her daughter asked, straining her eyes in an attempt to get a better look.

"He's come to us at last," she said again. "That man, my girl, is Michael Ryan, the son of my brother, Evan, and of Elizabeth Anne. It's your cousin. I'm sure of it. I'd know that walk anywhere. He walks just like his father did. Call out to him with the words, 'Erin Go Bragh' and see what his response will be," she said, her eyes starting to fill with tears. She so much wanted it to be true.

Mary Anne walked to the edge of the porch. Raising her hand in a fist over her head, she shouted the words as loudly as she could. Then she repeated the old Gaelic phrase, her fist pumping the air to accentuate each word.

The man stopped and looked directly at the two women on the porch two houses away. He smiled and, raising his hand in the air, gave a long, shrill whoop. Then he shouted, "Erin Go Bragh, my family! Erin Go Bragh! Ah hou! Ah hou!" and ran toward them.

PART FIVE

Epilogue: 1996—1997

List of Characters in Part Five

Sarah Catherine Ryan Edwards— the 3rd great-granddaughter of Timothy Ryan; from Monona, Wisconsin

    Daniel Peter Edwards—her son

Elizabeth Anne Delaney— the 5th great-grandniece of Elizabeth Anne Delaney Ryan

Mary Elizabeth Hughes Dawson—the great granddaughter of Patrick and Ana Ryan Hughes

Family Trees for Part Five in Appendix II

CHAPTER 44
...The crook'd staff must remain...

Dear Ms. Dawson,   *December 29, 1996*

This letter will seem very strange to you coming from someone you have never met. I got your name off of the internet from one of those genealogy sites. I think we may be related. Here is some background that may help you to know if you think we are.

When my sister and I were growing up and going out on a date or with friends, our dad would always say, "Remember whose kid you are. The choices you make when you are young will be with you all of your life." We got so sick of hearing it, but now I understand it a lot better. I find myself saying it to my son.

Recently, I asked Dad where he got that phrase. He said, "Those words have just always been in our family. I heard them when I was growing up, and I repeated them to you because I think they are right."

In addition to those words, we have something else that has been in our family for a very long time. It is a little pair of beaded moccasins. A curator at the Chicago Museum of Natural History identified them for my dad. He said they were Northern Cheyenne and were probably made some time before the Civil War. They were given to him by his grandmother, who was a little unsure about their specific history, except that they had been handed down in the family.

Dad also told us that there was supposed to be another family heirloom which he had never seen, but that it was very important to the family's story. He said that it was a stick used to herd sheep with, and that it came to America from Ireland. Dad said that some of his ancestors came from Ireland many years <u>before</u> the big migration of Irish following the Irish Potato Famine.

The family first names that have come down through the years are Elizabeth, Anne, Catherine, Ana, Sarah, Mollie, Zoe, Marie, Evan, Michael, Timothy, Patrick, Charles, Daniel, John, William, and Robert. The old surnames that I am aware of are Ryan, Hughes, Delaney, O'Rourke, and Connolly.

Do any of these names ring a bell with you? Does anything I have spoken about indicate that we may have a family connection? With that, I will close. Thanks so much for taking the time to read all of this. I will look forward to hearing from you.

Sincerely,

Sarah Catherine (Ryan) Edwards

Monona, WI

* * * * * * *

It was just after the holiday break. The class was on a field trip and moved through the museum at varied speeds. Some of the groups were all boys or all girls, with the exception of the pairs who were already identified as "a couple" by their classmates.

It was a nice museum in Cincinnati and had a wonderful section devoted to Native American artifacts from the Ohio River valley. A few items were included that came from elsewhere in the country and represented other Native American cultural areas. Many school groups regularly visited the museum, and this day was no exception.

"We only have about fifteen more minutes," the teacher said, as she walked among her students, who were strung out along the last section of displays. She paused at one of the cases. It was the only one containing items related to the Plains Indian buffalo culture.

One of her best students was kneeling down looking intensely at the display. She was a very pretty girl, almost slight of build, and her green eyes always seemed to light up when she learned something especially interesting. She was always respectful, but had a rather strong, independent streak which showed itself on occasion. Her family had lived in the area for generations, and the teacher had already taught the girl's older brothers.

"What is it that has you so absorbed?" the teacher asked.

"Oh, this knife! I've never seen anything like it. The tag says it is an unusual example of a Sioux knife, but that the handle is made from a naval peg. What would a naval peg be doing out in South Dakota, where this knife came from?" the girl answered.

"Hmm. That's a good question," the teacher replied, peering into the case.

"The tag says it came from Wounded Knee. That's the place we read about in that book. You know, the one where that guy, Black Elk, had a vision when he was a boy and saw all of the generations of grandfathers and grandmothers walking behind him. I really liked that book."

She paused and thought for a moment. Then she added, "<u>Black Elk Speaks</u>, that was the name of the book. I'll bet that knife has a great story to tell." The girl was still looking into the case, her eyes fixed on the strange-looking object.

"I'm sure it does, Elizabeth Anne. I'm sure it does," Ms. K said. "But you'd better start moving out to the bus now. It's about that time."

The teacher smiled as she watched the girl walk toward the front of the museum. *Good kids, those Delaneys.* She thought.

She bent down to look more closely at the object that had so intrigued her student. The explanation card next to it read:

Hand forged knife with what appears
to be a piece of naval peg for a handle.
Very unusual example of a Sioux knife.
Found in Jan. 1891 on the Wounded Knee,
SD battlefield.

Donated by the James O'Rourke Family

* * * * * * *

Sarah Edwards sat at her kitchen table. It was a Saturday afternoon and her son, Danny, had just been dropped off after attending hockey practice. People in the Madison, Wisconsin area loved hockey, and many girls and boys started their training in the sport quite early.

"Here's the mail, Mom," he said, setting the stack of envelopes and catalogues on the table. "Where's Dad?"

"He went to the store with your little brother. They'll be back in a few minutes. How did practice go?" she asked.

"Pretty good. I need to work on my backward skating. It's hard to switch," he answered.

He left the kitchen as his mother started to go through the mail. Her hands stopped at a letter which was addressed in slightly shaky handwriting. It was from Lawrenceburg, Indiana. She opened it and began to read.

Dear Sarah,   *January 10, 1997*

I was thrilled to get your letter. Thank you so much for taking the time to write to me. Let me say that I am sure we are related. My father said the same words to me as yours did.

I don't remember ever seeing those little moccasins you have, but I know exactly where they came from.

From all of the names you mentioned, I think that we are probably cousins. A few times removed, perhaps, but cousins nonetheless. There is no question in my mind that we had the same Irish ancestors.

I know their story pretty well. It has never been written down that I know of, but I heard most of it from my father, and it was told to him by his father. My mother emigrated from Ireland just before she married my father. Her name was Bridget. She made very sure that I knew about all of my Irish ancestors who came to America.

I want to say that when you mentioned the shepherd's crook, I started to cry. <u>I have that stick. I am looking at it now.</u> My parents actually met the original relatives who brought the staff here from Ireland. It came here about 1850.

Sarah, I would like so very much to meet you. But I no longer drive, so you will need to come to me. Could you do that? I hope so. I am alone. I lost my sons many years ago and my daughter and my husband as well. I have no grandchildren, and I have no contact with any other relatives on my side.

You must come here so that you can see this crook'd staff. It is very old, and I treasure it. You will, too. The crook'd staff must remain in <u>our</u> family. It means so much. More than any of us can imagine.

Oh, your letter was such a joy to read. I will look forward to your call.

Very truly yours,

Mary Elizabeth (Hughes) Dawson

Lawrenceburg, Indiana   812-555-2244

Danny Edwards came back into the kitchen. He was about to ask his mother if there was anything to eat. Instead, he stopped in the doorway. His mother was holding a letter to her breast with one hand and covering her mouth with the other. She was crying softly.

"What's the matter? Is there something wrong with Granddad or Grandma?" he asked, afraid to hear her response. He was a bright little boy and was, like his mother, always conscious of his surroundings and the feelings of others.

"No, honey. It's just this letter. It's a good letter, very good," she answered. "Some day you'll realize and understand just how good."

"Oh, okay!" he said, relieved that some family tragedy had not occurred.

"Can I go over to Nate's house 'til dinner?" he asked, the prospect of food no longer paramount.

His mother paused and wiped her eyes. She was still collecting her thoughts.

"Does he know you are coming, and is it all right with his folks?" she answered. Nate was Danny's good friend, and she already knew the answers. She asked anyway.

"Yeah! He said to come over after practice. Is it okay?" he asked again.

"Sure, go ahead. Have a good time, but just remember whose kid you are," she answered. Then she turned and looked directly at her son.

"Make good choices, Danny, because the things you choose to do when you're young...." she began to say.

"I know, Mom. I know. They will be with me all of my life." He finished her sentence, rolling his eyes just a little as he turned toward the door.

If you only knew. She thought. *If you only knew.*

She wasn't even entirely sure why she knew the words were true. But she knew that they were!

APPENDIX I:
MAPS

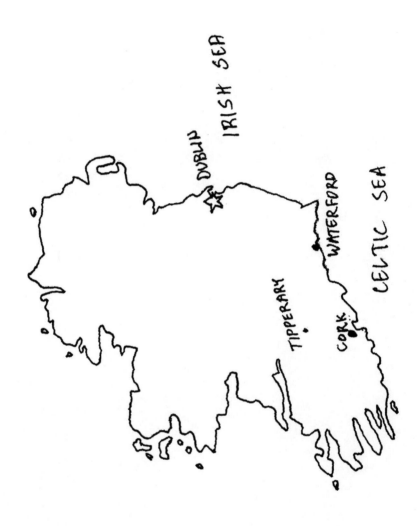

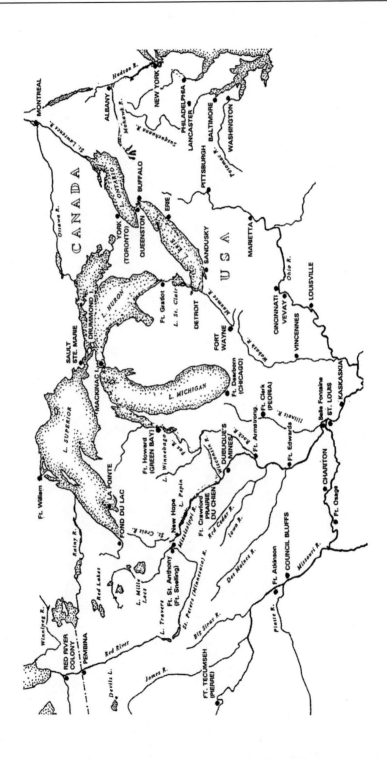

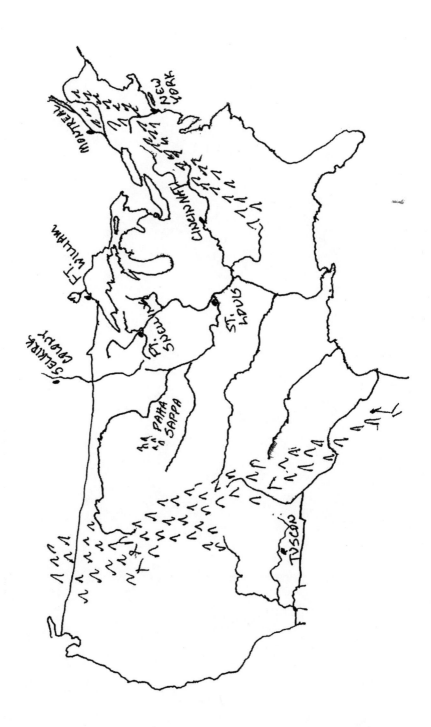

APPENDIX II:
FAMILY TREES

The Ryan, O'Leary, Hughes, and Delaney Families

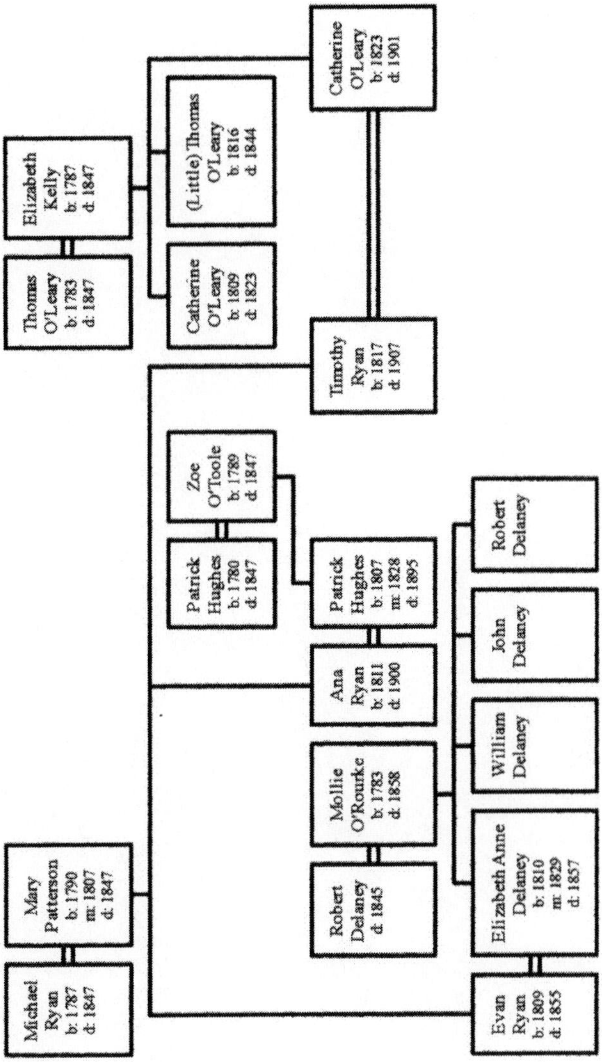

Descendants of Evan Ryan and Elizabeth Anne Delaney

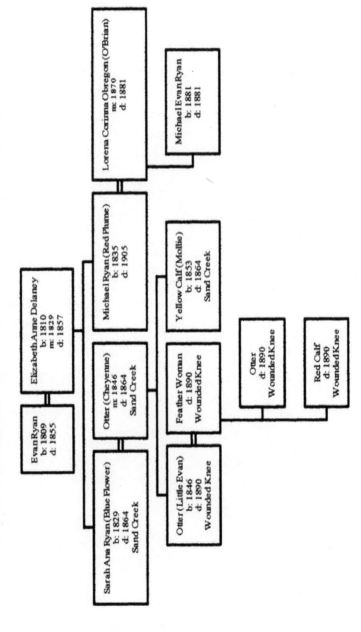

Evan Ryan
b: 1809
d: 1855

Elizabeth Anne Delaney
b: 1810
m: 1829
d: 1857

Michael Ryan (Red Plume)
b: 1835
d: 1905

Lorena Corinna Obregon (O'Brian)
m: 1870
d: 1881

Michael Evan Ryan
b: 1881
d: 1881

Sarah Ana Ryan (Blue Flower)
b: 1829
d: 1864
Sand Creek

Otter (Cheyenne)
m: 1846
d: 1864
Sand Creek

Yellow Calf (Mollie)
b: 1853
d: 1864
Sand Creek

Otter (Little Evan)
b: 1846
d: 1890
Wounded Knee

Feather Woman
d: 1890
Wounded Knee

Otter
d: 1890
Wounded Knee

Red Calf
d: 1890
Wounded Knee

Descendants of Patrick Hughes and Ana Ryan

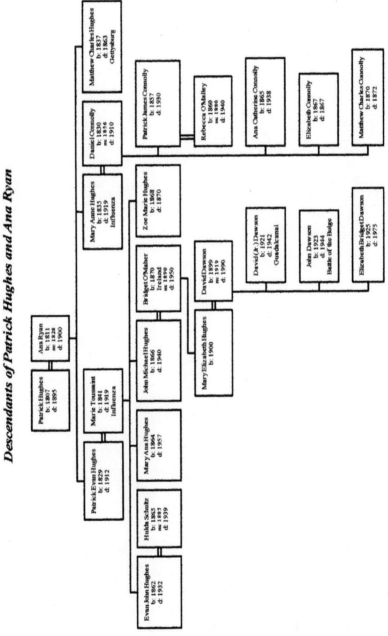

Descendants of Timothy Ryan and Catherine O'Leary

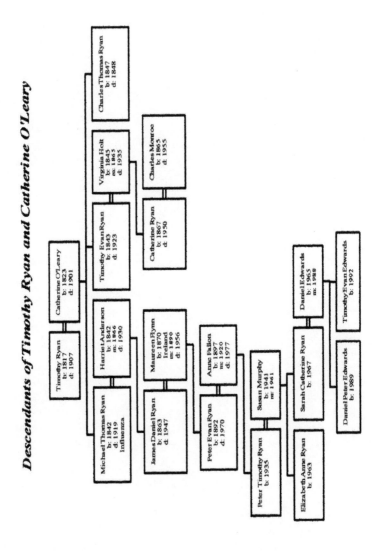

SUGGESTED READING

Anderson, Gary. *Kinsmen of Another Kind.* Lincoln: U. of NE Press, 1984.

Brown, Dee. *Bury My Heart At Wounded Knee.* New York: Holt, Rinehart & Winston, 1970.

Farb, Peter. *Man's Rise to Civilization.* New York: E.P. Dutton, 1968.

Gilman, R., Gilman, C., and Stultz, D. *The Red River Trails,* St. Paul: Minnesota Historical Society, 1979.

Goodman, N. & R. *Joseph R. Brown.* Rochester, MN: Lone Oak Press, 1996.

Grinnell, George. *The Cheyenne Indians.* Lincoln: Bison Book, 1923.

Hoebel, E. *The Cheyennes.* New York: Holt, Rinehart & Winston, 1960.

Hogan, M. *The Irish Soldiers of Mexico.* Fondo Editorial Universitario, 1998.

Hoig, Stan. *The Peace Chiefs of the Cheyennes.* Norman: U. of OK Press, 1980.

Llewellyn, K. and Hoebel, E. *The Cheyenne Way.* Norman: U. of OK Press, 1941.

Loewen, James. *Lies My Teacher Told Me.* New York: Simon and Schuster, 1995.

Mails, Thomas. —

    The Mystic Warriors of the Plains. New York: Doubleday, 1972.

    Dog Soldiers, Bear Men and Buffalo Women. New Jersey: Prentice-Hall, 1973.

Moore, John. *The Cheyenne Nation.* Lincoln: U. of NE Press, 1987.

Neihardt, John. *Black Elk Speaks.* New York: William Morrow, 1932.

O'Donnell, Edward. *1001 Things Everyone Should Know About Irish American History,* New York: Gramercy Books, 2002.

Sandoz, Mari. —

> *Cheyenne Autumn.* New York: Avon Books, 1953.

> *The Buffalo Hunters.* Lincoln: Bison Book, 1954.

> *These Were the Sioux.* New York: Dell, 1961.

> *The Beaver Men.* Lincoln: U. of NE Press, 1964.

Storm, Hyemeyohsts. *Seven Arrows.* New York: Harper and Row, 1972.

Tomkins, William. *Indian Sign Language.* New York: Dover Publications, 1969.

Utley, Robert. *The Lance and The Shield.* New York: Ballantine Books, 1993.

Wissler, Clark. *Indians of the United States.* New York: Doubleday, 1940.

SPECIAL THANKS

Cover layout by John LeBrun, Eau Claire, WI (He is one of the author's favorite local drummers and also manages the Tiyospayepublishing.com website.)

Cover photo of tipis by James Keip, Mazomanie, WI; used with permission. JWKEIPART.COM or poniespainted@ yahoo.com

All crook'd staff and knife photos by Tim Seyforth, Seyforth's Studio and Camera Shop, Chippewa Falls, WI and used with permission.

Moccasin photo by Carrie Moulds, Chicago, IL and used with permission. (She is a niece of the author and a descendant of Irish immigrants from Dublin.)

Irish sheep-herding staff made by James O'Rourke, Clearville, PA; see his work at Caneman2.com

Hand-forged knife made by Dan Winrich, Dutchman Forge, Fall Creek, WI.

Dog Soldier Staff made by the author many years ago in honor of all Veterans. They are the ones who defend our families and our land.

Northern Cheyenne moccasins are antiques owned by the author. In 1950 they were given to him by his grandmother, Hattie Belle Isgrigg (1869—1955).

ABOUT THE AUTHOR

Peter E. Roller taught American History to high school students for twenty-three years and earned both a B.A. and M.S.Ed. in that field. He was then employed by the Wisconsin Education Association Council for seventeen years as an organizer, a specialist in community relations, and as a facilitator for the advancement of teaching and learning.

He and his wife live in northwestern Wisconsin. They are historic reenactors and his wife's tipi is a nationally recognized and award winning example of a historically accurate Cheyenne/Lakota lodge.

He plays bass guitar and is well known in local music circles. (See lucycreek.net]

He is also an Eagle Scout.

ORDERING INFORMATION

Quantity discounts are available on bulk purchases of this book for educational institutions, reading clubs, gift purposes, or as premiums. Please contact Tiyospaye Publishing, 8965 Hwy. 12, Suite #44, Fall Creek, WI 54742 or http://www.tiyospayepublishing.com.

The author is available for personal presentations to educational institutions, clubs, and to adult or youth organizations. Contact him through Tiyospaye Publishing.

You can also order this book via the internet. Go to tiyospayepublishing.com for ordering directions. Credit cards and Paypal are accepted.

A Teacher's Guide is also sold separately.